SPIRITS & SUNFLOWERS

MALIGNED MAGIC #1

AUSTIN DANIEL AND A. D. ARMISTEAD

CONTENTS

CONTENT WARNING

Spirits and Sunflowers is a cozy contemporary MM fantasy romance, but there are some content elements that may be upsetting or emotional for some readers, including grief and loss, death of a spouse and of parents (off-page), and references to homophobia. In general, the book deals with healing after these experiences and we hope you find the story to be an uplifting resolution.

Thank you so much for reading and we hope you enjoy Spirits & Sunflowers as much as we did writing it!

-A.D. Armistead and Austin Daniel

CHAPTER ONE

ADRIAN

Adrian Sharp lit the tallow candles one by one, their glow rippling across the pale marble of the mausoleum walls. A dim circle of light surrounded him, flames flickering in the mist that gathered like clouds near the high vaulted ceiling. Pre-dawn blues faded into warm golds as the blazes sputtered and grew larger than their wicks should've allowed. He exhaled, lifting his hand to draw symbols in the mist and smoke, watching the clouds of incense split at his touch. The shapes flattened themselves against the marble, guttering the light from outside, warding the little building from any passing glances and sheltering his activities from the watchful eye of the International Arcane Order; he wouldn't want to alert the suits and spooks to the efforts of an unregistered necromancer.

He drew chalk over the remnants of last week's attempt, the lines now etched in the stone after six months of repeated motion. Adrian placed his late husband's wedding band in the center of the diagram, whispering the ancient words to summon his spirit back from the beyond; as the hum of magic flowed through his body and into the wards, it lifted the dust into the air. Sparkling particles of things long past.

For a moment, he felt the hairs on his arms prickling and standing at attention. The sigils shimmered once, twice, then dissipated. The light from outside returned to the mausoleum, the motes of dust glittering where they hovered.

Adrian's heart sank as he sat before the carved names on the altar, palms flat against the cold, unforgiving stone. What was the point of his gift if it couldn't bring back the person he wanted most to see? What was the point of being able to commune with the dead if the one person he needed refused to speak with him? What was the point of any of it at all?

He massaged his temples, eyes stinging. Six months of rituals in the cemetery, each one ending in inevitable failure and disappointment. Adrian plucked the ring up off the floor, affixing it to the golden amulet that hung about his neck, tucking it beneath his shirt and resting it against his heart. He'd try the sage and lavender again soon, go through his old notes, and see if there was anything he was somehow still missing.

Of all the burdens Seron Sharp had asked Adrian to bear, grief was by far the heaviest and undoubtedly the loneliest. It was agonizing waking up each morning and knowing that he would never again see Seron's tousled blond hair on the pillow beside him or see his crystal blue eyes brighten over his morning cup of coffee. Sometimes the very act of breathing seared Adrian's lungs like daggers.

It had to work, eventually. He had to be given the chance to say goodbye. Seron would've wanted to give him that, at least.

Wouldn't he?

He hadn't gotten the chance to say farewell. They'd said their vows, given their promises to each other, but only after Seron had breathed his last had Adrian been so much as informed that his husband's life had been in danger, let alone erased for good. Only when there was nothing left for him to do. It had been the worst of the problems Adrian had faced, and the one he most regretted being unable to solve, even with the power humming through his veins. Not even the specialist healer the Navy had called in—one of those spoken of in rumors who tended to patients behind closed doors, light flashing underneath the seams—had been able to do more than ease Seron's passing.

So Seron had been awarded a Purple Heart and Adrian a Gold Star. Adrian had accepted them both, alone on the stage in front of sympathetic faces. The cold medals didn't ease the emptiness in Adrian's actual heart, nor the anger burning in his chest.

He traced the letters on the plaque with his forefinger, turning to light the candles in his family mausoleum one by one, wondering what his ancestors would think of having his husband buried in their midst. Adrian didn't care. Seron had become a Sharp when they'd stood—against their families' wishes—under the linden trees and promised each other lives full of happiness.

Neither of them had imagined their time together would end so abruptly.

Despite the failure of the spell, Adrian told Seron the events of the week, kneeling before the sepulcher where his love was interred. He'd managed one entire day without so much as a sniffle! He'd found shreds of normalcy, flitting around the red-roofed halls of UC Berkeley, using a combination of work and willpower to find a sense of purpose beyond grief. It had taken six months, but it was progress when, before, everything had ground to a halt. Progress that Seron could be proud of if he were listening. If he could.

Anything that could fill the silence of the tombs. Anything that would make Seron feel close again.

"I miss you," Adrian whispered, palm on the unforgiving marble. "You brave idiot."

He left the wreath of lilacs and sunflowers at the base of the monument and slipped out of the building into the blinding sunlight once more.

Adrian locked the gate, glancing up as fellow cemetery-goers exited the mausoleum next to his. A man, slender and dark-haired, was dressed in an impeccably tailored burgundy jacket to ward off the chill of the spring morning. A little girl with hair as yellow as sunflowers held his hand.

"They really liked it, don't you think?" The little girl peered up at the back of the man as he locked their gate. Adrian had seen him several times, though never with the child. Late evenings and early mornings, they had passed each other like ships in the night.

"I think they were extremely impressed," the stranger answered in a quiet voice, a warm tenor that set Adrian's pulse racing. He turned, dropping to a knee to retie the little girl's loose boot strings. "And they always will be, because they love you as I do. Now." He finished with her boot and straightened her purple sweater. "Brunch."

"Neighbors first!" She dragged blossoms from the cotton bag on the ground and ran towards Adrian, bright and beaming, hand outstretched with a fragrant white peony. "Hello! I'm Tula and this is my papa. We're visiting my grandparents today. This is for you, and I can leave one here, too, so you can smell the same thing as who you lost. Can I go say hello?"

"Tula," her father chided.

"I..." Adrian took the flower, fingers smoothing over the fragile petals. "Yes. Alright. Thank you, Tula." She was bright and adorable and full of hope and life. Who was he to dampen her light? "I'm sure he would appreciate your company." He smiled at the child, holding the gate open for her. "He always enjoyed making friends."

"So do I!" She hopped twice, darting a grin at her father, then rushed inside, her voice echoing, "Hello, hello, hello!"

The man bowed his head solemnly, tucking the bag of greens and flowers over his shoulder. "I'm sorry for your loss. Thank you for your patience."

"Thank you for sharing her with him, even for a moment," Adrian slipped his hands in his pockets, studying his elegant profile. "It's like I said: he liked making friends." Somber features, a proud chin, and eyes that squinted thoughtfully, as though he could see more than was apparent. Emerald green, glinting in the misty morning light, with a red-tinged shadow towards the bottom of each iris. "I'm Adrian. I've seen you before."

A quirk of a dark brow. "Lucas," he answered, bowing his head. The little girl chattered behind the gate, the content of her conversation lost to the echoes. "She's developed a fascination," he murmured, tucking long-fingered hands into his pockets. "I worried at first that my pilgrimage was at fault, that I would turn her morbid, but she seems quite happy making her new—"

"Papa!" Tula came rushing out past Adrian. "Do we have the yellow flowers? He likes yellow better. I gave the white one to the old man with the tie."

Lucas peered into his bag, withdrawing a slender handful of daffodils. "Don't overstay your welcome, sunbeam."

"I won't!" She rushed back inside.

"How does she…" Adrian blinked, gazing at him. "There aren't any pictures of my family in my mausoleum."

Lucas shrugged, dropping his gaze. "There are in ours. I'm sorry. She gets over-excited." He grimaced. "Beautiful day, isn't it?"

"It is." Adrian pressed his lips together. "Thank you again."

"For what?" Lucas glanced towards the door. "Tula! Time to go!"

"But I want to hear about the siege and the sunflowers!"

"Their imaginations put us to shame," the man muttered. "*Now*, sunbeam."

The little girl skipped out, squeezing Adrian's hand. "Thank you! May I visit again? I like them very much."

"If your father doesn't mind," Adrian said quietly. Her hand was so small and sun-warmed in his. "I don't and I'm certain they would appreciate the company."

"Thank you." She dipped a ridiculous little curtsy. The father had passed some element of his formality to the child. "Would you like to come to brunch?" Tula asked. "The man with the nice smile said that you like quiches and that's what we're having."

Adrian flexed his hands in his pockets, his eyes stinging. "Perhaps next time," he murmured. "I wouldn't wish to impose." How had she *known*? Was she… He hadn't met many who could speak with the dead and to have such a skill at such an early age… And why would his own family choose to appear to her and not him? "Thank you, Tula." He inclined his head. "Lucas."

"Adrian." The other man bowed again, a rounding of his shoulders as he collected the little girl to his side and guided her away.

"But what about our other neighbors?" she asked plaintively.

"We'll come back," Lucas murmured, barely audible.

Adrian watched them go, frozen on the gravel walkway; Tula turned back twice to wave at him, even as her father hurried her along. As they left, Adrian thought he felt a breeze against his palm, sun-warmed and gentle, but it vanished as soon as the girl and her father were out of sight. Quiche and yellow flowers. His grandfather's white tie. The man with the smile. Sieges and sunflowers.

Quiet walks through a meadow near where they'd been stationed during their off-duty hours. Often, Adrian wondered if he would have been able to protect him if he'd stayed in the service, but he and Seron had reasoned that Adrian could do more good at the university where he taught students to design planes rather than flying them himself. More good for the future, perhaps, but it hadn't saved Seron. Adrian studied the flowers on Seron's grave, then drove home through the streets of San Francisco alone.

Adrian didn't return to the cemetery the next week—a conference took him away from his routine—but the week after, he brought a brightly colored bouquet of zinnias to place at the mausoleum gate next to his family's. Halpern: the name was starkly carved into the granite. He placed the flowers at the entrance, with a simple handwritten note expressing his condolences and his thanks and then he filled Seron's resting place with sunflowers. It was the least he could do.

By the time he emerged from his family's mausoleum, the sun was high in the sky and his stomach grumbled. Quiche. Perhaps he could pick one up from the bakery near his apartment, then open that bottle of brandy he'd meant to share with Seron. Adrian rubbed his temples as he locked the gate, exhausted, and heard the gate clank to his left.

Out of the corner of his eye, he saw Lucas rise from collecting the flowers, peering at the note. He glanced up. "Thank you." Lucas was alone and seemed more somber for it. He lifted the flowers gently, unlocking the gate. "My mother loved zinnias."

"I thought they were appropriate. They symbolize friendship," Adrian murmured, glancing down at where the grass was slowly infiltrating the gravel. He cleared his throat. "And I thought your daughter might like the colors."

"She will. I'll take a picture for her." Lucas stared resolutely at the gate. "How's your family?"

"Dead, I'm afraid," Adrian exhaled, raising a brow. "Not much change there. Yours?"

"Just so." Lucas huffed a dark chuckle, glancing his way. "At least I think so. I suppose I ought to check since I'm here."

"I imagine they'd be louder if they weren't." Adrian studied him. "Tula is well, though?"

"Very. She just moved up a level in her judo classes, so our schedule is sideways, but she's pleased." Lucas hesitated as though he were about to say something, then he hummed under his breath instead: a quiet lilting little tune.

"I suppose I should let you get back to it, then." There was no reason to keep the man for idle chatter, not when he almost certainly wished to be alone. "Have a good afternoon."

"Thank you." Lucas stepped past his gate, then turned around. "She didn't... I mean to say... You weren't here last week. I hope you didn't feel uncomfortable."

"Of course not." Adrian flashed him a slight smile. A tinge of sorrow, perhaps, that the girl had succeeded in connecting with Seron when he had not. "I was out of town. Thank you for noticing, though."

"Ah, well." Lucas shrugged. "I've seen you around here, too."

Adrian felt his cheeks warm as he turned away. It didn't mean anything, of course. Lucas had a family and their schedules had simply happened to align. No reason to think he meant anything more than that. Still, it felt good to be *seen*. To be spoken to without pity. "She has a talent," Adrian murmured. "It's not often that one is willing to share such things. I simply didn't expect it."

Lucas looked down at his hands. "A talent for storytelling, certainly." He cleared his throat. "She means well."

Adrian raised his brows. "I do like quiche. She was right about that." And everything else, but it wouldn't do to spook the man by recognizing the girl for the skills she undoubtedly possessed. That would only cause trouble. For her, for Lucas, and for the International Arcane Order. Best to let the matter go. He nearly let the conversation fall into silence, but he felt that strange warmth against his hand again, and it bolstered him. "I was thinking about getting some today."

Dark green eyes darted to him, then away again. There was a steady confidence Lucas exuded in the presence of his daughter that appeared to have dissipated in her absence, shifting into something more flighty. "Have you had it at Noisette? They have a nice seasonal at the moment."

"Once or twice." The last time had been when Seron was on leave, nearly a year before. Adrian swallowed, watching Lucas' fingers tense and release at his side: slim and dexterous. Where was Tula's mother? He'd never seen Lucas with anyone until the week before last. "Would you care to join me for breakfast after you've paid your respects?"

"Oh." Lucas peered down at the zinnias, his dark brows drawing together, then smoothing. "Ah." Another hesitation. A breath. "Very well." Another darting glance. "...would you like to meet my family?" he asked slowly, turning the flowers in his hands as he nodded to the open gate.

"If you'd like the company. You're certain I wouldn't be bothering you?" Adrian watched as thoughts visibly crossed behind those gilded emerald eyes, like ghost ships. Ephemeral and imagined. A blood moon rising over green waters. Perhaps he was spending far too much time in cemeteries.

Lucas shook his head. "No bother. A visitor will be a nice change of pace."

Inside, there were work lights covered by translucent plastic with shapes cut in them that sent prismatic fractals spinning across the smooth white marble. Lucas cleared his throat. "Mama. Papa. This is the neighbor Tula was telling you about. He brought you flowers; isn't that nice?" He lay them on a clean mantle before a cluster of framed photographs and lit a few small votives that smelled like coconut and fresh mango. "Tula's taken another belt, which is why she isn't here, but we'll come after her tennis match this weekend so you shouldn't need to wait long." He glanced back at Adrian. "I apologize. I've been rude. Ah... Adrian, may I introduce my parents: Marcus and Lida."

The place felt alive with the scents and the colors and the movement of the lights. And something else: something cold and warm at the same time that hummed electrically in the air, distinct and familiar. The tang of ozone just after a lightning storm. The earthy taste in the air that only persisted when the dead chose to make their presence known.

Beautiful and vivid, making the Sharp mausoleum seem all the more lonely and dark by comparison. Adrian thought he should've buried Seron under a tree, where he could see the sun, not deep within the cold, unforgiving stone.

"Hello," Adrian said softly, glancing between the portraits. Lucas had inherited his father's nose and his mother's eyes and smile. Drawings done by little hands decorated the small room. "Your granddaughter was kind enough to lay flowers for my husband two weeks ago," he added, stepping into the center of the room. Warmth touched his shoulder, like fingertips, then it was gone. Comfort and welcome given freely, without supplication. "I was only returning the favor."

Lucas had collected a small broom to brush off surfaces on the other side of the space, his brows drawn in concentration.

"Is there anything I can help you with?" Adrian watched him putter about, crossing his hands behind his back for lack of anything better to do with them. "Should I keep talking?"

"They aren't great fans of 'should'," Lucas answered wryly. "You don't need to. Unless... I don't suppose you follow sports, do you? I always forget to check the scores before I come." He poured out the water from the vase, removed slightly drooping flowers, and replaced them with fresh daisies, zinnias, and baby's breath, mixing Adrian's offering with his own.

"Oh. I'm afraid not. Unless they like swimming." Adrian stepped closer to the portraits, eyeing one with a young Lucas, his canary yellow graduation cap pulled down over his eyes while his mother laughed. "Refreshing. 'Should' and 'must' were two of my father's favorite words."

Lucas stepped back, lips curved just a touch as he adjusted the flowers. Gods, but he was handsome when he smiled. "It's simpler having boundaries and borders. I can understand that. Rules and repetition make it much easier to handle chaos." He touched the edge of a portrait of his parents, shifting it slightly towards the vase. "I was quite a stickler for a while. Drove them mad."

"I was in the military." Adrian turned towards him, admiring the way the amber lights made his skin gleam and eyes glitter. "It was precisely what my father didn't want, which made it all the more appealing."

"Ah. What branch?" Lucas asked.

"I was a pilot for the Navy."

"I was in the Naval Academy when they..." Lucas nodded towards the mantle.

"I'm sorry for your loss. Truly. It seems like they really care for you."

"They do. They did." Lucas patted the smooth marble twice, then collected his cloth sack. "Shall we?" he asked, nodding towards the door.

"I don't mean to rush you," Adrian murmured. "Take as long as you need."

The candles winked out as one. Lucas glanced at them curiously, then shook his head. "It's alright. I'll be back tomorrow."

"Suit yourself." Adrian turned back towards the portraits, a nervous buzz in his chest. "It was lovely to meet you both. I hope you don't mind me spiriting your son away for the time being."

"Spiriting," Lucas chuckled, a sound as dry and quiet as autumn leaves, and turned off the lights. The daylight reflected on the marble and seemed to flex the space. He touched the wall, patting it fondly, then stepped outside. "How long were you with the Navy?"

"Four years." Adrian couldn't help but notice the way the light caught at the stubble on Lucas' cheek and the sharp edge of his jaw beneath it. "Then I thought it was probably time to put my PhD to use."

Lucas locked the gate behind them, tucking his hands at the base of his spine. "In what?"

"Aeronautical engineering." Adrian smiled slightly, studying his profile. "Not as much of a shift as you might think. I teach at the university nearby."

"Teaching how a machine works is very different from flying one. In your case, at the very least, your feet are significantly closer to the ground." Lucas moved the way a dancer might, in a ballet about a battalion. Quick and smooth at the same time. Rigid and not, his fingers flexing to catch the breezes as they passed. "Or perhaps I'm mistaken about how the lessons work."

"I always wanted to fly," Adrian admitted, finding himself eager to share. There was something about Lucas, the way his gaze touched and retreated, that created a space around him where anything could be said. Perhaps *needed* to be said, if only to close the distance. "But I like being able to set my own schedule. I inherited my father's single-engine when he passed and now I can fly it wherever I like, whenever I care to." He gave Lucas a small smile as they passed rows and rows of headstones. "I'm rambling about myself when I hardly know anything about you."

"It's hardly rambling; I asked." Lucas dipped his head as they passed beneath a low branch, reaching to touch it and make the leaves quiver. "Anyway, you know everything about me that's interesting already."

"I don't think that's the case." Birds were chirping merrily from the blossoming fruit trees as Adrian pulled his sunglasses from his pocket. "I'm already considering nearly a dozen questions I could ask you and that would scarcely scratch the surface."

"Nearly a dozen?" Lucas snorted quietly. "Are you planning a novel?"

"Should I?" Adrian lifted a brow. "Maybe I'll take notes, then. The first question is very important: how do you take your coffee?"

"With my hand, generally." Lucas' lip curled in a smirk.

"See, that particular response told me all *sorts* of things about you." Adrian grinned as they neared the parking lot. "I'm growing more and more curious by the moment."

"You must be starved for entertainment." Lucas rolled his eyes, lifting his gaze to the clouds masquerading as streaks of white in the endless blue canvas above them. "Have you heard of the internet? It's chock full of *actually* fascinating things."

"*Someone* doesn't enjoy answering questions." Adrian lifted a brow when the other man answered by humming a tune under his breath. "That will make for a very quiet brunch. Unless, of course, you'd prefer we stick to my favorite subject."

"Aeronautical engineering? I know nothing about it except that there was a fellow who, at some point, realized air moved both over and under a bird's wing." Lucas glanced at him sideways, tucking his chin to his chest. "*Fine*. I will answer... three questions. And then we can talk about you. Agreed?"

"I think I'd like to change the order of operations you've proposed." Adrian plucked the keys to his hybrid from his pocket and twirled them around his forefinger. "Let's talk about me, give me a chance to percolate on those three questions I've been so generously allotted, and then we can circle back again. Yes?"

"Or we could fail to circle back entirely." Lucas peered at his keys, then glanced away. It was a strangely enthralling challenge to try to hold Lucas' gaze for any length of time; his eyes were like hummingbirds, flitting color that never rested for long in any one spot, but gleaming each time they paused long enough to be studied. "And you'll have an opportunity to percolate on that, as well. We are thinking of the same Noisette, yes?" Lucas asked, plucking his keys from his pocket with a jingle. "Yellow awning, across from the yoga studio and the park, near the old sawmill?"

"The very same." What a curiously formal man. Even more strange was how easy it was to fall back into conversation; Adrian had been almost certain that skill had withered over the last months. But here he was, playing verbal chess with the promise of more at breakfast if the man didn't vanish into the breeze. "I'll see you in ten?"

Lucas nodded once and, without another word, he was walking across the mostly empty lot to a sturdy, unassuming gray hatch-back, the only color on the car from the clusters of little stickers on the rear passenger side window. Lucas folded himself inside and the muffled sound of talk radio gurgled from the car's speakers as he pulled away.

Chapter Two

ADRIAN

A drian skimmed his palms over the surface of the wheel, exhaling shakily. It was just brunch. Only a meal and a cup of coffee with someone new, someone who could be a friend. Still, he felt weighted down, rooted into place. He held his breath, counted to ten, and exhaled. There was no betrayal in brunch. Simply quiche and sunshine with someone who knew what it was like to grieve.

By the time Adrian found a parking spot near the café, he had largely assured himself that Lucas was not going to be there. But he was: perched on the edge of a booth beneath a picture of a French vineyard, dusting crumbs from the table into a napkin beside his metallic order number card. Lucas glanced up, a small crinkle at the corners of his eyes his only acknowledgment, and returned to sweeping up the collection of crumbs and twisting his napkin packet to keep it closed.

The café was as Adrian remembered it: the scents of coffee and bacon warring for supremacy, the grind of beans and slurp of foam, the modern covers of folk songs playing dimly beneath the low chatter of customers and employees. He waved, willing a smile across his lips as a tide of nostalgia threatened to overwhelm him. His therapist had said it would be a good practice to visit some of the same places he'd gone with Seron under different circumstances, but he wasn't sure he was ready. If Lucas hadn't been there, he would've ordered his quiche and a cappuccino and taken it away to eat on the little balcony of his apartment and stare down at the city like a gargoyle, where no one could see him. As it was, he couldn't in good conscience stand Lucas up, so he ordered a pain au chocolat and a spinach and ricotta quiche along with his usual cinnamon-sprinkled cappuccino and took his placard to the table Lucas had claimed.

"So." Lucas turned his cup precisely, ripples in the dark black coffee. "You can start with the mustache."

"Is that a question, a compliment, or a request?" Adrian pulled out the chair across from him, smoothing his facial hair with his thumb, doing his best to slip back in to the facade of elegant socialite to hide his nerves.

"You said you wanted to talk about yourself. I'm telling you where to begin." Lucas lifted his cup, curving his fingers around the smooth ceramic. "It's a very particular look."

"'*Particular*', he says," Adrian idled, accepting his cappuccino from a passing waiter. "What he means is 'dashing'."

"If you enjoy black and white films about thieves and ruffians and fencers, yes."

Adrian smiled gamely over his cup. "I won't be tricked into wasting one of my three questions on trivialities and simply take it as a 'yes, Adrian, it suits you exquisitely.'"

"Hm." Lucas' lips curled into a smirk as he glanced down at his cup; thick, dark lashes over bewilderingly green eyes. "Very well." He sipped. "Does it take ages to get into that shape?"

"No, not any longer. I've had plenty of practice."

"Do you have off days with it?" Lucas asked and sounded genuinely curious about the silly question. "Ones where it refuses to come to a point or curl symmetrically?" He widened his eyes, a sly lilt entering his quiet voice. "Do you have to call in sick?"

"You tease, but if that ever occurs, I would consider it." Adrian rested his chin on his fist, blowing steam from his cup. "One must keep up appearances."

Lucas nodded once, the hummingbirds of his gaze taking flight again as he sipped, dried his lips on the back of his knuckle, and set the cup back on the table. "One mustn't, but one may."

How was he supposed to hold a conversation if he couldn't ask the man questions? How was he supposed to distract himself from the fact that he'd been just here, some months before, with someone so very different? Adrian pressed his lips together, frowning. "Do questions about Tula count against my quota?"

Genuine pleasure bloomed across Lucas' expression. "Certainly not."

There. That hard-won smile set his heart racing. Perhaps more similar to Seron than he thought, even if only in the way Lucas made Adrian's pulse skitter. "Judo *and* tennis?"

"She bores easily. And she's active." Lucas quirked a brow. "She also fences, if you must know."

"I must."

"She placed second in her division. You have to see—" Lucas broke off, laughing, fishing his phone from his pocket to show Adrian a picture. "The boy who placed third looked as though he found a finger floating in his soup."

Indeed he did: red-faced, red-haired, and scowling with his bronze, as Tula held up her silver trophy higher, her hair in braided pigtails. Lucas looked delightfully smug. "A whole hand in his soup, even. You must be proud."

Lucas nodded. "Impossible not to be. She routed him in three moves, nothing extraneous. It was a beautiful thing to see." He smirked, "I have a video. He actually stomped on his helmet. I was crying, it was so funny."

"Would you show me?" Adrian tilted his head to the side, sliding the phone back across the table towards him. "I could always use a laugh."

Lucas' odd little hums weren't quite answers. Still, he flicked through his camera roll and leaned the device against the napkin holder so they could watch a tiny Tula snapping her épée through the air like a maestro and the boy throwing a temper tantrum as the referee ushered him away. Snorts and guffaws rattled the speakers as the image shook at the end. "He's a little monster. His parents looked exhausted, poor things," he chortled, slipping his phone back into his pocket. "Of course, they named him Brutus. What did they expect?"

"Ah. Yes." Adrian didn't know a thing about children or what should be expected with regards to them. "I suppose they got what they asked for." Still no mention of Tula's mother? Were they separated? "You don't seem exhausted."

"That's kind of you to say." Lucas ducked his head, turning to peer out across the street. "I'm sure it's at least partially because she has a better name."

"That can't be entirely it. I was a terror and I have an excellent name." Adrian studied the man's cheek. He wondered whether it was soft or rough, what it might be like to touch... He blinked quickly, banishing the thought as quickly as it'd come.

"Were you?" Lucas focused on him, curious again. Alighting on the branch of their conversation once more, poking about for treats. "How so?"

"I enjoyed picking fights." Adrian shrugged, smiling over his cup. "And I hated rules."

"Ah, nothing wrong with picking a fight, so long as it's fair and you don't get caught." Lucas winked, returning his attention to his coffee cup. "Some of Tula's best friends have emerged from spats."

"For me, the goal was always to get caught." Adrian had always hoped it might get his father to notice him. "And I took a perverse pleasure in being the underdog."

"You were lacking attention, were you?"

"Well." Adrian raised a brow. "What makes you think I ever stopped?"

"Nothing at all." Lucas chuckled, turning the cup ninety degrees again. "That explains this," he tapped his own lip. "And *flying*. No one becomes a pilot to hide."

"There you are! Figured me out entirely and it took less than half an hour!" Adrian thanked the waiter when he brought their food. "Should I be on my way, then?"

Lucas snorted softly, shaking his head. "I know better than to think I understand anyone. Besides, that's not why you invited me here." He adjusted his small plates in front of him as precisely as the cup of coffee. A slice of vegetarian quiche. A pair of poached eggs in a ramekin. Lucas lifted the ramekin and slid one of the eggs into his coffee. It made a slurping sound as it was engulfed.

"Why did you—" Adrian stared at the mug, horrified. "Are you *trying* to be shocking?"

"What?" Lucas idly stirred the cup with the spoon, yolks spilling up through the black liquid. "I wasn't implying I knew why. Only saying it wasn't to summarize you. Why are you alone?"

"Why am I..." Adrian lifted a brow, his breath catching in his lungs. "What a curious thing to ask."

"You have a lot of friends, I imagine. You're obviously an extrovert, and yet I've never once seen you coming or going with anyone in tow."

"To a *cemetery?*"

"It's where you go. Why shouldn't someone join you? I've always found the grounds very soothing."

"This isn't precisely the line of questioning I was expecting," Adrian muttered, picking at the edge of his crust with the tines of his fork.

"What were you expecting?" Lucas asked. And then the strange man lifted the coffee and drank the horrid egg concoction.

"I suppose I hadn't given it much thought, to tell you the truth." Adrian tried not to grimace as Lucas swallowed. "I hadn't seen you with anyone until the other day, either."

"Yes. But I am not a brash, dashing ex-pilot engineer from a well-to-do family with a mustache that demands attention." Lucas set his cup back down and tapped his nose. "Nor am I particularly fond of crowds. Did you have a falling out?"

"A falling out?" Maddening and perplexing. "...with *whom*?"

"Your friends. The ones you've leaned on through the years, who you've doubtless given swells of support to." Lucas lifted his brows, turning the cup again. "It's reciprocal, you know. Friendship."

"What do you mean?" Adrian exhaled sharply. "It's wearying, being pitied. I'd rather be alone for this particular—What does it matter to you, in any case?"

"You wouldn't rather be alone." Lucas pierced him with a steady, unrelenting drill of a study. So he *could* hold Adrian's gaze, after all, when he was inclined. "You have a total stranger sitting here because you wouldn't rather be alone. I could be a serial killer. You need to tell them that you would appreciate support. Grief takes time. It's best with assistance."

"...this is a very convoluted manner of asking me to go." Adrian bunched his napkin in his lap. "You could've just said you didn't want to come."

The drill of emerald ceased, broken by a confused blink, then darted away. "I overstepped."

"You did."

"I apologize." Lucas frowned, peering into his cup. "Now you see why I do not have galleys of friends dogging my heels."

"I thought it was because you were a serial killer." Adrian relaxed his hands, summoning a tone that hopefully resembled levity. "Hard to keep friends if they keep disappearing."

Lucas laughed, a sharp bark, lips pulling to one side. "Touché." He squinted across the street. "But I have a lovely trophy collection."

"What parts? Teeth? Hopefully nothing with skin. Harder to preserve."

"Have you seen the grimoires at the Musée d'Arcana in Paris? Whole bindings are made of skin and hair. I find it fascinating." Lucas glanced up, clearing his throat. "Time-consuming, though, I imagine. I've too many appointments to keep. What with the tennis and the judo."

"Indeed, far too time-consuming. Fathers are never serial killers." Adrian raised a brow. "You forgot the fencing. Suspicious."

"I didn't forget. I expected you to remember." Lucas smiled slightly, glancing back at his cup. "Teeth, definitely. College savings from the tooth fairy."

"I'm not sure your daughter will have any teeth left if that's where her college fund is coming from. Not with tuition the way it is, in any case."

"As if the tooth fairy makes sure the teeth are *hers*. It's a racket, all black market trading. We just toss a bag full of molars beneath her pillow every night and no one asks questions." He collected his cup, resting it against his collarbone. "Apropos of nothing, what shape are your incisors in? We get docked for cavities."

"All of my teeth are in impeccable condition," Adrian chuckled, low, his tensions easing again somewhat with the lighthearted, if macabre, banter. "You wouldn't want to rid the world of this flawless smile, though."

"You'll have to let me know when you're ready to start grimacing regularly." Lucas bowed his head, breathing in the steam. "How's your... whatever that is?" Lucas asked, nodding towards Adrian's cappuccino.

"*Delightful.* I don't intend to ask about yours."

Lucas smiled, sipping his concoction serenely. "You are down to two. Don't think I haven't been keeping track."

"*Two?*" Adrian glared at him. "And what was the *first?*"

"You asked why it mattered to me." Lucas took a bite of his quiche. "That is a question."

"One you didn't even answer properly. It hardly counts." Adrian sniffed, sipping at the foam, enjoying the way the bubbles popped on his tongue. "You're a very difficult sort of person."

"I've heard that." Lucas peeled a slice of scallion from his quiche and nibbled at it. "Is it a problem?"

"Not necessarily." Adrian took another swig, leaning on the table. "I enjoy challenges. Though I suspect you already gathered that much from your psychoanalysis."

Like twittering ravens on an electric line, the way Lucas' brows wiggled above his downcast eyes; Lucas finished the scallion and peeled a roasted bell pepper free. "I enjoy them as well."

"And am I?" Adrian nibbled on the edge of his chocolate croissant, the pastry flaking under his fingertips. "Difficult? And... Before you answer, that's a question about *me*, not you."

"Parsing," Lucas murmured. "I consider almost everyone difficult. I don't consider it an insult."

"Alright." Adrian returned to picking at his breakfast, even though he was starving. "But you did come, after all. So I must not be *so* terrible."

"You didn't ask if you were terrible. You asked if you were difficult." Lucas glanced up, emeralds catching the light. "I much prefer you to Brutus, for example." He paused. "Thus far."

"Oh, flattery will get you everywhere," Adrian sniffed, biting into the ribbon of chocolate. "Are you considering that two, regardless?"

"I appreciate semantics." Lucas smirked. "And rule-breaking."

"I thought you said you were a stickler for them?"

"I *was*." Lucas tapped his nose. "And *that's* two."

"*Damn it.*" Adrian narrowed his eyes at the smug-featured fellow. "I won't waste the third."

"Good. Now." Lucas pointed to Adrian's jacket. "Where did you get this?"

"A little boutique just off Valencia, if I recall correctly."

"You're wearing it wrong."

"...sorry, what?"

"You're supposed to..." Lucas rolled his eyes. "There's a reason the back cinches. It corrects the line."

It seemed like such an odd observation to make, but Adrian just lifted his brows. "Do you want me to—" He caught himself, grinning. "No. Never mind. I didn't quite finish that one."

Lucas snagged another bite of his quiche, chewing, watching Adrian with narrowed eyes. "Close call."

"I've decided upon it, by the way." Adrian had to admit, talking to Lucas was easier than he expected, even given the strange rules on questioning. Their conversation was as easy and light and lovely as the man himself. "Are you curious what I mean to ask you?"

"I imagine I won't have to wait long." Lucas set his fork down and sipped his coffee, sitting back. "What would you like to know?"

Adrian hummed, peering at him curiously, trying to gather *anything* from his expression. Anything at all that might give a hint to Lucas' answer before Adrian's precious question was asked.

"Would you mind if I accompanied you to Tula's tennis match tomorrow?" He smiled slightly. "Watching her triumph over larger children would be even more entertaining in person, I imagine."

"...You want to go see a children's tennis match?" Implacable. Watching him. "Or you want to know if I would mind?"

"I'd like to go with you, yes." Adrian raised a brow. "May I?"

"Why?"

"I already told you."

"Adrian..." Lucas said his name like a sigh. It was a surprisingly beautiful sound, even when it was bemused. "I'll talk to her tonight and see what she says."

Adrian beamed, digging into his quiche. "I suppose that satisfies our arrangement."

"You're lucky I'm a serial killer. Most fellows wouldn't entertain the notion."

"Which notion?"

"Allowing strange men from cemeteries to invite themselves to their daughters' sporting events."

"We've had brunch now." Adrian lifted a brow. "I'm hardly strange."

"Fair enough." Lucas bowed his head over his coffee cup. "I had forgotten the power of the almighty brunch."

"Is there another invitation you'd prefer to the ones I've made?"

"I'd prefer if you wore that jacket the way it was intended. I'd prefer if you told your friends that grief takes time and they should suck it up and support you." Lucas wrinkled his nose. "If you want to come and watch my daughter sweep the court with ragamuffin children, I have no problem with it so long as she is amenable to the suggestion."

What was with the repeated mention of the jacket? Was Lucas just a stickler for fashion? So was Adrian, really, but he'd grown lax since he'd lost Seron. Or was there something else? He could hardly ask the man. Adrian slipped the jacket off his shoulders and buttoned the back, before sliding it back on. "And for the record, they do support me. My friends." He exhaled slowly. "They always seem so damned *sad* around me, though. It gets tiring."

"Did you tell them that?"

"Of course not."

Lucas tilted his head to the side, silent but for the slurp of curdled egg yolk in black coffee.

"No wonder you wouldn't tell me how you took your coffee." Adrian wrinkled his nose.

"Would you like to try it?"

"Under no circumstances."

"My CO used to pour raw eggs in and let them cook in the boiling coffee. Two each morning. A complete breakfast in a cup."

"You didn't have to emulate him," Adrian sniffed. "Mine wore socks with sandals. Horrifying."

"I was trying to try things without judgment at the time. I was grieving." Lucas shrugged. "I enjoyed it."

"Did you try other things without judgment?" Adrian studied that careful, measured expression. Every word considered, every move mastered. "When you were grieving, or otherwise?"

"A wide array." Lucas smiled slightly, spinning the coffee with his spoon. "I highly recommend it."

"I've become rather attached to my peculiarities." Adrian finished his quiche and pushed his plate aside. "I wasn't certain you'd answer my question, given I've asked my quota."

"I said three *about* me." Lucas rolled his eyes, finishing his coffee, the cup clicking as he set it back on the table. The residue of the yolk still clung to the side of the white ceramic on the inside, making Adrian's stomach churn. "Do try to keep up."

"You should get brunch with men you met at the cemetery more often." No betrayal in brunch, Adrian reminded himself silently. He raised his brows, smiling slightly over his glass of water. Exceptionally pleasant to be seen. "Because they're dashing and it would please your parents."

"Tell me something I don't know." Lucas meticulously sliced his quiche into strips sideways with his fork. "Unfortunately, I've found that men who linger in cemeteries often smell funny and have a predilection for horror films."

"Oh, *horror* films, no."

"Oh, *yes*," Lucas assured him with a slightly evil grin. "Or they wear a whole assortment of talismans that bear no meaning to them."

"Then are you meaning to say I smell funny? The other two certainly don't apply, but I hadn't thought you'd gotten close enough to tell."

"I've grown more cautious over time," Lucas said, smirking. "You don't know me well, but I tend to say what I mean."

"...Do you intend to make a repeat of this particular exchange, then?"

"Which part of it?"

"The one where we order food and I watch you slurp eggs from mugs?"

"Oh." Lucas peered at his plate. "I'm not averse to the notion. Are you expressing an interest?"

"Would I ask if I weren't?"

"Possibly."

Adrian popped the crisped edge of his croissant in his mouth. "I like quiche and company that's just the right side of macabre."

"Very well," Lucas agreed.

Adrian smiled, dropping his napkin on his plate as he was filled with a sense of relief. "Well. That was as tasty as I remember." He tilted his head to the side. "Do let me know about the match, hm?"

Lucas held out his hand, lifting a brow. "Phone."

"A man of few words." Adrian fished his phone out of his pocket and unlocked it, handing it over. "There."

Lucas tapped on the screen with his thumb, then called himself, handing the phone back. "It's at twelve-thirty tomorrow. If she says yes."

"Twelve-thirty." Adrian nodded, putting it away. "And it's Sharp. Please don't put me in your phone as 'Adrian Cemetery'."

"I've been walking by your family's mausoleum at least once a month for ten years," Lucas smiled. "I'm familiar with your surname."

"Fair enough." More often than not, Adrian felt he haunted the remains of his old life like a specter, every interaction shaded a slightly different hue than when Seron had been alive. There was still a tight coil in his chest, telling him that coming here was wrong, sitting here, eating and chatting with a stranger under the blooming trees. But Lucas' smile warmed him in a way he hadn't thought was still possible, as did the simple acknowledgment that he'd been noticed.

There was no betrayal in brunch, Adrian reminded himself, closing his eyes and breathing in the scent of the sweet blossoms of spring. Seron would have been glad to see him in the sunshine, thawing out after a cold, dark, lonely winter.

CHAPTER THREE

ADRIAN

Adrian's boots clicked against the polished wood floor of his condo as he paced. The place felt empty, echoing. Thin tendrils of guilt tightened around his abdomen, turning coffee and pastries and the little bit of egg he'd eaten into bricks in his stomach, as he stared at the fridge and the little crayon drawings Seron's niece Palanna had sent as a response when they'd asked her parents if she'd be their flower girl. She'd worn little auburn braids and a dress the color of ocean waves on a sunny day.

It had been so simple to relax for a moment, to forget, to allow himself to talk without the tightness in his chest that had accompanied every day for the past months. So easy to flirt with a random stranger who'd shown him a sliver of kindness.

Had it not been enough, those minutes under the bright awning? Taking the flowers from Tula's hands like he'd taken them from Palanna years before? Their energies were the same—laughing, giddy expressions, and wide, curious eyes—even if that was where the resemblances ended. He'd only had the pleasure of meeting Palanna twice. Once at his wedding, once at Seron's funeral; Seron's sister hadn't been overly pleased with their match and then, once Adrian had fought her on where they would bury Seron's body... Well, that had ended that. He wasn't likely to see either of them again. He'd thought if he kept Seron near, buried him using the old methods, a part of him might still be close. But either it hadn't worked, or the man was set on ignoring him. Each time he visited the sepulcher, Adrian maintained a small flicker of hope that his husband might deign to speak with him. Each time he left, that light was dimmed, leaving only disappointment in its wake.

He passed his liquor cabinet with a grimace. At least the brandy would dull the knife in his chest that made breathing next to impossible. Adrian poured himself a glass, letting the alcohol burn, noticing a small, measured improvement in the tightness of his throat. Another little step in the direction towards normalcy, he told himself, dragging a blanket to the balcony to sit and watch the sun travel across the sky.

San Francisco had never been Seron's home and now he was locked in a marble tomb here with people who would've hated him for marrying another man, all because of Adrian's selfishness. Seron had hardly spent much time in the city when he'd been alive, though he had enjoyed their apartment overlooking the swell of the Pacific; he'd said the ocean and the sky bound the whole world together, and that each breath held a tiny taste of home; that he could hear whispers in the wind if he listened hard enough; that raindrops and snowflakes were kisses from the people he missed, and would be left over long after everyone they'd ever met was gone. Ashes into sunflowers, everything returning to the sky and the earth and the sea.

At his funeral, the priest had said Seron had been too good to remain on this earth long. Adrian was certain the berobed man said something similar about everyone, but in Seron's case, it had been especially true. Seron had been wounded protecting a little girl and her family from shrapnel when an IED exploded, one of his squad had explained, and had died from the sepsis that had followed, even when they sent in the best of the best to try and save him.

He wondered if the little girl Seron had saved had smiled like Palanna and Tula. For an uncomfortably long time, a small, terrible part of him had wished she had died, if that would have meant that his husband could have come home on his own feet instead of in a casket.

Selfish. Adrian had always been selfish. His father had said it enough times and Adrian had proven it just as many. He took a sip of the brandy, not tasting anything other than fire, but at least it distracted him from the burning in his eyes.

The sun was falling again when he rose from his perch. Little steps. It was all he could ask of himself. His hands had stopped shaking.

Inside, a single text message blinked on his phone's notification screen: numbers and letters, an address. No note. Nothing but the name attached to the message. The Raven from the Cemetery.

Raven? Adrian traced the edge of the screen with his finger. Lucas hadn't forgotten, for what it was worth. And Tula had apparently approved.

Little steps.

He unlocked the phone and tapped out a response: *Do either of you like flowers?* Adrian rolled his eyes. That was far too stupid and sentimental. He deleted the message and wrote another: *Thank you.*

Minutes of silence. Then three little dots followed by the utilitarian reply he should have expected from the man: an emoji of a thumbs up followed by a black bird.

Of course. Adrian sighed, scrubbing his hand through his hair. *I'll see you tomorrow, then.*

Nothing. He could picture the man nodding as he had in the parking lot, walking away from his device without a word. Maybe humming a wordless tune under his breath as he considered, noting the information and tucking it away for safekeeping.

When it was beyond clear that was all the response Adrian was going to get, he slid his phone away across the countertop, picked up the book he'd been trying to read for months, and began his evening ritual of staring at the same two pages until his eyes blurred and he fell asleep on the couch.

The tennis club buzzed when he arrived, cars hunting for parking spaces in the narrow lot of the large blue warehouse that housed the courts. Inside, it was freezing and smelled like rubber. Parents shuttled children to and fro. Adults without children carried rackets and bags, signing in on tablets or reserving their courts for later. Through the wide windows overlooking the bright green courts, Adrian could see groups of twos and fours playing and hear the crack of the balls as they bounced. At the far end, three courts were packed with tiny boys and girls running in a circle, holding their rackets over their heads, while a small set of bleachers was sparsely filled by observers. He spotted Lucas even from this distance, standing on the top riser, leaning against the wall, arms crossed, eyes on the court. He stood out more starkly, still and studied beside shuffling figures and chattering couples. The Raven from the Cemetery. He certainly appeared avian, perched high above everyone else.

Adrian shifted his bouquet of gladioli and scattered greenery to his other arm, crossing the odd rubber ground with more confidence than he felt. He let the chatter wash over him, filling him with the sort of serenity he'd always found in crowds, and ascended the creaking bleachers, holding out the brightly colored bouquet for Lucas, hoping the warmth on his cheeks wasn't visible. "They're still warming up?" he asked softly, watching a girl a few inches taller than Tula dive to return a ball. "The parking lot was pretty full; I had to circle a few times."

"So did everyone, apparently," Lucas muttered, peering at the bouquet curiously. "We're still waiting on two kids." He sniffed at the flowers. "I told them we should just start and they can shuffle in another bracket but that wouldn't be equitable." He looked up. "She'll like these. Did you eat anything? I have snacks."

"A late breakfast, but I imagine I'll get hungry." Adrian glanced around the stands, crossing in front of Lucas to take a seat next to where he stood. "How long do these things typically last?"

"Days. You didn't bring a pillow?" Lucas smirked, resting the flowers atop the beige cloth bag and fetching a small reusable bag of baby carrots out, offering them to Adrian. "About two hours if we're lucky and we get started soon. The bathroom's upstairs next to the gift shop." He sighed, softening as Tula cackled from the far court, spinning in circles next to a few other children. "You don't have to stay the whole time. She's delighted you wanted to see her play at all."

"Truly?" Adrian raised a brow, studying him. "To be fair, she has seemed delighted by most everything, during our short acquaintance."

"True enough," Lucas snorted, smiling fondly as he checked his phone absently.

"Do you want me to stay?" Adrian asked softly. Why was it seemingly so difficult to maintain Lucas' attention? "If you've changed your mind—"

"You're fine."

A sharp whistle pierced the air and the children ran to stand on one of the white lines at the edge of the court as the last two stumbled to join them with frazzled-looking parents.

Lucas sank to the bleacher beside him, hands clasped loosely between his knees as he watched.

The players were between the ages of four and six, most of them with rackets that looked too big for them, and the rules had been softened for their age group. Halfway through her opening game, the little boy Tula was playing against fell and started crying. Without a second thought, Tula abandoned her racket, leaving it to crash against the ground, running to the other side of the net to hug her opponent.

Lucas hissed under his breath, staring daggers at the referee who attempted to intervene, but his daughter was skipping back to her side of the net, smiling encouragingly, before he had a chance to go down and argue with the woman in charge.

"She has a tender heart, your girl," Adrian murmured, glancing at him with a smile. "Is she always like that?"

"No one is always like that. She once poured her spaghetti in my lap and screamed until her throat was sore." Lucas smirked, resting his chin on his hands to watch the end of the match. "Fortunately, she often leans towards compassion."

"Are you sure you didn't deserve it?" There was something comforting about Lucas' aloof, quiet demeanor. Unassuming, largely, as though he expected to slip through life unnoticed, watching from a distance. "Maybe she didn't like the spaghetti."

"She was infuriated at the time, as I recall, that she wasn't allowed to watch a third straight hour of Eamonn the Elf."

"Eamonn the—" Adrian chuckled, the smell of fresh flowers wafting towards him. "That *would* incite one to violence, wouldn't it?"

"She was displeased. We have since reached an accord." He leaned forward in his place as Tula set up to serve. She faulted on the first but aced the second through before the red-cheeked boy had a chance to swing his racket like a baseball bat and promptly land on his rear. "That's my girl!" Lucas grinned fiercely.

Tula tumbled back to the lower rung of bleachers after she won her first match, waiting with her friends while they sorted the brackets for the next sets.

"Halpern," a woman's voice snapped sharply.

Lucas glanced down at a scowling woman climbing up the bleachers towards them. "Monica," he greeted her with equal warmth. That is to say: none.

"Did you see that travesty?" Monica asked, gesturing back towards the court.

"Take a long walk off a short pier," Lucas murmured in much the same light and easy tone as some would say 'hello'.

The woman's face darkened, her hands clenching. "It's wrong for a girl to put boys down like that. It's her place in this world to lift—"

"I will lift you into the parking lot if you don't stop talking to me." Lucas smiled mildly. "And if you try speaking to my daughter today as you did last month, I will let the coach know, and we'll see how many more opportunities your son has to lose."

"I'm not particularly well-versed in the arena of youth sporting events, but it appeared to me that they sorted it out themselves on the court," Adrian said, lifting a brow. "And by your reasoning, I imagine it's *your* place to allow children to stand up for themselves. Builds character, I've heard."

Monica turned dark brown eyes on him, narrowed and irritable as live wires. "No one asked you."

"Three." Lucas stared at the back of his hand.

"I will talk to the coach myself."

"Two."

"You set her straight, Halpern, or someone will."

"One." Lucas slowly unfolded, rising to his feet, and the woman huffed, stalking back down to the front row of the bleachers at the other end from the children. He watched until she'd taken her seat, then eased back down. "Thank you for trying. She's just mad her son lost."

"That woman is a walking discrimination suit waiting to happen," Adrian muttered under his breath as he stared at her from across the court. "All over tennis? They're what... *Five?*"

Lucas chuckled wryly. "Welcome to the wild world of children's sports." He glanced at Adrian. "Tennis has always been a violent business. Two French kings died as a result of the game. At least in this case, no one is likely to perish."

"Maybe some of them should," Adrian muttered, snapping a carrot in half with his teeth. "You know, my father would've—" he stopped himself, clearing his throat. "It's probably best I don't suggest emulating that man."

A quick flick of a curious gaze, a lift of a brow. "You're in a fine fiddle today." Lucas leaned back against the wall, crossing his arms, as other people's children ran about the courts and Tula cheered along with her friends. "What would your father have done?"

"He certainly wouldn't have instilled a false sense of superiority in me because of my gender," Adrian sniffed. "I slipped during a swimming meet once and hit my head on the diving board. Took a fairly bad concussion. The coaches had to call off the competition entirely to get my father to take me to the hospital." He shrugged helplessly. "I suppose I shouldn't speak to how others decide to raise their children. I feel a tinge of pity for the boy, that's all."

"You should. He hates tennis," Lucas murmured, and Adrian followed his gaze to Tula's blond braided pigtails dancing as the girl cheerfully played some sort of hand-clapping game with the same boy she'd bested in the first round. "He spent a whole lesson one time blowing bubbles with his racket because the coach didn't want him to feel left out while the others practiced. It was rather lovely." He hesitated, then rested his hand lightly on Adrian's shoulder. "I'm glad you weren't decapitated by a diving board." In the cold of the courts, the air conditioning working itself into a froth battling the heat of the afternoon outside, his hand felt unnaturally warm. When he took it away, Adrian could feel the outline of his fingers for a lingering moment.

"My husband, Seron, used to say I treated children like smaller adults," Adrian said quietly, not entirely knowing why. "I didn't think it was at all strange to do so but... they're not entirely the same. Children say what they want; they're damned good at it. And they forgive."

"Adults don't forgive?"

"...not all of us." Adrian glanced down at his hands, missing Lucas' hand on his shoulder. "Not half as well as we might like."

"You are very critical of yourself." Lucas peered at him. "For someone so fond of themselves."

"Hush," Adrian gave him a half smile. "Don't let me hear you say such things about me."

"Alright. Who would you forgive, that you haven't as well as you'd like?"

"I..." He cleared his throat as an icy pang of grief left him breathless. Adrian frowned. "I shouldn't have brought it up, perhaps."

"Why not? You don't know me. I don't know anyone you know. Think of me as your priest. I'm very good at keeping secrets."

Adrian believed him; Lucas sat there in profile, concentrating on the crack of tennis balls and the skid of sneakers, but he was also listening to Adrian, not only hearing him.

"Did I overstep again?" Lucas asked after a moment, his hand returning to rest gingerly against Adrian's shoulder.

"No, you..." Adrian measured his breaths, focusing on the expansion of his diaphragm and the pressure of Lucas' palm. "A priest, is it?"

"Or if not that, a more agnostic confessor." Lucas glanced at Adrian's way, pursing his lips just so.

"You do that quite often, you know."

"Do what?"

"Make that face." Adrian lifted his brows, reaching to pluck a fallen petal off of Lucas' lap. "Bemused and mildly irritated."

Lucas stilled like a cat. Waiting. Watching; his gaze focused on some middle distance where he might have seen everything or nothing. "I suppose I am both by turns." Lucas' gaze sharpened, focusing on him as it had the day before, as though he were peeling back the layers to stare directly into Adrian's mind. The feeling was unnerving, making the hairs on his arms stand up on end. "At very exciting moments, I even ramp it up to amused and excessively irritated."

"What do you find *very* exciting, I wonder? People who threaten your daughter, certainly." Adrian tilted his head to the side, feeling something odd tickle his senses. Did Lucas possess the same gifts as his daughter? Or was Adrian just being overly sensitive? "Monica seemed to elicit the less pleasant option of the two."

"That was my amused face," Lucas asserted, deadpan. "You couldn't tell?"

"Oh?" Adrian quirked his brows. The sensation he'd felt briefly had already dissipated. Overly sensitive, definitely, but that tracked. Adrian had become overly sensitive in a thousand other ways these past months, why not magically, too? "Then I wonder how you look when you're irritated."

"No one's lived to tell the tale," Lucas whispered dramatically. "You'll have to let me know what it looks like. If you survive."

"I'm made of stern stuff," Adrian told him with a wink, holding the flower petal out to him. "I might surprise you."

"Might you?" Lucas accepted the petal, turning it over in his hands as he looked back down at the court. "I suppose we'll have to wait and see."

"You seem incredibly patient." Adrian followed his gaze, watching Tula bounce to her feet again, racket in hand. "I hope you don't mind."

The little girl looked up at the bleachers for the first time since he'd arrived, wearing a broad toothy smile as she waved at them delightedly. "*Marcet sine adversario virtus*!" Lucas called.

Seneca the Younger. Adrian recognized the words only due to the impatient days he'd spent with his Latin tutor as a boy, learning the language that underpinned vast swaths of magical theory and alchemy, carefully sounding out the syllables of the famed statesman's philosophy on Stoicism. The man quoted Seneca off-hand? Not only knew the Latin—'virtue dies without an adversary'—but seemed to have imparted the knowledge of both the language and the phrase to Tula, who spun, half-hopping, and gave them a thumbs up before skipping to her starting line.

"Mind what?" Lucas asked.

It took a moment for Adrian to recall what they'd been discussing previously. It wasn't common for people to teach their five-year-olds Hellenistic philosophy. But then again, Lucas was proving to be less and less common by the moment. "I meant to say: I hope that you don't mind waiting to test my mettle with your deadly expressions," Adrian explained, clapping lightly as Tula served an ace. "I appreciate you letting me tag along again. It's nice to be around people who don't expect anything of me."

"On the contrary, I expect a great deal. All your teeth, for instance. Free training in engineering. What else... Potentially a kidney."

"A *kidney*? Oh, you've upped the ante."

"You only *need* one." Lucas smirked, his gaze fixed on the court. "What if I get hungry?"

Adrian lifted the bag of baby carrots. "I'll trade you. Carrots for my organs."

"No take-backs." He stood up, whooping as Tula scored another point, then settled back in. "Besides, I have higher-value snacks. Date balls. Marshmallow squares. Carrots are for chumps."

"He offers me chump snacks," Adrian sniffed, "and I brought you both flowers."

"Both?" Lucas glanced at him, a perplexed lift of his brows.

"They *were* for both of you." Adrian huffed. "Now I'm not so sure."

"Oh." Lucas' cheekbones were more pronounced with his lips pursed in confusion. His emerald eyes became hummingbirds again, darting and flitting. "...thank you."

"You could tell me the kinds you like so I'd know," Adrian suggested, flexing his hands in his pockets. "For next time."

"She likes peonies." He narrowed his eyes, focusing on the side of Tula's head. "And weeds."

"...and you?"

Lucas exhaled slowly. "I'm past the age of public matches and performances."

"What do you mean by that?"

"I..." Lucas blinked rapidly, turning the petal between his fingers again. "I don't know why you'd want to—"

"You already sussed me out." Adrian pressed his lips together. "I'm alone and I'd rather not be."

"Yes, but... I don't need to be *bribed*. I'm happy to spend time with you." Lucas frowned. "Not—That is—At least until your usual companions become less obtuse and can muster up the courage to go with you to visit your husband." He cleared his throat. "You aren't a burden."

"Oh." Adrian grinned, peering back at the court. "It doesn't need to be *bribery*. You could just—" He swallowed, cheeks warming. "Ah. Well. If you don't want me to—" Had he presumed something about Lucas' interest? His inclinations? Was he being overly sensitive *again*? "Thank you, regardless."

"If I don't want you to what?" Lucas asked under his breath.

"It doesn't matter." Adrian risked a glance in Lucas' direction. He looked so befuddled that Adrian might as well have told him that the ceiling was actively falling on them.

"...right." Lucas stared at the petal, his head snapping up as others cheered around him. The second court over had finished their match. "I—Would you look at that backhand? Terrible form. You'd think they were only five. How will they ever get into the Olympics?"

"How indeed." Adrian followed his gaze back to the children wrapping up their games. What he wouldn't give for a hint of insight into the man's thoughts. Was it so strange for him to want to... What? Have someone to speak with he didn't know from before? That was all it was, right? A desire for company? A reason to interact with humans again outside of work who didn't handle him as though he might break? He smiled as the little blonde girl gave her opponent a hug and a high five after she won her second match and skipped towards her father.

"Did you see?" Tula cried, leaping onto Lucas' lap.

"I did." Her father smiled, smoothing her hair back from her face, and tucking wisps back into her braid. "Well played."

She grinned. "You said I get ice cream. Hi, Mr. Adrian!"

"After the match." Lucas bounced her, his expression softening as he held his daughter.

"I'm done, though."

"Everyone else isn't," Lucas reminded her patiently.

"Mr. Adrian, do you want to get ice cream? I won all my matches."

"I saw! Very impressive." He couldn't help but return her sweet, earnest smile. "Though I liked best how you helped the little fellow who fell, I think. That certainly seems worthy of ice cream, once they're all finished up."

"Adrian brought you flowers, in confidence of your success," Lucas informed her.

"For me?" Tula asked, beaming and slapping her palms to her cheeks. "They're so pretty!" She hugged the bouquet. "Thank you, Mr. Adrian!"

"You're very welcome." Adrian nodded. "Thank you for letting me come watch you play, and for the invitation to brunch the other day. It was very sweet of you."

"I'm sweet! Did you hear, Papa?" She gazed up at Lucas, practically squealing in excitement. "I'm sweet and I have flowers and Mr. Adrian's coming to ice cream!"

"I'm sitting right here," Lucas murmured dryly, rubbing his ear with a dramatic wince.

"If you don't mind, of course." Adrian turned to him. "Do you, Lucas?"

"I—No. It's fine." He patted Tula on the head. "Don't you want to sit with your friends, sunbeam?"

"Can I bring my flowers?"

"May I," her father gently corrected her grammar and Tula rolled her eyes, wearing an expression very similar to one Adrian had seen her father wear multiple times already.

"*May I* bring my flowers?"

"Yes."

Tula hopped to her feet, skipping away to show off her prize. By the time the matches were over, half the blossoms had ended up in the other girls' hair and her own.

When they arrived at the ice cream parlor, Tula made a point of telling every single person she met that Mr. Adrian had given her the flowers, pointing at her head, and Adrian was granted an additional scoop for his generosity.

"—and then Mabel told Anabelle that Patrice thought her socks were an ugly color, so we all agreed to wear yellow on Tuesday and I want mine to be the same color *exactly*."

Lucas studied her over the strawberry scoop of his cone. "Mustard yellow."

"Yes," she chirped.

"Wonderful," Lucas sighed.

"You aren't a fan of mustard yellow?" Adrian scraped off the smallest morsel of his cinnamon ice cream and tapped his forehead with the tip of his finger. "Noted."

"It's a perfectly fine color, but it doesn't suit everyone." Lucas bit a slice of frozen fruit from the cream.

"But you made that whole dress out of it for Ms. Estrada," Tula pouted.

Lucas squinted at her. "You want a dress by Tuesday?"

She smiled brightly, licking whipped cream off her spoon. "I won *all* my matches!"

"You know Cymbeline Estrada?" Adrian let the mingled salted caramel and cinnamon scoops melt on his tongue. "And you made her a *dress*? A yellow... You know, believe I saw that one in person!"

"Oh gods, did you?" Lucas asked, horrified. "She made me do that to the sleeves; I told her it looked as though she'd been stung by bees."

"She was exceedingly pleased with how it turned out. Wore it to a charity gala, if I recall correctly." Adrian smiled sincerely, impressed, sugar on his tongue. "That was yours?"

"Possibly." Lucas shook his head at Tula's impish grin. "I'm not sending you to school in silk brocade."

"Okay." She grinned. "Can I go play Ms. Pac-Man?"

Lucas huffed, fishing for change from his pocket to pour into her palm. "Nefarious."

"So you know Cymbeline," Adrian repeated as Tula skipped to the arcade. "I'm surprised I haven't seen you before; I visit her fairly regularly."

"Do you? I don't *know* her. She liked some of my designs and had me stitch a couple of things for her. That's all." Lucas peered at him. "Odd company for a professor to keep: philanthropists and celebrities."

"I suppose it would be if I weren't somewhat of a philanthropist myself." Adrian shrugged. "To my surprise, my father decided to keep me in his will. No sense in keeping a family fortune if you've no family to speak of."

Lucas watched him quietly, a small furrow between his brows. "I'm sorry."

"It was a bit of a relief when he passed, as horrible as it sounds." Adrian pressed his lips together, exhaling sharply. "I'd hoped for some sort of closure before my father died, but... One can't have everything."

"No. I suppose one can't." Lucas had broken a piece of his cone off and was nibbling on the edge like a mouse. "Do you want to talk about him?"

"My confessor, eh?" Adrian shook his head. "No. It's too early in the day to speak much about my father and I haven't had nearly enough brandy. Perhaps another time."

Lucas hummed under his breath, his eyes narrowed slightly with unspoken questions, then returned his attention to his ice cream. "Aside from the obsession with flouncy shoulders, she was very nice. Cymbeline, I mean."

"She is." Adrian raised a brow. "Is that what your work is, then? Making flouncy shoulders for celebrities and philanthropists?"

"Precisely. Shoulders only. I leave the rest to the peons."

"Good for you. Delegation." Adrian swirled his spoon, catching ice cream as it melted along the sides. "And you enjoy it?"

"Usually." Lucas squinted. "I enjoy it more when people wear my work as intended. But one can't control everything."

"They'd be foolish to try." Adrian studied his expression. Nonchalant, but still somehow on edge. Comfortable being discomfited. "I wouldn't mind seeing your work if you were in the mood to show it."

"You've seen it." He sniffed. "You ruined the line of my jacket."

"Your... You mean the one I wore to brunch?" Adrian blinked, lifting his gaze. "Why didn't you *tell* me?"

"I told you what the belt was for."

"I fixed it when you—"

"I noticed. It was much better."

Adrian sighed, rubbing his temples. "Have you been holding that against me?"

Lucas pursed his lips. "That would be churlish."

"I like that one; I wear it all of the time. It's surprisingly durable for how comfortable it is and just wide enough in the shoulders."

When Lucas was proud, his eyes softened and glittered. Who would have guessed? "Of course." He plucked at the paper wrapping of the cone. "Did you pick up anything else?"

"It's remarkably breathable and I'm rather fond of the way you drew attention to the stitching on the collar—"

"From the boutique, Adrian. *Philomela*. Did you pick up anything else?"

A shiver went through his spine at the sound of his name on Lucas' lips. Was... Damn, but he liked the shimmer of those green eyes and the way his lips barely curved when he smiled. Maybe not mere companionship. Maybe... Adrian blinked, trying to recall the question. "I... not that day. Just the jacket."

"Hm." Lucas eyed him critically. "You would look good in one of my suits. The three pieces." He tilted his head to the side. "Though it might end up distracting your students. You could stop by the shop."

"Next Saturday?" Adrian asked quietly, meeting his gaze. "I'll try not to mess up your lines, but I'd feel better if you were there to correct me."

"...as you will." Lucas lowered his gaze back to his dessert, but that pleased half-smirk lingered on his lips. "I can schedule you for a fitting during judo."

"I'd like that," Adrian murmured, feeling a blush warm his cheeks. "If it isn't too much trouble."

"I wouldn't have offered if it were." They sat together in the ice cream parlor with the tinny sound of the jukebox warring with the arcade in the back. Lucas dabbed his lips with a napkin and folded it into a small square. "Anything exciting coming up this week?"

"I'm not certain what your definition of *exciting* is, but I'm giving a public lecture at the Central Library on Thursday. I think there are supposed to be demonstrations for the kids, too," Adrian added, then cleared his throat, returning to the ever-growing puddle in his bowl. "That is to say, if next weekend is too distant a date for you, you're welcome to come. The both of you."

"I think demonstrations meant for university students might be a little over Tula's head," Lucas murmured.

"No, I meant the little ones. The students at the engineering school are running an event, wind tunnels and paper airplanes and the like." Adrian shrugged, smiling over his spoon. "I'm only tangentially involved; they did all of the work."

"What is the lecture on?"

"Oh! I'm talking about my research for about ten minutes, but the focus is to get the public interested in science and engineering, so... More stories about flying, less science."

Lucas hummed low, inclining his head slightly. "I'll talk to Tula about it and see how the week takes shape." He glanced towards the games where Tula was balanced on a stepping stool beating at the buttons with her palms. "Thank you for the invitation. And the company. And the flowers."

"You're welcome," Adrian exhaled slowly, reaching his hand across the table. "I *like* you, Luke. I'm not certain if I'm ready, or... if you're—" He broke off, lifting his gaze to try and discern anything from the fellow's guarded expression. Interested? Available? Not just humoring a grieving man as a charity project? "In any case, it's no trouble."

Lucas studied his hand for a long beat; the man's eyes were as indecipherable as ancient glyphs carved into dark green tablets, a thousand flitting thoughts all in foreign tongues. Perhaps more Latin, Adrian mused, or perhaps Adrian had misread the entire situation and the poor man was just a straight single father trying to be kind.

Then Lucas rested his hand atop Adrian's. "When you're more certain. If you are. We'll see." Lucas smiled slightly. "Yes?"

"Yes," Adrian agreed, the sensation of sunbeams warming him to his toes. Not a misunderstanding then. He thought of the quote Lucas had called like a battle cry to his daughter and remembered a fragment of his studies from that dark, lonely library of his youth. Seneca the Younger and the Stoics and their prime virtues.

Wisdom, courage, and moderation. Perhaps it was a clue, a step towards unlocking the mystery of the man who was now holding his hand so gently. "Of course. I'll let you know."

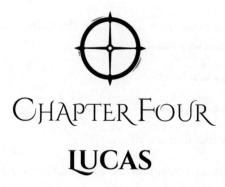

Chapter Four

Lucas

Tula was as giddy as a fairy, wiggling and dancing through the rest of the day including her bedtime routine with the remains of her bouquet clasped tight in her hand. Petals had trailed her throughout their little house as she sang into the blossoms. Lucas chuckled as he swept them up in the dim lights after he'd put her to bed.

Flowers.

Why had he never thought to bring her flowers? Ice cream and dance parties and make-your-own sundae nights, but flowers... Maybe because he'd thought of them for so long as a tribute to the dead and Tula was very much alive, even if she did hear the whispers from the other side.

He should have known better than to call her his angel.

Lucas' heart gave a pang as he finished rinsing the dishes and loading their dishwasher, then rested a hip back against the counter in the still quiet of the evening. Adrian had been sweet to think of her. Of them both.

He slipped a petal from his pocket, thumbing it. Soft, but not fragile, still smelling faintly sweet.

Adrian called him Luke.

No one called him Luke.

No one gave him flowers, either.

It wasn't that he'd been hurting for company. He had plenty of attention, when and where he chose it. Apps were exquisite things. Like ordering a pizza, Lucas could time a rendezvous with a perfect stranger who wanted nothing from him other than sweat and sighs and slick, with enough time for a shower before he went to collect his dollop of sunshine.

He didn't have *time* for more, he told himself. Not with his business growing alongside his daughter.

So why was he considering this... This... He sniffed the petal, frowning in the dark. Because Adrian seemed so sad and lost and lonely. Because Adrian had defended Tula when Monica had been a menace. Because Adrian spoke to Tula with such kindness.

Because Adrian was handsome, damn him. Ridiculously handsome. Infuriatingly so. As though he'd been concocted in a machine purely to tantalize Lucas' various fantasies. Gentle and strong at the same time. Sculpted but smooth. And that *mustache*. He laughed to himself, shaking his head. That mustache told him that Adrian might be at least as vain as Lucas himself was. For better or worse.

Was that enough?

Maybe he was overthinking this. He knew he did sometimes. After all, the man was still in mourning. A little time and attention wouldn't hurt either of them if it could be managed with minimal harm. Tula liked him. It would be good for her to have exposure to different kinds of people and different experiences. Engineers and pilots and professors.

Lucas walked through the house, turning off lights and checking the doors and windows, the bells that warded evil spirits from the entrances, and the symbols and Latin spells etched in chalk and power that he'd hidden behind shelves and under the rugs to shield and absorb the resonance of the gifts used inside their home. The gifts they shared, he and his daughter. The gifts that made him and Tula who they were, yet also made them vulnerable to the world that feared them. Just in case, Lucas unbound the talisman from his wrist that masqueraded as a braided leather bracelet and spun it in each room, recycling whatever trace energy they'd left behind to be stored in the raw garnets and sapphires.

When he finally climbed into bed, he looked up the lecture Adrian had mentioned and sent the link to a few of the parents from Tula's class. If they were going to go, they might as well take some of the kids together and make an outing of it. That way it would feel less like anything that could be categorized as a date because it definitely wasn't that.

What's this? was the lightning-fast response he received from Anara Murphy, mother of three, owner of a little flower shop a few blocks away, and the only other person with any sense in the Parent Teacher Association. Three little dots appeared and a moment later, a screenshot of Adrian's face came back to him with a winking emoji. *A little something for the adults, too. I think I've seen him before. Always orders sunflowers.*

He knew. He'd seen the bundles carried into the neighboring mausoleum many times, from a distance. Lucas rested his head back against the headboard and sighed.

'I like you, Luke.' Simple, sweet words. 'I like you.' He couldn't remember the last time he'd heard them. Quiet and vulnerable, an offering. 'I'm not certain if I'm ready.'

No. Not a date. Just a lonely man who found some hope in Tula's bright gaze and Lucas' lack of pity.

Lucas wondered what Seron must have been like to engender that much devotion and heartbreak. Someone to match the fellow he'd married, he supposed. Handsome and clever. Good.

Lucas was not a good person. He tried, sometimes, but goodness had never come naturally to him. His parents had been good. Selfless, generous, and pure-hearted like their granddaughter.

Lucas could ask Tula, he supposed, what she'd learned about Adrian's late husband, but that was grotesque. He couldn't use her gifts that way. He never wanted her to be used for her magic, never wanted her to think that was appropriate. And she had already told him far more about her ghostly friends than he wanted to know. Lucas rubbed a hand over his face. Two more times in the last week, he'd had to remind her that she couldn't run around *sharing* the stories about her deceased friends...

In any case, Lucas wasn't going to be drawn into Anara's web. Not on this one. Fantasizing about the sexy widower scientist would only lead to disappointment. Lucas could see for himself that Adrian wasn't ready. And Lucas wasn't sure he was either. Not for what Adrian might need if he were to ask... Comfort. Affection. Something steady and supportive, not just a casual fling. That was more than he'd tried in years. And yet. What harm would it do to watch a handsome man who bought sunflowers talk about clouds?

Lucas: *Did you want to bring the kids? The library isn't far away.*

More ellipses, followed by a quick, disappointing message.

Anara: *I've got a spin class booked for Thursday. Miss you, though! Maybe the zoo this weekend? Malcolm has been asking to go.* Another pause, then more typing. *Do you know what's up with yellow?*

Yellow? Oh. *Solidarity,* Lucas answered. *One of the girls at tennis was being teased. Do you need fabric assistance?* He didn't particularly like the idea of going just him and Tula; there was safety in numbers. But she was so excited about the idea. *Zoo Sunday?*

Anara: *Yep! Reggie's already put it on the calendar. Morning, so we don't miss Melanie's nap?*

Lucas: *Morning so we can have those orange banana smoothies for breakfast.*

Anara: *Yes!!! See you then!* Another brief pause. *Say hi to the handsome professor for me!*

Lucas narrowed his eyes at the tiny image of her at the top of the screen.

Lucas: *Say hi to the handsome spin instructor for me.*

Anara: *Should I give him your number?*

He huffed, rolling over to plug his phone in and turn off the light.

Lucas: *Goodnight, Anara.*

It buzzed again, shortly after he sent the message, showing a picture taken from a website of a handsome blond athlete standing shirtless in front of a bike.

Anara: *I'll find out if he's single for you. Don't worry.*

Lucas grumbled as he turned his face to the pillow and willed himself to sleep.

After a short while, the door to his bedroom creaked open and Tula stood under the frame, holding a stuffed deer. "Papa?" she sniffed, rubbing her eyes with her fist.

The half-drowse he'd been slowly sinking into abandoned him entirely. He eased up onto his elbow, watching her backlit from the hall light. "What's the matter, sunbeam?"

"You're still here." Her bottom lip trembled and she hugged her little creature tighter to her chest. "I had a dream they came to take me away and I hid under your bed and—" A wail broke loose as she shuddered, hair falling loose around her shoulders. "You weren't *here*."

"Where else would I be?" He sat up further, patting the bed beside him. "Come and check."

"What if you're a ghost?" She blinked at him, eyes red-rimmed and watery. "I don't want to know if you're a ghost."

"I'd tell you. I promise." He wiggled his fingers. "Come squeeze."

"Okay," she whispered, slipping across the floor in her bare feet to climb up on the bed next to him. She sniffed, reaching out her hand to touch his. "You're still here? Really real?"

"I think I am. Are you? Let's make sure. Is your favorite color still purple sparkles?"

"And pink swirls," she agreed, curling up against him. "I was afraid... I don't want you to go anywhere." Tula turned to him, eyes wide from her nightmare. "Okay?"

"I'm not going anywhere for a long, long time if I have any say." She was so small and soft. He pressed a kiss to her hair which still smelled faintly of lemons from her bath. "I don't want you to go anywhere either." Too harsh. He'd been too harsh with her. Trying to make her understand... "You know I'm not angry with you?"

"'Bout what?" She lifted her chin. "The mustard yellow dress with the ruffles and the little beads that look like petals?"

Far, far more detailed than their last discussion and nothing to do with her gift. He shook his head. "No. I'm not mad about that. Or about anything. I just want you to be careful, so that neither of us has to worry about anything happening to the other."

"About the magic?" Tula sniffled, hugging him close. "Can I not see my friends anymore?"

"Of course you can. You just need to stop talking to your living friends about your other ones. They need to stay separate. And now," he cursed himself, cuddling her closer. "Now isn't the time. I'm sorry. You're safe. I'm going to keep you safe, no matter what."

"Okay." She squeezed him tightly, shivering in his hold. "You'll stay and I'll stay and nobody will get taken anywhere?"

"Exactly." Come hell or high water. "Would you like to stay here? Or do you want to go back to your bed with Mugsy?"

"Mugsy and I wanna stay." She cuddled up to him on the pillows. "Can we?"

As though he could deny her when she was red-cheeked and sniffling. "Do you want to listen to the train noises?" Lucas asked quietly, tucking her beneath the covers and settling her and her stuffy cozily. "Or do you want to tell a story with me?"

"Story," she nodded. "About the fairies in the forest?"

"Very well. Once upon a time, when the trees were big and the sky was small, a little village of the oldest creatures lived beneath the mushroom caps in the forest."

"And they made their hats from rose petals and their pillows from dandelion fluffs." Tula sighed, snuggling closer to him. "And the girls wore mustard yellow with sequins and had tappy-toe shoes."

With *sequins* now, too. He smiled down at her. "They ran and jumped and played in the moss of the forest, collecting abandoned shells to gather dew drops in, and the hummingbirds would come to them for their wings to be shined."

"And the dragonflies and butterflies and fuzzy little moths?" Tula yawned, her eyelids half-closed.

"All of them. Shiny, shiny wings. Scrubbed to a gleam, so that the sunlight and the moonlight turn them all the colors of the rainbow as they fly," he agreed quietly, rubbing soothing circles in her hair.

"And when it rains they put on their boots and dance in the puddles and slide down the leaves like water slides." She glanced up at him. "When are we going to go ride the water slides again?"

"When the weather changes, so that the puddles are warm." He hugged her. "I need you to rest now so we can dream together, okay?"

"You have to sprinkle fairy dust on my eyelids." She tilted her chin expectantly. "So I have sweet dreams."

"Another helping of fairy dust coming right up. You have to close your eyes so they'll come out. You know how shy they are." He waited for her to snuggle against him, soft blue eyes hidden behind resting lids. "Dear little fairies, will you come again to bid our sunbeam goodnight? She has so much to do tomorrow and your dreams always delight." He whistled quietly, drawing energy from the air to warm his fingertips, which he brushed gently against her closed eyelids. "Thank you, fairies. We'll see you again tomorrow."

"I love you, Papa," she mumbled against his shoulder. "Night, night."

Mornings were chaos as per usual, with Tula struggling to find the match to her pink tennis shoe and then remembering belatedly to tell him about the snack day they were supposed to provide. Lucas dropped her at school with two bags of sliced apples and carrot sticks and then headed to his studio.

He'd named his studio *Philomela*—the Latin word for the evening songbird—because his mother had always called him her nightingale.

Peace and quiet...

No. Never that. There were calls to be made, negotiations for fabrics and supplies, and his assistant had hired a new seamstress who didn't entirely understand his aesthetic yet, so he had to go and teach her the methodology of his stitches. By the time lunch rolled around, Lucas realized he still hadn't eaten breakfast, but he'd had three cups of coffee and his hands were starting to shake.

"Taking a walk," Lucas announced, slinging his coat over his shoulders and slipping out into the crisp spring air.

A heavy fog lay over the streets, the city brash and sharp. He loved days like this when it seemed like he could wear the clouds on his sleeves. But Lucas was restless. He kept thinking of silver eyes in the stark lighting of the ice cream shop, and the way Adrian's hand had felt beneath his own. Lucas had meant to comfort, and he had, but he hadn't considered the reciprocal effect.

He had liked touching Adrian. He had wanted—suddenly and devilishly—to keep touching him. To see if the muscles in his forearms continued up to his shoulders. To feel them under his hands. He'd wanted to make the man blush again. Laugh. Shiver.

Lucas puffed out a breath, fishing his phone from his pocket as he headed up the hill towards the market square.

On the app, little green dots mapped the options for relief all around him.

He missed cigarettes for the first time in six years. Coffee would have to do instead, along with a little physical stimulation. Lucas swiped through the active profiles in his vicinity, discarding the available men for various reasons. Too bulky. Too skinny. Too much leather. He couldn't remember if he'd been this choosy before he'd gone to app-based meet-ups. He recalled, dimly, a time when he'd simply swanned into a club at midnight, had two drinks, picked someone willing, and swanned out again. Before his bedtime had become nine-thirty and the idea of being out after dusk made him exhausted just thinking about the next day.

There. A classically handsome brunet with blue eyes and an easy smile. Low maintenance. Low expectations. He sent a message and bit into his sandwich.

Hey! The reply sailed back when he was halfway through his iced coffee. *I'm off in half an hour. Buy you a drink? Coffee, smoothies, or something more potent?*

He stared at his cup. *Coffee*, he answered, accepting that he might just not fall asleep tonight. He sent the address of a coffee shop a few blocks away that he rarely went to. *This work?*

Yeah, sure! Does 2 work?

Lucas glanced at his watch, sighing. Later than he'd have liked, but needs must. *I'll see you there then.* He paused. Too punctuated? *Looking forward to it.*

Me too. With a smiley face. The things he did for release. The shirtless picture that followed shortly after softened the blow slightly. A tattoo of a constellation on the man's chest and a pleasant little trail of hair disappearing below his belt. *See you soon!*

Forty minutes. Lucas scrubbed a hand through his hair and finished his sandwich while he checked availability for the closest motel. He'd long since grown out of trysts in bathroom stalls and back alleys. And the *park*. He'd *enjoyed* the park when he was younger. The sense of danger. The risk of being caught. He couldn't risk that now for a stranger. He had a little girl to get home to.

Still, Lucas skimmed through his photo albums to find a semi-recent selfie of himself where he found the angles and shadows pleasing and his face wasn't in the frame, and sent it in answer with a wink. These were the letters of courtship now: emojis and headless torsos.

As he passed the time and wandered towards the café, he fielded some calls from his cell and checked in on the boutique's sales numbers. He recognized the smiling, brown-haired fellow immediately, chatting with a female barista with ear gauges as she brewed his espresso. The man had a pleasant voice, a warm tenor, with a bright, cheerful laugh. His choice of attire, though, left something to be desired; the black tee shirt and jeans weren't fitted, and the fellow was carrying a gym bag that said 'Patient Paws Veterinary Clinic' with a little embroidered bone underneath.

"Let me cover your coffee?" Lucas offered as he joined him at the counter, offering a hand. "Lucas."

"Rhys," he grinned, his smile widening as he studied Lucas appraisingly, pulling out a quarter. "Flip for it? Your call."

"Heads," Lucas lifted a brow, fighting a smirk.

Rhys flicked the coin high up into the air, catching it on his palm and flipping it down onto the counter, whistling low. "Well, I guess it's my lucky day." Washington's profile gleamed against the marble. Rhys slipped his wallet back into his pocket. "I should've gotten a double!"

"There's still time," Lucas chuckled, fishing his billfold from his pocket. "Long day?"

"Early morning, but they always are." Rhys seemed to smile as easily as he breathed, running a hand through his short-cropped hair and across his clean-shaven face. "That's a nice jacket you've got on. Really sharp."

"Thank you." A compliment on his work always warmed him to his core. Lucas ordered a plain Americano and tucked his thumbs into his pockets. He was never entirely sure what to do with his hands at this stage. "I do try for sharp. It's better than dull."

"You succeeded today, at least." More of that affable, easygoing smile. "You've got good taste in coffee, too. That's three for three," Rhys murmured with a sly little wink. "Quite the streak."

"I'm going for a hat trick," Lucas murmured, tongue in cheek, and collected the coin from the counter, offering it back to him. "You're the lucky one. I can only hope that some of that might rub off on me." He sighed, wincing. "That sounded better in my head."

Rhys hummed, stowing away the quarter with a low chuckle. He shook his head, laughing. "It's alright; you're already a much better conversationalist than most of my company."

"And I don't have fleas." Lucas was sure his smile wasn't as natural or warm as Rhys', but he was who he was. "Never have. Not even once. It's a point of pride."

"How'd you know about...?" Rhys blinked, capping his cup with a lid, glancing down.

Lucas nodded to the incriminating embroidery. "I suppose you could have that bag for some other reason, but..." He plucked a long wiry hair from Rhys' sleeve. "There were other clues."

"That's my girlfriend's!" Rhys laughed as the tuft of hair was safely deposited in the nearest trashcan. "She's a very nice border collie. Sweet as can be."

"Does she know where you are right now?" Lucas asked, sipping his coffee as they left the counter. "I've heard they're very territorial."

"They're also very forgiving." Rhys smiled, starting to wander over to a coffee table before Lucas stopped him.

"Do you want to go somewhere else?" Lucas asked and Rhys followed him like a retriever out of the shop. "Unless you want to get a lot of extra attention."

"Oh, okay!" Rhys nodded, looking slightly befuddled. "Sure."

Lucas glanced at him out of the corner of his eye. "Preferences? I'm verse, so—"

There was a slight furrow between his brows that hadn't been there before. Rhys hoisted his bag onto his shoulder. "Very to the point."

Lucas opened his mouth, shut it, tilted his head. "I've found if I don't lay my boundaries out in advance, they usually don't matter. Is..." He was handsome. Built. Nice. No. Not nice; *affable*. That was a talent Lucas had never possessed, being effortlessly likable. "You're new to the app."

"I..." Rhys' gaze dipped. "That obvious? Really?"

Lucas wished it weren't, but now that he'd seen that, he couldn't unsee the rest. "You just got out of something, hm? What? A couple of years?"

"Five," Rhys said quietly, suddenly preoccupied with the sidewalk.

"Five." Lucas hissed softly. "...Do you want to talk about it?"

"You know, I was hoping not to?" Rhys' lips pressed together in a tight line. "We can get back to your boundaries if you want."

Lucas lifted a brow. "No bondage, no piss play, and I'm not going to call you 'daddy'." He watched the man's expression steadily darkening. "There are *dating* apps, you know. Some of them are even fairly good, I hear. New algorithms."

Rhys huffed quietly. "I'm not a complete Luddite."

"I wasn't accusing you of being a Luddite. You're far too good at selfies for that." He bumped Rhys' shoulder. "I met a fellow on this one one time who, I kid you not, fully expected me to blow him in a photo booth. It's fairly singularly focused."

"...did you do it?"

Lucas snorted, rolling his eyes. "No."

They stepped out into the crosswalk as the walk sign turned on; Rhys tucked his hands into his pockets. "Have you been doing this long?"

"About seven years," Lucas admitted with his most winning smile.

"Christ." The color seemed to drain from the man's face. "And that's... Sorry, that was incredibly judgmental of me. I'm sure you have your reasons."

"I do." Was it that terrible? Why? It was honest. Economical. Simple. "What exactly did you think you were signing up for?"

"I mean, I guess I knew, but I didn't..." Rhys hummed, shaking his head. "It's alright. I can... I don't mind if that's all you want from me."

But this was substantially more than Lucas wanted from his afternoon. He sighed. Rhys made him sound like a villain. A pathetic villain. "I'm not in the habit of—" Lucas sighed and held out his hand. "Give me your phone."

"...why?"

"I'll list some of the apps that will suit you better."

Rhys fished it out of his pocket, touching Lucas' wrist when he placed it in his palm. "I'm sorry I wasn't what you were hoping for."

"Likewise." He opened the note app and made a list. Then made a second list marked 'avoid'. He didn't look up. "Try not to put yourself in situations you're not one hundred percent invested in," he murmured. "There are people who will take your offered inch a few thousand miles. That would be unfortunate. You seem like a nice man."

"So do you," Rhys said softly, squeezing his hand as Lucas handed his phone back. "It was still nice to meet you. Phone?"

Lucas glanced up. "...why?"

"Danny took all of our friends in the breakup." Rhys looked desperately sad, but the expression smoothed away again after a moment. "I wouldn't mind picking up a new one."

Why did all these men have pitiful companions? On some level, perhaps Lucas understood why Adrian's friends didn't accompany him to the cemetery, but standing stalwart by Rhys through his breakup shouldn't be so complicated, should it? He offered his phone even though he had plenty of friends, more than enough, and not nearly enough time for all of them. "He sounds like a winner."

Rhys shrugged helplessly. He typed in his number quickly, returning Lucas' phone. "Good luck with your hunting."

Lucas shook his head. Not his day. Not his week. Not Rhys' fault. "It's no trouble. Now you have a new friend. One who doesn't know Danny from Fred." He saluted him lightly with his phone before tucking it away. *Hunting.* Gods, but that sounded uncomfortable and ill-worth the effort. Especially given the implication that he'd be after someone who was trying to escape him. The thought soured on the back of his tongue. Adrian wasn't trying to escape him, he thought, and nearly texted the man before he stopped himself. Not looking to escape, but not looking for Lucas either. Not really. Better to just go back to work. "All's well that ends well, as they say."

CHAPTER FIVE

ADRIAN

There weren't any mustard yellow peonies at the florist's when he visited Monday morning, so Adrian simply doubled his order of sunflowers, scribbling out a note for Tula explaining why. *The man with the smile liked these. I hoped you might, too.* He'd bought brightly colored zinnias for Lida and Marcus Halpern. Lucas was the most challenging and Adrian was quite certain he liked being so, but eventually, Adrian settled on a bird of paradise. An entire potted plant for the Cemetery Raven, the man who had designed his favorite jacket without Adrian even knowing. That had to mean something, didn't it? He scribbled out a second message to go with them, promising that the flowers weren't a bribe and set the trio of brightly colored gifts and their matching cards before the gate to the Halpern mausoleum, then slipped into his family's vault and knelt on the cold marble before his husband's tomb. Drawing the chalk lines and setting out the candles, chanting in Latin until mist filled the room. Nothing. *Still* nothing. Nothing Adrian could see, in any case, but a part of him still hoped Seron was listening, wherever he might be.

"He's not much like you," Adrian admitted quietly. In some ways, that was a relief. Seron had loved the world and everything in it and, while Adrian had adored his wide and easy grins, sometimes he'd wondered if it was selfish to deprive others of Seron's warmth by keeping him to himself. People who needed his light more than Adrian. Seron had been too good. Too giving. It had rankled, on occasion, making Adrian feel as though he weren't truly deserving.

Selfish. He'd always been selfish. It hadn't bothered him before Seron.

"I like him," Adrian continued, thinking of Lucas. "Even though it feels..." He bowed his head until it nearly touched the cool stone. "I lost a part of myself when I buried you. I'm not sure what's left of me to give or if it's cruel to you or him or both to even try." He flattened his palms against the marble, feeling the thin strips of grout between the tiles. "I never knew how much lonelier it would feel after having and losing you. I can't *sleep*. I can barely eat. Even now, I'm disappointing you." Adrian grimaced, closing his eyes tightly. "But you would hate to hear me say that." He cleared his throat. "He has a little girl, made of sunlight, like you. Did you meet her? Did you—I know I told you I didn't want children. I didn't consider it when you asked." Silence spurred him on, even as his voice shook. "I enjoy seeing her smile. I never gave it much thought, but perhaps you were right. I suppose I should be used to that by now."

No response. Not even the warm presence Adrian had felt in the Halpern mausoleum. Empty and blank, just like the space that stretched before him save for the little pops of yellow petals.

Had Tula spoken to Seron? Or were her talents something else entirely? The details she'd mentioned seemed too specific to be coincidental, but perhaps... Maybe if she had looked into *Adrian's* mind, instead...? Telepathy was a more common ability than necromancy, certainly. Because the alternative—that Tula could do what Adrian did and Seron had reached out to her, without any ritual or supplication—meant that Seron wasn't willing to talk to *him*, specifically.

Adrian wasn't certain which was worse: being unsuccessful or being abandoned.

He stood, slow and measured, knees aching, pressing a kiss to where Seron's name was engraved, readjusting the sunflowers on the dais just so. "I love you," Adrian murmured, "I wish I could hear your laughter again. Perhaps one day you'll let me." He traced the divets in the stone, as cold as the day outside.

The lecture had gone moderately well. Adrian left the podium as the modest audience of students, parents, and children clapped politely. He had included videos of the miniature rockets and planes his seniors had made for extra credit a few semesters ago. A few of the little ones cheered at the footage of the real rocket launch from the previous fall. They could all touch the stars, if they were only willing to reach for them, he promised, with what he hoped was a reassuring grin, then lost himself among the dispersing crowd.

The exhibits and demonstrations had been set up earlier in the day, manned by several students he'd taught in the previous semesters. Adrian was proud of their work, each child's excited smile attesting to the purpose of the outreach event.

He heard Tula before he saw her, cavorting with a gaggle of other children as they tried to make their paper airplanes go farther or faster. From there, it was easy to spot her father where he leaned against a wall nearby, arms crossed like a protective statue.

"Interesting and inspiring, as usual." Admiral Kristina Zielinksi stepped to Adrian's side, surveying the activity. She was a sturdy woman, even now that she was out of active service, with cropped dark hair and dark eyes that seemed a touch somber even when she was not. Warrior's eyes, Seron had called them. She'd seen too much, as had he, and it never quite left her. She turned that gaze on Adrian, resting a hand on his shoulder. "It's good to see you doing these again."

Another well-meaning reminder that Adrian was less than he'd once been. He summoned a smile for her. "Thank you for coming; you look well."

She nodded, eyes scanning the booths. "You have a good crop of students this year."

"I do, yes." He tilted his head. "Do you intend to stay for long?"

"I came for the lecture." She eyed the children whooping as they waved colored scarves, catching the wind beneath them. "I think I may have aged out of the demonstrations."

"Anyone can make a paper airplane." Adrian patted her hand where she still applied a light pressure to his shoulder. She let go with a little grimace. "Where's your spirit of competition?"

Kriss chuckled, nodding to the man sitting on the floor with a youth lifted over his head. "I think Tremaine has that well in hand." She sobered, glancing back towards him. "We've missed you, you know."

"I... Yes." Adrian dipped his head, frowning. Not this conversation again. "I'm sorry I haven't been around as much."

"There's no need to apologize." Kristina sighed deeply, her hand returning to his shoulder. "We were thinking of you on your anniversary. We tried to call."

"...I didn't feel much like talking to tell you the truth." Adrian pressed his lips together, trying to remain steady under her scrutiny. "Are you still going to the museum opening?"

"Of course." She kept watching him as though he were about to fall apart, and with the renewed weight of her hand on his shoulder, he thought he very well might.

"Mr. Adrian, up!" A tiny hand tugged at his pant leg. Tula peered up at him, wiggling her fingers above her head. "Up like a rocket!"

He stared down at Tula, blinking. She was effervescent, giggling up at him with hope and delight. Helpless, Adrian slipped his hands under her arms and lifted her above his head, her arms outstretched as he turned in a circle. "Hello again, little one." He set her lightly on her feet again and tapped her lightly on the tip of her button nose. "Did your papa make you a new dress to match your friend's socks?"

She giggled, tugging at the bright yellow sundress she wore over her leggings. "And a hat! I didn't bring the hat. Papa says it's rude to wear hats inside. I don't know why. Do you?" Before he could answer, she continued, "Did you really fly all those places and take all those pictures? Papa says you have a plane. Can you show me? I want to go up and kiss the clouds. They're so pretty."

"Maybe one day, if it's okay with your papa." Adrian squeezed her shoulder. "Tula, this is Kriss. She's one of my oldest, dearest friends."

"Oldest, certainly," Kriss muttered wryly.

"Uh-huh! I remember! How's your head feeling?" Tula asked, staring up at Kriss cheerfully.

"My head?"

"You hit your head when you fell off that cliff, right?"

Kriss stared at her.

"And the smiling man picked you up? No? He said you have a scar on your cheek from it. Here." She poked at her own flushed cheek. "Do you feel better now?"

"...yes," Kriss answered quietly, touching the faint line of the scar that stretched down to her jaw. "I feel better now."

"Good!" Tula turned in a circle, looking between them. "Do you like my dress?"

"It's beautiful. It suits you very well." Adrian turned to Kriss with a slight smile, nerves tightening his stomach. Kriss was out of the service now, but her last posting before she'd been promoted out of the field had her working with the International Arcane Order, rounding up magically gifted individuals like Tula. Supposedly, the tower system was meant to teach spellcasters to hone their talents, but in Adrian's experience the towers were more meant to keep mages separate from the general population than to help their charges master the art of the arcane. Adrian had come from a long line of magical practitioners who had successfully dodged the registration process, but the risk of discovery was ever-present. He was grateful to talk about something—anything—else. "She'd give Cymbeline a run for her money, hm?"

Kriss hummed under her breath, watching Tula curiously. "For a certainty. How did the two of you come to be acquainted?"

"We're neighbors!" Tula beamed, throwing her arms around Adrian's waist in a hug. "Mr. Adrian gave me flowers and he gave my grandparents flowers and he said we could come and play today!" She spun as the college students began demonstrating with the remote-controlled airplanes. "I have to go! Bye, Ms. Kriss! Bye, Mr. Adrian!"

"Bye," he began, but Tula had already run off. The girl was sunlight, distilled, and brought to life. "She's excitable, that one," he murmured, watching her go. "What were we speaking of?"

"Neighbors?" Kriss quirked a brow. "Did the Hendersons move out?"

"Oh, no. We... At the cemetery. Her father's parents are buried next to..." Adrian tucked his hands into the pockets of his slacks. So Seron had spoken to Tula. He was *there*. Adrian's heart thrummed. Seron was there, after all this time, and Tula could hear him, see him, listen to his stories... And the gods only knew what Kriss must be thinking. He tried for a bashful grin as he met her eyes. "I told her some stories, which is how she knew about your scar. A lot of questions."

"What a dreadful story to tell a child." Kriss looked a little alarmed, but her concern seemed to be with Adrian and not Tula. "You're still going?"

"Yes, why wouldn't I be?" Adrian asked. "He was my family. I can't just leave him. In any case, it's on my way to work."

She nodded slowly. "That's all true."

"And you have qualms."

"I have no qualms," she disagreed. "I have concerns. I'm concerned about you. I hate to think of you spending your time in cemeteries telling war stories to children. Just... come to the house this week-end. We can..."

Adrian closed his eyes, wishing very much to be elsewhere. "I have plans this weekend."

"Plans." She exhaled slowly, squeezing his shoulder. "Alright. Next time. I'll send you a—"

"Professor Sharp?" Lucas' voice cut through. "Do you have a minute?"

Adrian shifted out of her reach, bowing his head. "Next weekend. I promise." He forced a smile, turning towards Lucas. "I believe I do." Adrian glanced at her. "Yes?"

Kriss nodded. "I'll call you. At least text me back this time, please, or I'll be forced to investigate."

"Yes, Admiral." Adrian dipped his head with a small smile. "I will." If only to avoid further inquiry. "Take care of yourself."

"Until next weekend." She patted him gently, nodded to Lucas, and headed over to where Tremaine was throwing paper planes at the remote-controlled ones.

"Bad timing?" Lucas asked under his breath.

"Perfect timing, actually," Adrian disagreed softly. "I'm glad you're here."

"You saved me from watching a documentary about the extinction of whales and we managed to turn this into a school project. I'm glad I'm here, too." He crossed his arms at his back. "Would you like some air?"

"Please." Adrian sighed heavily, feeling as though he might crum-ple. "She worries. Means well, but..."

Lucas nodded towards the double wooden doors. "I like this library. I haven't been back to it in a long time. The domes." He pointed up as they slipped from the conference room into the main lobby. "The stained glass. It feels like a church, only the opposite of stifling."

"Not a religious man?" Adrian hummed, grateful to be away from the crowd. "Interesting for a confessor."

"I try to be interesting. Thank you." Lucas peered above them. "Speaking of which: fascinating lecture."

"You liked it?" Adrian couldn't help the grin that spread to his cheeks. "Truly?"

"No. I'm just in the habit of lying to new friends, and this seemed like the best way to continue that pattern."

"New *friends*." Adrian brightened considerably. "I've been promoted from 'near stranger'?"

"You've spared me dying whales. A promotion was deserved." Lucas glanced at him out of the corner of his eye. "Did you actually fly through the eye of a hurricane?"

"Twice," Adrian told him. "I wouldn't recommend it. Your daughter asked me to take her flying."

Lucas exhaled a long-suffering sigh that seemed to resonate through the whole of him. "I'm sorry. She... Hm. She's developed a fondness for you. She'll forget about it after a while if you don't bring it up."

"I was going to ask you if you'd allow it," Adrian admitted, studying his expression. "Name a date and a place. It wouldn't be too much trouble."

"Thank you." Ravens on a line again, the way Lucas' brows flicked. "That's very generous. But she doesn't—I hope you don't take this the wrong way, but it seems like too much of an imposition." He tucked his chin to his chest. "I do appreciate the offer. Truly."

"If you change your mind, let me know." A slight, but expected disappointment. "I wouldn't mind an excuse to fly again, and am happy to take you both up."

"You don't need an excuse. You have a plane." Lucas looked at him curiously. "If you want to fly, you can fly."

"I suppose that's true." To share the sky with someone again, even if they were five and fascinated by everything... Perhaps that itself was part of the appeal. To see the world below with unjaded eyes. "I overstepped. I apologize."

"It's not overstepping. It's just..." Lucas shook his head. "It's *early* stepping. Not over." He spread his hands. "She attaches to people quickly. She doesn't handle it well when they move on. She doesn't understand."

"I'm sorry," Adrian murmured, closing his eyes. "I should've realized—I'm sorry."

"Please don't be. There's no reason you should have to think about these things." His fingers touched Adrian's elbow lightly. "I thought—I'd thought that bringing her around to see my parents more often might help her orient to the idea of people being there and then gone. That's backfired."

"Why would it work, when she can *speak* to them?" Adrian met his gaze. "She just told me about something there's no way she'd know. Not unless she'd conversed with—"

It was like watching doors slam shut. Lucas' jaw tightened. His eyes darkened. "Thank you for the invitation." He looked down at the wrist opposite the one on which he actually wore a watch. "Look at the time. Very nice seeing you. Have a good night."

"Lucas," Adrian hissed. "Stop. *Please*. I need to know—Why would he talk to her when he won't—I've tried *everything*." He flexed his hands in his pockets. "I had thought I failed, until—"

"Failed what." Lucas stared at him, cold and hard as steel.

"Her talents aren't unique." He glanced around the empty courtyard. "Rare, but not unique. I'm sorry I frightened you."

"I don't frighten easily." Lucas lifted his chin, looking as though he might start spitting bullets. "This is my amused face."

Adrian studied him, heart sinking. *Friends*. He'd said, just a moment ago, that they were. "I'm gifted, too. I don't mean her any harm, I swear to you."

Lucas was quiet and still, the slight tension of his jaw the only sign that anything was amiss, but he was different than Adrian had seen him before. Coiled, like a snake. "I won't talk about this here."

"You're right." Adrian nodded once; his pulse raced, thundering in his ears. "I shouldn't have—*Damn it*, can you forgive me for—?"

"Tonight. I will see you tonight. Where we met. You can explain yourself. Once." Lucas rolled his shoulders back. "Then we'll see. I'm taking her home. Is that going to be a problem?"

"No." Adrian's eyes began to sting, his throat tightening. *Selfish*, the word rattled in his mind like a sharp hiss. "No, of course not. You're safe with me, Luke. I promise. I've made a mess of this, but—"

"Eleven." Lucas turned away from him, heading towards the doors. "You have one opportunity to explain why I should trust you."

"I'll be there," Adrian murmured, mortified, his fingers quaking in his pockets. Why had he said a damned thing about the magic she possessed? He turned away before he could meet those sharp, too-observant eyes, trying to tell himself he wasn't fleeing as he walked quickly through the little herb garden and down the stairs toward his car, hoping no one noticed the flush on his cheeks or the shine in his gaze before shutting the door firmly behind him.

CHAPTER SIX

LUCAS

The gleam of the wards usually eased him. That faint glow beneath the doormat and within the meticulously engraved Meranti wood of their front door let Lucas relax, safe and secure, in their home, with the knowledge that they were protected by charms and technology as much as possible.

Tula scowled as she thumped her backpack on the front bench with gusto. Sometimes she reminded him too much of her mother: full of fury and fire; thank the gods her tempers were a rare occurrence. Not like Teresa's had been. Those had been actual fires, literal and figurative, and her tantrums had forced his whole family to move multiple times. Teresa—with her angelic looks and demonic temper—had not listened to his parents when they tried to teach her the simple lessons they'd taught Lucas with ease. To keep her powers hidden. To only cast in warded areas. To clean her resonance and any evidence of her casting thoroughly when she did. To maintain control of her emotions and not let them get the better of her. Lucas' parents had been training him to hide who and what he was from the day they realized he could read their minds.

Their parents, he corrected himself. They'd considered Teresa a daughter. They'd wanted him to think of her as a sister. They would be disappointed in him for distancing himself from her, even if it were only in his thoughts.

Lucas gazed down at Tula. "I understand that you didn't want to leave early. There's no need to act out." It had seemed so straightforward when they'd taught him the rules. Practice only within secured wards. Don't speak of your gifts. Keep your head down. Why couldn't Tula understand? Why hadn't Teresa? What was he doing wrong? He touched her shoulder gently as she started to stomp off. "Tula."

"You made my friend sad." She sniffed, crossing her arms. "I could tell."

"*I* made *him* sad?" Lucas pressed his back teeth together, seeking patience. "I am doing what is necessary to keep you safe. I *told* you not to speak of your visions to anyone—"

"I didn't tell. I asked a question—"

"Of a *Seeker*." Lucas knelt in front of her, holding her arms. "The woman you were talking to was a Seeker, Tula. If she has guessed... If she has deduced, as Adrian did, what you are, then we will have to run. Do you understand?"

"Ms. Kriss is *nice*. And Mr. Adrian was so sad when we left. I *saw* him, papa."

"Tula. Listen to me." He met her eyes sternly. "She might have been nice tonight, but that's only because she did not know *what we are*. You *cannot* take risks like this. Do you want to be taken away? Is that what you want?"

"*No*. You said... You said you and me would always be together and they'd never—" Tula's eyes grew wide and terrified. He never wanted to frighten her, but what else was there? He'd tried reasoning and cajoling and bribing and all that had led them to now.

"I will do everything in my power to make sure that that's true, but I can't do it alone. I need you to help me. I need you to work very hard to keep those worlds separate. Can you do that for me?"

"But I want to talk about my friends. I want to talk about the smiling man and Mrs. Canterwell and the cat that lives in our attic." Her eyes shone in the low light of their study. "Why does that mean they'll take me away?"

"We've discussed this, Tula." She was still too young for him to tell her about the Mage Wars. She was too full of hope and light for him to darken her with the years of battles across the world, the front lines awash in fire and blood and chaos, the Aether Rend that had nearly broken reality... Maybe if he told her, she would understand. Or maybe the knowledge would simply dim her, frighten her... No. Lucas hugged her, searching for a way to make her realize how she needed to be more careful. "Many people without our gift... They don't understand us. And what they don't understand makes them afraid of us. I'm sorry. I know it's hard. I know it doesn't feel fair. This is what we have to do, to stay together and to stay safe. You can tell me about all of your friends. Right now, though, we're in danger until I sort this out. Can you be brave for me?"

"I don't know." Her bottom lip began to tremble. "Where are you going, papa?"

"I'm going to do everything I can to keep us here, protected, with all your friends. If I can't—" He touched the yellow bow in her hair. "If I can't fix this, then we're going to leave tonight when I return.

We'll find somewhere new and we'll start over. We'll be together and we'll be okay."

"*No!*" She shouted, squeezing her tiny hands into fists. "I don't *want* to leave!"

"I don't want to leave either, sunbeam, but I would rather leave with you than lose you."

Tula closed her eyes, hugging herself as tears began to spill. "I don't want to pack the bags. I don't want to go. I like it here. I made a *promise.*"

Twice. They'd practiced packing their go bags twice and never used them. She had no idea what it was like to run, uprooting everything over and over again. He had wanted to protect her from that. From all of it. He kissed the top of her head. "A promise to who, sweetheart?"

"I said I wouldn't say. Not even to you." She wrinkled her nose. "*Especially* not to you."

"Tula," he warned. "You can't keep secrets from me. We have to tell each other everything. You know that."

She frowned, staring at her hands and then at him, sniffing. "Okay, papa. It was Mada and Grandpop. Please don't tell them. I *promised.*"

"Mada and Grandpop and I had traveled twice by the time I was your age," he told her, dabbing at her tears. "They won't be mad at either of us for staying safe. What I'm trying to teach you is what they taught me." He held her, resting his cheek on her head. "I wish they could help you the way they helped me."

"They do help me. They want to help you, too." She sighed softly, sniffling in his arms. "Where are you going tonight? Can I come? I can help."

"You can help me by packing your bag and getting it into the shell room." He kissed the top of her head. "I'll call Miss Lisa to come and stay with you. I want you to get your special phone—the one we keep in the dollhouse—and if I call, you answer. Alright?"

Tula gazed up at him with sadness where only sunlight should have been. "Okay."

"Tula, I love you. I love you more than anything in this world. You're my daughter and I'm going to keep you safe. I'm sorry that it's scary right now. I wish that it weren't."

"You're going to come back, right?" Tula squeezed his arm. "You promise?"

"I will always come back for you." Come hell or high water. "I promise. We keep our promises, don't we?"

"Or the fairies will come and take away all the ice cream sundaes and cookies and rainbow sprinkles." She wrinkled her nose. "Are they going to take away my sprinkles for telling you about my secret with Mada and Grandpop?"

"I don't think Mada and Grandpop would want you to keep things from me, love. They wouldn't ever want to put either of us in danger." He ran his hand over her head, smoothing stray golden hair. "And the fairies understand that as well."

"Okay." Tula leaned against him, holding on tight and breaking his heart. "I'll pack my bag. Can we have a banana split when you get home?"

"With strawberries and sprinkles." It wasn't fair; she was right about that. She was harmless, gifted with sight and wisdom beyond her years. To let the Seekers get their hands on her would be like allowing a wild boar to carry a fragile glass artifact. They would destroy her even if they didn't mean to.

The Seekers, however benevolent their public campaign was made to appear, were careless and possessive. Teresa was proof enough of that. She'd been wild enough before, but the last time Lucas had seen her... She'd returned from her years in the tower changed. Raw. Unwieldy. Dangerous. He couldn't let them do that to Tula, who only wanted to listen to stories from her friends and left joy in her wake like rose petals.

Adrian owed him answers and evidence. If he was what he said he was... If. Then there was a slim chance that they could survive this without upending Tula's whole world. "Don't forget your tooth-brush, sunbeam."

"...can I pack my ponies?" Tula asked, hope and hopelessness warring in her expression. "I think they can fit in my backpack if I take out my crayons."

"You can put your crayons in my bag, okay?" He squeezed her shoulder as his phone began to buzz in his pocket. "I need to do a little work. You let me know if you need me, hm?"

"Okay, papa." She hugged him tightly again, sighing in his arms, before trotting off to her bedroom, backpack in hand.

Tula had said the Admiral was 'nice'. Not so nice that one of his father's old contacts in the Resistance hadn't immediately recognized both the photo and the name when he'd made the quick call on his way to collect Tula. "Miss Kriss" Zielinksi was linked to over twelve collections and a couple of disappearances. Lucas would be damned if he'd allow Tula to be added to that statistic.

He answered his phone when he heard the door to Tula's room close. "Yes?"

"You're safe?" Lucas had been a child when he'd first met Rothco, and even then the man had been grizzled and ancient. Sitting in a rocking chair that was as worn as he was, his beard dusty and gray. Nice enough, for a hermit on the edge of nowhere. Rothco had been a good friend to Lucas' parents and had served, often, as a point of contact when they were trying to get a mage with a complicated case somewhere new and safe. His voice sounded like sandpaper on stubborn wood. "And the kid?"

"Behind our wards, yes." Lucas glanced down the hall and carefully shut the office door. "I have some due diligence scheduled; I'll let you know how it goes."

"Lucas," Rothco grumbled across the line. "I know you've got the touch, but erasing a Seeker's mind—never mind a U.S. Admiral's—is a tall order."

"No. I know that." Lucas scrubbed a hand through his hair. "I'm just... clarifying some additional facts."

"You bring that little ice cream cake to me, you hear. You and her both. I'll introduce you to some nice folks. Friends of your parents." Hundreds of them, living off and between the grids, holing up and away like Rothco or taking the fight to the IAO and making everything harder for everyone else. "We'll keep you safe," Rothco told him sternly.

"I don't want her to grow up like I did," Lucas hissed. "That isn't why I called you." He would speak to Adrian. He would find out what the man knew and how much danger they were in. He would make a plan. He would keep her safe. It didn't add up. If Adrian was who he said he was, why would he associate with—be friends with—a woman who had spent much of her career locking people like them away? "We've got a good life here."

"You do until you don't. That's how it always is." Rothco cleared his throat—a hacking sound that rattled the phone and threw static through the line. "Even before the registrations," he added morosely. "You live among the sheep, it's only a matter of time until they turn on you. They've got knives under that wool."

Every time he spoke with the old man, Lucas was reminded how lucky he was that he could pick and choose when he heard the thoughts of others. A lifetime of never being able to shut them out had made Rothco deeply paranoid and cynical. Lucas grimaced. "They're not sheep, Roth. They're just people."

"I know you're out of the game, but you're not seeing what I am. There's been an uptick in roundups in the past few years and from what I can tell it's only going to get worse," Rothco grumbled. "I owe it to your folks to keep an eye on you, but it's damned near impossible to do if you don't let me help you."

"I don't need looking after. I've kept her off their radar. I'll keep her there and free."

"She's not free now. She's just fooling herself into thinking that those friends of hers won't turn her over to the precious International Arcane Order at the first opportunity. 'For her own good.' Bullshit. For theirs. And they all just go along with it. And that, Lucas, is why they're sheep."

"She won't be free with your friends. I remember," Lucas grunted. "I remember running and looking over my shoulder. I remember being asked to do things that no child should be asked to do."

"They shouldn't, no." Lucas could almost see Rothco's nonchalant shrug from the other end of the line as he said it. "But that's the lot of every mage in this world until we change it for them."

"I'm changing it. I'm changing it for her."

"Until she ends up in one of those towers getting all the re-education they can throw at her."

"That's not going to happen." But he had come too close this time to tripping up. He'd trusted and trust was always a risk. He knew that too well. "I'm teaching her everything Mada taught me. I stayed out. Tula will, too." A little knock at the door to his office drew his attention away from his phone call. "Yes, tulip?"

"Are you going to talk to Ms. Kriss?" His daughter stood in the doorway in her yellow dress, hand against the frame. "The smiling man said she was nice and brave and strong and he saved her. I *saw* it. He saved her and she's friends with him and Mr. Adrian and—"

"Tula." The smiling man. Adrian's lost love. Lucas grimaced. "Just because someone is nice to one person, that doesn't mean they'll be nice to you."

"But she *was* nice to me." Tula was like Teresa in so many ways, Lucas thought tiredly. The complete opposite in others, yes, but the stubbornness...

"Thought you said you were teaching the kid," Rothco rumbled in his ear.

"I've got it. Thanks for the heads up, Rothco."

"If you find you're willing to reach out to someone who can help you, just call. I can have people on your doorstep in an hour."

And wasn't that a cheerful thought? "I'll call if we need it. Stay safe."

"You, too."

Lucas watched Tula as he hung up and pocketed the phone. "Tula, we've discussed this before. It is a Seeker's *job* to take us away from the world like they took your friend Eloise."

That made Tula's lip tremble, but the girl didn't relent. "She didn't take away Mr. Adrian."

"We don't know what she knows or why she does what she does. We don't know her. She's a stranger, Tula. This isn't up for discussion. You need to listen when I tell you things. You need to learn. I can't—" He rubbed his temples. "There is a way that the world is. Your wishing doesn't change it."

"...are you going to tell Mr. Adrian?"

"I am going to do what is necessary for us to be safe. As I always will." He looked across the room to her. "No matter what. Do you understand?"

"Yes, but I asked about Mr. *Adrian*."

Lucas gritted his teeth. "You aren't listening to me."

She placed her hands on her hips. "*You're* not listening to *me*."

"We may be forced to leave everything we know because of your *carelessness*," he hissed, rising to his feet. "Tell me you understand."

"*No!*" She stamped her foot on the ground. "You're not listening to me at all! Not even a little bit."

"Control your temper."

"I don't *want* to." Her eyes flashed a dangerous sapphire. "I don't want to control anything and hide and *lie*."

"I do not very much care what you want and what you don't want right now, Tula. You put us in danger and you're refusing to take responsibility for your actions. It's unacceptable."

"*You're* unacceptable, Papa." She wrinkled her nose up at him and the lights began to flicker.

Lucas crossed to her in two steps, unwinding the leather strap from his wrist as he moved. It glowed, absorbing the energy that was leaking off of her like mist. "You will not use your gifts for harm. Control yourself."

"You're not *listening* to me." She shivered, staring at him. Tula blinked, then her shoulders slumped and she began to wail. "I'm sorry. I didn't mean to ruin everything. I didn't mean to—I just wanted to make a friend."

He waited for the last of the light to absorb into the leather before he knelt to touch her, lifting her chin. "We all make mistakes, Tula. What matters is that we acknowledge them, take responsibility, and learn."

"I shouldn't have said the thing to Ms. Kriss." She nodded, her cheeks wet. "I don't want her to take me away."

"I don't want her to, either, sunbeam. Her or anyone else." He dropped his fingers with a sigh. "I'm not mad at you. I'm frustrated with the situation. Okay?"

"Yeah..." she sniffed. "Can you play me a fairy song before you leave?"

"I'll trade you a fairy song for a hug." He opened his arms. "Can you forgive me?"

She nodded solemnly, stepping into the circle of his embrace. "And me, too?"

He brought her close, patting her back. "Always. Always, Tula." He kissed the top of her head. "I love you. Do you know that?"

"Yes." She peered up at him. "You tell me every day."

"Do you know how much?"

"As high as the stars?"

"And as deep as the universe." He touched her nose. "I'm not going to let anything happen to you."

"Only the good things." Tula squeezed him tightly. "You'll let those things happen, right? Can we go to Disney World again? You can be Prince Charming and I'll be your fairy godmother princess, okay?"

"Okay." The life he'd built for them. The business he'd built. The pride he'd felt in his work. He could do it all over again, as many times as he needed to.

CHAPTER SEVEN

ADRIAN

Adrian pulled up to the cemetery at ten-thirty and tapped his fingers on the steering wheel, breaths already unsteady. He could leave now. Peel out of the parking lot and go back to pacing his empty apartment alone. Haunting his halls like a ghost. He could leave well enough alone. He had endangered them—all of them—by talking about what he and Tula could do. Even if he hadn't *seen* anyone... Hadn't *sensed* anyone in that little garden... It had been a risk that could destroy any chance that Tula would have at a normal life and any hope Adrian might have at finding a semblance of happiness again. He wouldn't have... He *shouldn't* have... One never knew when the Seekers were listening. Their very identities were protected and safeguarded, so they could better catch and restrain their magically-inclined quarries to lock them away where they might never again see daylight. That was their purpose. Their place. Logging the gifted, protecting the known world, since the Mage Wars had nearly torn that world asunder.

Tula wanted to touch the clouds. She looked at him with stars in her eyes. She called him her friend and he had put her in danger. Adrian pressed his forehead to the steering wheel, closing his eyes tightly and willing his breaths to even again.

The two taps at his window jarred him up, where he found Lucas peering through the driver's side window. Adrian rolled the window down. "Where?"

Lucas nodded towards the gates, lifting his flashlight. "Alright?"

Adrian rolled his window back up, tapping the ignition button and locking his door with a beep. "Is this where you take my teeth?" he asked, only half-kidding.

"If I need to." There was no faint smile to accompany dry wit. Lucas walked away, not looking back or further acknowledging Adrian's presence until they were well into the empty, dark cemetery. Adrian fiddled with his keys in his jacket pocket; the jingle sounding like a car crash in the silence.

"You told me you have a gift," Lucas murmured, finally.

"How do you think I survived my stint in the Navy? Flying through a hurricane?"

"Skillful flying." Lucas still wouldn't look at him. The yellow glow from the flashlight showed just enough of him to let Adrian know that he was tense, all his loose, dangerous grace tightened like a spring. "And if that wasn't it, you're an idiot for talking about it in public. You don't strike me as an idiot."

"What do I strike you as?" Adrian asked, not entirely wanting to hear the answer.

"Pained." Lucas scowled into the dark ahead of them. "Generous. Starved for light. Clever."

"You're kind."

"Rarely."

Their boots crunched in the gravel, the beam from Lucas' flashlight scaring a lounging cat from its place beneath a bench. "I didn't mean to—Tula brought it up in front of my friend and it took me by surprise. I haven't been thinking clearly lately." He pressed his lips together. "As you might imagine. I'm sorry, Luke. I'll be more cautious."

He shook his head. "First, you will prove that what you say is true."

"That I'm a practitioner?" Adrian tightened his jaw. He supposed he hardly had anything left to lose. "...Alright."

Lucas turned the flashlight off, stepping back. "In your own time."

"Now?"

"Now or never."

Adrian closed his eyes, touching the flex of power that had been a part of him since he was smaller than Tula, then pressed his palms together and drew them apart. His magic flowed through him, currents of electricity making the hair on his arms stand on end as lightning—violet and blinding—crackled between his fingertips. Bright enough to see, even through his eyelids. He let the energy dissipate, cutting off the source like the gate to a sluice. It was a relief to cast, to let his carefully curated masks slip, if only for a moment. So much trouble to conceal something so wonderful. "Does that satisfy?" Adrian asked, blinking the shadows of residual colors from his vision as the scent of his power buzzed around them, thick as smoke.

Lucas' expression was impossible to read in the shadows. "And you speak to the other side."

"Anyone can do that. But I hear them answer when they wish to, yes." Adrian lifted his chin, crossing his hands at his back. "I can't do anything if they don't want to be heard."

"What did you fail?" Lucas wondered. It was difficult to tell in the dark, difficult to see his expression, but he sounded... calm. Impossibly so, given how Adrian felt like his pulse was visibly throbbing in his neck. "You said that you'd failed."

"There are certain preparations one can make after someone has passed, that make it easier for their spirit to return." Adrian swallowed, dropping his gaze to the dark, dew-covered ground. "I thought perhaps he *couldn't...* But Tula has spoken to him. So it's me." He'd been able to convince himself before, that perhaps Tula had just been lucky. That it was Adrian's thoughts she'd read... But it was clear from the story she'd spun earlier... Adrian hadn't seen Kriss fall and get the scar along her jaw, but Seron had. His muscles were molten; it was a wonder he could stand at all. "I didn't fail. Seron isn't gone or silenced; he simply doesn't want to speak to *me*."

Lucas was quiet for a while, accompanied by the rustling of the leaves. "You want her to speak to him for you?"

Adrian pressed his thumbs against his eyes to stave off the stinging. "I handled this poorly. I'm sorry, Luke. I was overwhelmed once I realized my suspicion was accurate and then I wanted you to hear it from someone who wouldn't hurt her."

"My daughter told you and some random woman at the library. Do you really think I didn't know?" Lucas scowled. "She talks to the woman who died two doors down. They feed pigeons together. What do you want with her? That's what I need to understand."

"Why would I want *anything* from your daughter?"

"That is what I am asking."

"Nothing," Adrian whispered, biting his lip. "I don't know *why* he won't answer me. I don't know why he wouldn't... He left me here *alone* and doesn't even have the decency to—" He exhaled a shaky breath. "It hurts me and I don't understand, but if he doesn't wish to speak to me, I'm not going to go through a child. I know what it feels like to be valued only for what I can do with my gifts; I would never wish that on anyone, especially not Tula."

Lucas watched him, silent, for a long beat. "What is that woman to you? The one at the library."

"The one I was speaking with when you approached me?" Adrian lifted his brows. "Why?"

"I don't remember inviting you to ask questions." Lucas hissed, stern and quiet. "Who is she to you?"

"An old friend." Adrian shifted uncomfortably under the man's gaze, flexing his hands in the deep pockets of his jacket. "What do you wish to know about her?"

"Does she know what you are?"

"Kriss—"

"—is a Seeker," Lucas snapped. "A sniffing dog. And you led her right to my daughter, so I will ask again: does she know what you are?"

Adrian hissed low, shaking his head and massaging his brows. "How did you find out?"

"I am asking the questions," Lucas reminded him firmly.

Adrian winced. "She would be court-martialed if anyone found out I was having this conversation with you."

"Do I seem like I care overmuch what her consequences might be?" Lucas lifted his chin. "Far worse could happen to my daughter. Do I need to ask again?"

"No." Adrian peered down at his boots, sighing. "We served together: Kriss, Seron, and I. Escaped relatively unscathed from one too many scrapes. She grew suspicious of the wrong man. I corrected her."

"So, he wasn't gifted."

"In many ways, Seron was, but not in the way you mean."

"But you are." Lucas watched him narrowly. "And she knows this, and yet you remain unregistered. Explain."

"I was certain she meant to report Seron, then me," Adrian told him, his heart beating rapidly in his chest. "She never did. She decided the risk I posed wasn't worth the punishment I'd receive for subterfuge. She tried to convince me, for a time, to turn myself over," he admitted. "I declined. My family has contained gifted individuals in every generation for centuries. They made it through the whole of the Witch Trials and the Aether Tear with no one the wiser. It hardly seemed like the time to start when the registrations began. Kriss respected my wishes."

Lucas peered up at the drooping branches of the tree above them. "Does she suspect Tula?"

"From tonight? I don't know, Lucas," Adrian admitted quietly. "I wouldn't think so. I covered for Tula as best I could. I've had my suspicions for a while. It only became clear to me tonight as a last piece in a puzzle."

The fog flexed around them like a living, breathing thing. Lucas held out his hand, his expression unreadable. "Would you mind if I verified what you say?"

"...verify." Adrian lifted his brows. "How?"

"You have your rare gifts. I have mine." Lucas waited for a long moment, the moon's gleam peeking through the fog to make the angles of his features seem sharper. "I can repel falsehoods. I can find memories. Or I can cleanse them."

"'Cleanse' them?" Adrian repeated warily.

"As if they'd never been," Lucas told him, as though remarking on the weather. "If need be."

Erasing memories? Finding them in the first place, but washing them away as well? It was a terrifying gift. And Adrian suddenly had a very clear understanding of exactly why Lucas had reacted as he had. No Seeker would ever have let him be if they'd known. He would have been locked away, or worse, used for that ability. No doubt he feared the same for Tula, that someone would want to take advantage of her connection to the world beyond. "...do you intend to cleanse mine?"

"If. Need. Be." Lucas flexed his hand. "If it helps, I do not relish the practice."

Adrian winced. All semblance of warmth was gone. "You under-stand the amount of trust in you this requires? I'd be giving you control over my *mind*. I hope you understand my reluctance."

"I am entrusting the safety of my daughter to the next words that you speak. Consider it an even trade."

Adrian extended his hand, his heart racing. "A trade, then. I hope it eases your nerves."

His thumb closed over the tips of Adrian's fingers with all the pressure of a single feather drifting through the air, and then the wash of crimson petals that hid themselves in his eyes began to gleam like fire-lit gems. "Speak and speak true," Lucas murmured, his voice little more than a whisper, caressing Adrian's mind. "Tell me what you know of her." Tender. A supplication.

And Adrian found himself speaking. Of every interaction since he'd met Tula. Each little glimpse. The familiarity of the way she spoke, hints that she shared his specialty. The resonance he'd felt in their family's crypt and the cold in his own. The words Tula had spoken at the library, more verbatim than he'd realized he could recall.

He felt his ears pop when Lucas let go of his fingers, a wave of dizziness washing over him as the man caught his elbow. "I've got you. You're alright."

Adrian exhaled, slumping in Lucas' arms, leaning on him for support. Not entirely unpleasant, that experience of being seen. Of being known. "That's..." He couldn't *feel* anything missing. Adrian cleared his throat. "That's a rare and dangerous power you have, my friend."

"It is," Lucas agreed softly, the velvety texture of his bespelled voice replaced by weariness. "As I said: I've run enough."

"I'm glad I was able to bring you some measure of satisfaction." Adrian inhaled deeply, almost able to taste the spices on his skin. Could he blame Lucas, for trying to protect his family? Would he have not done the same? He leaned into Lucas' arms, grateful for the contact. Gods, he missed being touched. *Held.* "...do you intend to stay?"

"For now." Lucas exhaled, slow and careful, as though he were trying to blow out all the air in his lungs, then took a small sip of softening night air as the fog abated. "Tula will be relieved."

"Does she have someone to teach her how to use her more unique talents?" Adrian met his gaze steadily, watching the shades of emeralds shift in his eyes.

Lucas ran his tongue over his teeth as the sky became visible once more. "She seems to be perfectly capable of using them. It's the not-using them where she struggles."

Adrian tucked his hands into his pockets. "...I could teach her to tune the spirits out. If you think it would help."

"I'm not sure she *would*, even if she knew how."

"It's nice to have the option."

Lucas considered him out of the corner of his eye. "Is it safe for her to spend time with you when your friend is in opposition to our existence?"

"I wasn't planning to mention it to Kriss or practice in public spaces," Adrian told him quietly. "I'm offering, if you'd let me."

"I'll consider it." Lucas shifted back. "Feeling steadier?"

"Yes, I... just don't know what you want from me anymore, Luke."

"...what I want?"

"I wasn't sure—" Adrian glanced away. "Was whatever you saw—all you heard—enough?"

"It was not as terrible as I had feared, between what the two of you had previously explained. Still. I would prefer that my daughter and your friend did not cross paths again. Can I have your word?"

Adrian nodded, beginning to feel like a bobblehead on a dashboard. "As much as it's in my control, yes."

"Alright. Come here." Lucas led him over to the bench nearby and held out his hand, his palm cupping starlight, making it pool between his fingers.

Adrian shuffled to sit beside him, body leaden. "Wait until after they bury me to take my teeth, will you?"

"Don't be ridiculous; digging your body back up would be an enormous additional effort." Lucas wiggled his fingers. "Here, please."

Adrian placed his hands underneath Lucas', the darkness making the blood-red bruises in Lucas' irises look like twilit shadows. "What do you—"

Lucas drew his hand slowly up and the starlight coalesced between their palms, swirling lazily into a sphere; Lucas placed the small, cool orb in Adrian's hand. As he watched, the moonlight shifted to a brilliant sunset, coalescing into a tangerine in his palm. "You need to be more careful. For yourself and Tula." He frowned. "I saw that your intentions are pure and you don't want anything to happen to her."

"Of course not." Even the thought made him feel ill. "She's just a child. No one deserves to be locked away for things they can't control." Adrian considered the summoned tangerine. He supposed it was a peace offering, of sorts. He peeled it with his fingernails and let the fruit burst on his tongue, closing his eyes to savor the taste of summer.

Mind manipulation was a rare talent indeed, and one that would certainly land Lucas in the Seekers' custody, even without the lifetime of subterfuge. No. It was better for Lucas to be out in the world, even if he had to fight to protect his daughter.

Running. There were more ways than one to keep someone safe.

Moonlight filtered through the rising mist, casting an eerie glow through the cemetery. Adrian reached for the amulet he'd worn since he was a boy, slipping it off over his head. The gold chain became visible once it rested in his palm, the pendant of a lion rampant, jewel-encrusted and glittering. He held the heirloom out to Lucas, watching him study it in his hand. Masking and protection. His teeth buzzed with arcane energy as soon as he removed the artifact, but the feeling soon faded. "This was a gift from my father when I was a little younger than Tula. I don't need it as I did then. Perhaps it might help."

Lucas eyed his hand, the red in his eyes shining like rubies as he considered it. He traced the etchings between the gems. "Enochian. So many have lost touch with the old arts."

"You come from a family of practitioners, yourself?" Adrian asked, tracing the creature's mane. "Do you know how to activate it?"

Lucas touched the center emerald and it began to gleam, setting each of the succeeding jewels glowing until the lion turned in the center and faced east. He flexed his hand, drawing moonlight to pool as shimmering liquid in his palm and the wards within the crest hid his power like a lead wall. "I've read about warding crests, but I've never seen one this extensive."

Adrian smiled, watching the lights dance along the angular features of Lucas' face. "It's kept my family safe through many a witch hunt. I'd be glad if it continued to do so for yours."

"...you're sure you don't need it?" Lucas asked quietly, not looking at him.

"I've developed other ways of getting myself out of trouble." Adrian pressed it into Lucas' palm, feeling the warmth leave him. It felt right, knowing it would soon be in the hands of someone it could protect. Who Adrian could protect, by proxy. "It should be hers."

"Thank you." Lucas smoothed his fingers over the lion's mane before he tucked it into the inner pocket of his jacket. "I'll see to it she knows its value and its history."

"As long as it helps protect her, I'll be satisfied." Adrian touched his shoulder. "Would you walk with me for a while? Perhaps to somewhere less dour?"

Lucas nodded. "We should leave before someone comes to investigate the resonance." He peered up at the sky as though looking for the flicker of the Seekers' satellites. "There's a fairly edible taco truck not far from here."

"I didn't realize your teeth were that sharp," Adrian murmured, tongue in cheek.

"Sharper, when the need is there." Lucas stepped away, unwinding a length of cord from his wrist and tying careful knots, each one glinting for a moment before it darkened. "Do you want to eat or do you want to be clever?"

"Can I not do both?" Adrian tilted his head to the side. "I haven't seen that sort of talisman before. What are you doing?"

"Clearing resonance," Lucas murmured, swinging the knotted strand as they walked. "Nothing so storied as your legacy inheritances, but they work in their way."

"As long as they do." Adrian felt the gentle tug on his power as the wayward magical resonance remaining from their casting was recaptured in Lucas' strand of fabric. "You're a secretive sort of man, aren't you?"

Lucas snorted. "I'm an alive sort. Alive and free. Secrecy goes hand in hand with the others." He paused, peering at Adrian. "One would think."

Adrian hummed to himself. "There's something to be said for having friends in the right places."

"I have friends," Lucas sniffed. "I keep them by keeping them separate."

"And what about me? I'd hardly call myself separate, now."

Lucas narrowed his eyes. "Friends don't make friends consider fleeing into the night."

"Ah." Adrian dipped his chin, feeling foolish. "So I've already lost that designation, have I?"

"Every mage I've ever known has been a risk to me. There's no reason to take it personally." Lucas turned away, scanning the quiet cemetery. "Everyone else, it seems, is brash and careless. One by one, they are collected and taken away. To be known is to be a name in someone else's witness statement."

"We don't need to continue this if you'd rather not. I don't want to be someone's burden." Adrian grimaced, searching for some-thing—*anything*—in his expression that would give away what Lucas felt. "But if it's all the same to you, I'd prefer not to forget you. Either of you. And if you can trust me again, I would like to earn your friendship back."

Lucas' gaze had been drawn away again, across the headstones and between the weeping trees. "My parents believed things could change. They kept just ahead of the Seekers. Constantly travel-ing, finding people like us, helping them secure safe houses and new lives. They were always off somewhere, doing something the International Arcane Order wouldn't like. Protesting. Orga-nizing. I went with them when I was growing up. Then I reached my rebellious stage, but how are you supposed to rebel against rebels?" He frowned across the manicured lawn, droplets from the sprinklers catching the starlight like tiny bulbs. "I spent the last two years of their lives arguing with them. Politics mostly, but... oh, about everything. I missed my father's last birthday to be in an Academy demonstration. I chose to. I didn't call them. I knew they didn't want me in the Navy; it was too dangerous for far too many reasons. They were proud of me anyway. Isn't that the *worst*? When you're trying to get someone to see you as an individual, as an adult, as different, and all they want to do is love you?"

"I wouldn't know," Adrian admitted quietly. "Seron was the first person who cared to see me for who I was and not just someone to carry on the family name." He placed his hand on top of Lucas'. Warm, slender fingers. A comfort, quiet and steady. "I understand not being what one's parents might have hoped for, though."

"It's more difficult than you think: protecting exceptional children. I didn't realize until I had one of my own." Lucas frowned. "I try to give her space to breathe—to be who she is—but I feel like I spend more time covering her light than not. I wonder if she'll look back and think I didn't care for her because of that."

"Oh," Adrian exhaled, squeezing his fingers. "I don't think she will. She adores you."

"When I was five, I adored mine," Lucas chuckled wryly. "Then I hit puberty and became a menace and it took them being gone to make me see how damned foolish I'd been."

"I'm not certain there's a single teenager who isn't a fool," Adrian sniffed, his nose running. "Even if she's a menace for a time, eventually she'll realize you tried your best. Hopefully without you dying, yes?"

"I suppose it wouldn't make too much of a difference to her." Lucas rubbed his hand over his face. "In ten years, she might well prefer to have me safely stowed somewhere out of the way."

"...has it always been just the two of you?" Adrian asked softly, lifting his gaze. Never a word about any of the rest of her family. Not a mention of Tula's mother. "Am I allowed to ask that?"

"...I took her in shortly after she was born." He squinted at the branches of the tree above them, falling in alongside Adrian. "There was a little while her mother was vacillating about whether to keep her. Two years of visits and then that was it. She was gone. No goodbye, nothing." Lucas frowned. "She left the country, I think. Sometimes I forget that Tula remembers her. Months will go by, then she'll ask."

"I'm sorry." Adrian dropped his gaze. "It's little wonder you were hesitant with me. If it makes you feel better, I'm not precisely the type to vanish in a puff of smoke."

"No, it doesn't seem that you are." Lucas touched the wrought iron as they passed through the gates to the parking lot. "You're feeling steady enough to drive?"

He was lightheaded, still, from Lucas' invasion. "After some food, I think. I've never had someone... delve before. It's disorienting, to say the least."

"So I've heard." Lucas shut his eyes, sighing quietly. "Alright. I'll drive."

"Are you sure you're well enough to do so? We could walk, if you'd prefer. It's not a terrible evening for a moonlit stroll."

"I'd like to put some distance between us and whatever resonance I might have missed." He paused at his car, glancing over. "I promise not to steal your teeth."

"For now, in any case." Adrian nodded, crossing to the passenger side door. "If I didn't trust you, I wouldn't have allowed you to root around in my mind."

"Trust for trust." Lucas slipped into the driver's seat. "I don't *root*. I'm not an amateur. I call."

"Oh?" Adrian took his seat and turned to him. "Do tell."

"You can't possibly want me to discuss magic theory right now."

"Why not? I'm curious. It's a fascinating topic and you, as you said, are not an amateur."

Lucas huffed, setting his car into reverse and backing out of the space. "It's been a very long time since I discussed it with anyone." He pulled out onto the winding drive leading to the main road. "I ask for what can be provided and it rises to the surface, like bubbles in champagne."

"And you see them? Or only hear what I say aloud?"

"I can see memories, but I have to leave the present to do so. I've only done that a few times. What you shared was enlightening enough." Lucas glanced at him as he drove. "They'll take me away from her if they discover what I am."

"I know." Adrian frowned, the stoplights washing them both in a ruby glow. "They would use you for it. I wouldn't wish for that, or for your girl to be raised by others. You know that, right?"

Lucas nodded once, watching the road again. "I heard you before." He kept time to some song in his head, tapping his thumb on the wheel. "I was harsh with her. She's young enough, she wouldn't be held responsible. It's my fault; I should have taught her better. I should have been more careful."

"It doesn't seem in her nature to be careful, Luke. I imagine it'd be like trying to divert a river from its path." Adrian studied the shape of his fingers, how they skimmed across surfaces, never gripping too tightly. "You're a good father. Better than most, I imagine."

"You haven't seen enough of my parenting to make that assessment."

"I've seen how you are with her. How *she* is with *you*. You care very much. That you're second guessing yourself is evidence of that." Adrian leaned back in his seat. "Perhaps you're right, though; I don't know anything about parenting."

"That isn't—" He shook his head. "Honestly, I don't think anyone does. In the end, you always do something they'll see as wrong."

"Or vice versa," Adrian murmured, turning towards the window.

"I shouldn't think—Ah." Lucas hummed, a pleasant lilting half melody. "Yes. I imagine, from her perspective, that might..." He pulled into a little gravel lot beside a brightly colored food truck. "Do you want to talk about them?"

"Them?"

"Your parents." Lucas set the car in park and turned to him; the ruby gleam in his eyes was gone, leaving only shadows and the subtle sheen of emerald in its wake. "You've mentioned them a few times. As your confessor, I'm here, should you wish to."

"My father was a bigot and my mother was never there." The words were more acerbic than Adrian had meant them to be, but it was an old, old wound. "It doesn't matter anymore. My father is dead and my mother is doing what she does best: being entirely unavailable."

"I'm sorry." Quiet, but without pity. "I would hesitate to disagree; it seems to matter to you."

"More than I'd like," Adrian sniffed. "I hoped they'd put aside our differences to attend my wedding; they didn't."

"Expectations have a way of garnering dissatisfaction," Lucas murmured solemnly. "And yet sometimes they are unavoidable. I'm sorry they weren't there for you."

"That's alright. It made my decision not to attend my father's funeral fairly simple. And my mother, in turn, shunned Seron's. So." Adrian tilted his head to the side. "Shall we?"

Lucas silently bowed his head for a moment, then stepped out of the car. The night was brisk and the air smelled strongly of onions and spice.

Adrian followed on his heels, trying to put his father out of his mind. Lucas ordered most of the menu and carried chips and salsa to a squeaky little table while they waited for the feast. "Eat the salsa; you'll get scurvy without vitamin C."

"Scurvy." Adrian selected a chip. "Do I look ill to you?"

"You did earlier."

"Flatterer," he muttered.

"You're welcome." Lucas curved his hands over his knee. "...I don't think I would talk to you."

Adrian drew his attention from the way Lucas' fingers laced together, trying to catch up to what he'd said. "What?"

"If I could have heard from my parents, the way Tula does? If I could, even now..." He shook his head, his voice tightening. "I don't think I'd ever leave. I'd just stay there with them until I was part of the marble." He laughed darkly, rubbing his knuckle to the corner of his eye. "They only talk to her, you know. No messages for me. They tell her stories. They talk to her about her gift. And I've recently learned that they specifically ask her not to tell me what they talk about. It's fair, I suppose. She has the right to her relationship with them. And I... It's part of it, I think. If I can't talk to them, can't see them, can't hear from them, then I can't fool myself into thinking they're still here. They want me to acknowledge that they're gone."

"...you're saying Seron is trying to protect me?" Adrian whispered, letting the salsa burst on his tongue, tangy and just spicy enough to make him sweat. "I thought... He knew I was angry with him and he didn't want to—I don't know."

"Maybe you're right." Lucas wrinkled his nose. "I don't imagine anyone enjoys talking to someone angry with them. I don't know him; I couldn't begin to guess why he does anything. I'm just saying: I can see a reason why my parents talk to Tula and not to me, and why Seron might not answer you."

Lucas was right; Adrian *wouldn't* leave the mausoleum if Seron answered him. What meaning did the rest of the world hold for him when he could be loved, instead? If he could speak with him again, hear the sound of his laughter echoing against the marble? "Have you ever been in love?"

Shadowed green eyes flicked to him curiously. "In? No. In the general vicinity, yes. But I've... No. I haven't been."

"In a general vicinity." Adrian raised a brow. "Your parents?"

"For a certainty. I have been a great observer of love." He smiled wryly. "Does that count? I can recognize it fairly well in others."

"Is that so?"

"It's a talent I have honed: people-watching. Listening."

Adrian quirked his brow in question.

"Not like that," Lucas chided with a rueful shake of his head. "Not since I was quite young. It is not so simple or pleasant to know what someone is thinking. There is no tact or kindness in a thought; only unrelenting opinion. I prefer to be the one with the opinions. Mine are the ones that matter, after all." Lucas preened as he said it and Adrian couldn't help but smile at that. "I won't say that it hasn't... enhanced my skills at reading faces. I did have assistance in that regard for a time. One can do what one can do." The sharp angle of his shoulder lifted and dropped in a shrug. Lucas looked up into the sky again. "How long were you married?" he asked, changing the subject.

"Two weeks ago, we would've been married five years. We'd been together a few years before that." Adrian nibbled on the spiced salsa. "It doesn't sound like very long, but I can hardly remember what I was like before. Testier, probably."

"So. Similar to now, then," Lucas quipped.

"I'm not *testy*," Adrian sniffed, glancing sharply at him. "When have I been testy towards you?"

"Right now." His lips curved sharply. "You should see yourself. You have a full furrow. Careful with that; you could permanently wrinkle."

Was Lucas... teasing him? Gentling once more? Then again... He had shared more in the last hour than in the entirety of their acquaintance. He'd looked after him, stayed and supported him. Perhaps, no matter what he'd said, he'd never stopped being Adrian's friend after all. "How dare you." Adrian narrowed his eyes, trying to keep from smiling in relief. "I would *never*. Take it back."

"Gods and monsters, you've made it worse now. You've aged a good ten years in the last minute. It's horrifying."

"*Horrifying*. First I'm sick; now I'm old and horrifying," Adrian grumbled as the man's smile bloomed. "It's a wonder you can stand to look at me at all."

"I don't frighten easily, I've told you." Lucas covered Adrian's face with his hand, a muffled laugh escaping him. "Do stop. You're testing my limits."

It was a beautiful, unexpected sound, and Adrian couldn't help but join him. He rested his cheek on Lucas' palm, watching his eyes glinting in the moonlight. "We're sitting on the side of the road in the dark. Have we devolved into teenagers?"

"Do you have a pack of cigarettes and some purloined vodka?" Lucas asked. "I left my boom box at home."

"I guess we'll need to start over again." Adrian shifted his chair closer to him. "I'm more of a brandy or whiskey man, in any case."

"Excellent choices, both. I recall getting very ill from a bottle of crème de menthe." He stuck his tongue out, still laughing. "To this day, the scent of mouthwash stymies."

"Not toothpaste, too, I hope."

"Switched to the baking soda variety a while back." Lucas rolled his eyes. "There were a few weeks where Tula thought she was supposed to make gagging noises when we brushed her teeth."

"So the crème de menthe incident was relatively recent, then?" Adrian quirked a brow. "Might I ask the occasion?"

"I had the bright idea to use all the liquor in the house rather than simply pouring it out when we remodeled." He shook his head. "Not that there was much to begin with, but I'd been carrying that green bottle for four moves. Never again." Lucas' smile softened. "There." He tapped Adrian's forehead gently. "Much better."

"You have a wonderful smile, you know?" Adrian wanted to gather his hand close and cup it to his cheek. Would it be welcomed?

Would he scare the man again? "I wouldn't mind seeing it more often."

"No?" Lucas hesitated, the expression faltering as it was named, his gaze dancing away again. "I'll take that under consideration."

"Do I..." Adrian pressed his lips together. "I should've asked, before... Do I make you uncomfortable?"

"No. Hold that thought." Lucas slipped from his seat to collect two trays laden with tacos and plates of meat and vegetables. "Yes," he seemed to change his mind as he set the trays on their table. "Yes and no. Where do you want to start?"

"I want to start with what that means." Adrian frowned again, watching him steadily. "I'll stop if you—"

"Stop what?"

"...flirting with you?" A heat rushed to his cheeks and he was glad he'd moved away. "I'll stop if you'd like."

Lucas dropped his gaze, hiding behind lashes and shadows. "...I wasn't sure that was what you were doing. I wasn't sure you meant to."

"...I wasn't, either," Adrian admitted quietly. "I'm still... not in the best place. I like you, though. Do you want me to stop?"

He watched those lips curl into a wry crescent. "Not particularly," Lucas huffed, knuckles pressing together at his knee. "I elected not to read into it. Given..." He glanced around them. "Circumstances."

Adrian lifted his chin. "I know. I know." He traced a line across Lucas' fingers carefully. "It feels as though it's a sort of betrayal. But I was hollow before I met you and Tula, and now I—" He scrubbed a hand across his face. "I don't know."

"I see." Lucas turned his hand over so that their palms met. Warm and smooth. "I'm disinclined to be a party to something that makes you feel like you're betraying him. Even if you aren't."

Heat rose to his cheeks as Adrian traced the tender lines at the inside of Lucas' wrist. "Is it alright if that's all I can be for now?"

"It's alright." He was soft and pliant in Adrian's hold, flexing gently. "Even if that's all it ever is. I can handle quite a lot of grayscale, but I don't want to confuse Tula."

"That's more than understandable." Adrian closed his eyes. He felt as though he'd swallowed a thousand butterflies, their wings fluttering in his chest. "I thought I might melt into the floor when she asked me to hold her. I didn't think I liked children."

"No?"

Fingers in his hair for the first time in months, gently combing it back from his face. Soothing. "Don't stop," Adrian whispered, leaning into the touch, his voice raw. "Please, don't stop."

"As you will," Lucas murmured. "It's alright, Adrian. It hurts. It might always hurt. But it's alright. You're here and you're good."

"I'm—" He nodded slowly. It surprised Adrian to hear him say so after the night they'd had. "You think so?"

"I've seen you. In here." Lucas tapped his head lightly.

Adrian hummed an exhale. Ridiculous. The man must think him ridiculous, overcome by the simple act of being touched. "You're good, too. I hope you realize this."

Lucas chuckled. "Never mind 'good'; I'm fucking fabulous. Absolutely delightful." His fingertips raked Adrian's scalp lightly. "You'll get there."

"An aspiration." Adrian rolled his eyes, voice shaking from some ungodly combination of laughter and tears. "For if I don't succumb to scurvy."

"An excellent point. Tomatoes. Peppers. And protein from the beef. You'll be back to fighting form in no time."

"Soon enough," Adrian agreed, shifting close enough to nestle against the curve of Lucas' shoulder. "I'll take your word for it."

CHAPTER EIGHT

LUCAS

They played chess in the parking lot on sunny days when Tula was at her tennis lessons. They took walks around the university campus during the odd lunch hour. And Lucas *liked* him. He liked the way Adrian's hands felt when they brushed his own, like spiderwebs, here and gone, leaving a lingering impression of where they'd been. All their visits were like that. Short, with sensations that carried on well after they parted. Once a week. Every so often twice. Some unplanned mornings where they ran into each other at the cemetery and lingered for a moment to trade stories or make plans. And it was... nice.

He'd never been good with people. He'd never been good at playing a part or pretending to like what he didn't, or keeping his opinions to himself. But it was easy with Adrian. Sometimes the man balked, and a moment would pass where Lucas would prepare for Adrian to bail... only he didn't. Not because he was being polite, or because he needed anything, but he just found his way through like a pilot in a storm.

Which Adrian was.

He was a pilot still very much in the midst of one of the worst storms of his life.

Lucas could remember the first couple of years after his parents had died with perfect clarity. The misery. The unexpected heart-breaks from the tiniest stimuli. A smell in the air. A photograph. A Christmas tree. *Holidays*. Oh, those were the worst. So many memories piled on top of each other.

"What are you doing for Independence Day?" Lucas asked as Adrian picked up their takeout containers from the counter. It was a cool day, the sky a glorious expanse of powder blue dotted with floating orbs of cloud, like cotton balls, and they'd elected to share their lunch hour al fresco.

"There's an air show I was thinking of going to with Kriss."

Her name set Lucas on edge. He still couldn't understand what Adrian saw in the woman that made him willing to risk being near her, but it wasn't his place to say anything. As long as she kept a wide berth from him and Tula, Lucas would hold his tongue on the matter.

Adrian's fingers brushed his as they took their bags. Warm and calloused. "Do you have plans yet?"

"We usually go to the fairgrounds. Pop balloons. Throw rings onto bottles." Now that he was saying it aloud, Lucas realized it sounded like a silly suggestion, but he'd committed. Adrian hadn't asked about Tula's ability for weeks. That was respect. For her. For them. He'd earned silly suggestions. "Maybe you'd like to join us, before or after your air show. Put some cavities in your teeth to protect yourself."

"From that devilish tooth fairy. I'd nearly forgotten." Adrian smiled, touching his shoulder. "I'd love to go with you if Tula doesn't mind the extra company."

"You do have to let her win all the games. It's emotionally debilitating."

"You didn't *lead* with that." Adrian narrowed his eyes, but his smile didn't disappear. "I'm not sure my pride can take it. I'm very accustomed to winning, you know."

"Yes. I'm well aware. I've met pilots before," Lucas informed him with a roll of his eyes. Every day, Adrian seemed a little brighter. "I'll trade you some rice for some naan."

Adrian traded him without a second thought. "I'll lose to her and be happy about it, so long as I get a gigantic, ridiculous, multicolored stuffed creature out of the affair."

"That's between you and her. I don't negotiate about her stuffed animals. That's way above my pay grade." Lucas dipped the bread into his curry and nibbled from the soaked edges. "How are the students this semester?"

"The summer session is rather peaceful. Just labs and seminars, working on grants, and putting together papers. I've got a conference coming up in a few weeks in Spain." Adrian scooped some of his curry onto the pile of rice, their feet touching under the park table. "I'll be gone for sixteen days."

"Spain in the summertime. My only work travel takes me to France in the rainy season," he laughed. "Have some paella for me."

"It's going to be *broiling*." Adrian chuckled, shaking his head. "I'll eat my fill and send you pictures. I'm going to miss our time together."

"Are you?" Lucas bit a little more naan, chewing it slowly. So would he, though he couldn't admit that aloud. "We'll always have cell phones," he offered with a smile. "It'll be like you never left. Except you'll be a lot hotter and they'll force you to take naps."

"Hotter?" he asked, watching Lucas closely.

"You know what I mean."

"Siesta time is beach time." Adrian winked, but he reached out across the space between them, wiggling his fingers. "I'll call you. Every night, if you'd like. Just like I never left."

"You don't call me every night now." Lucas lifted his brow.

"I could," Adrian chuckled. "To keep you from missing me too much while I'm away. Preventative measure."

"You think I'm in danger of that, do you?" Lucas asked wryly, folding his bread to scoop another mouthful of curry. "Pining?"

"Terrible danger." Adrian lifted his brows, sipping on his mango lassi. "By the time I return, you'll be pale and wan, haunting your halls like a Victorian widow. Who will make sure you don't get scurvy if not me? Your poor teeth might become necessary donations for Tula's college fund."

"I think you're getting us confused. I have saved you from scurvy too many times to mention. I don't require assistance with the matter myself."

"As you wish." Adrian dipped his head, seeming more than a little disappointed. "You will keep me abreast of all of the kindergarten gossip though, won't you? I'm not sure I'll be able to contain myself if I don't know which colors are the best and who dared to try and trade carrots for brownies at lunch."

"So what you're saying," Lucas murmured, trying not to stare too long at the way Adrian's lips pursed around his straw, "is that *you're* going to miss *me*."

"I told you I would." Adrian rolled his eyes, swirling his straw in his drink absently. "I haven't gone a full week without seeing you for two months. I enjoy our time together. Is that so unexpected?"

"...no." Grayscale. Gray. No expectations. No commitments. Just... "I enjoy our time as well," he admitted. "I wouldn't be averse to you calling. When you like. For the sake of kindergarten gossip."

"Wonderful." If the man was trying to conceal the smile that blossomed behind his fork, he failed utterly. Warm as the beaches of Barcelona, a sweet little quirk of his mustache. "I'm pleased to have reached an accord."

Friends, Lucas reminded himself sternly as he watched Adrian swallow. They were friends. Grayscale friends. Something as ephemeral as fog. "...what's the conference about?"

"High-efficiency materials for supersonic travel." Adrian lifted a brow, taking a bite of his curry. "That's what the title says, in any case. Mostly it's an excuse to sit at the beach and drink and expense the whole endeavor onto one's grants."

"I always suspected that was what conferences were for," Lucas murmured, tongue in cheek. "Sangria." Adrian was unreasonably handsome. No one was supposed to look like that in real life. Even models were edited before going to print. "Supersonic sangria, perhaps, although that sounds like a recipe for a hangover."

"And nausea, certainly." Adrian chuckled. "Most of the attendees bring their families and spend a few days sightseeing afterward. It's a nice racket."

"I can only imagine."

"It will be good to go. I have a friend coming from the UK and another from France. It's been too long."

"How long?"

"A few years. Time got away from me." Adrian sighed, closing his eyes and leaning back. "It's been doing that lately."

"I'm pretty sure they sped up the clocks a couple of years ago. You'll have to let me know if it's slower in Spain."

Adrian tapped his foot under the table. "I'll test my watch if you like, darling."

Darling. Lucas blinked slowly, staring at the swollen grains in his takeaway bin as they absorbed the curry. Flecks of red spice amid the green. It was only a word. It didn't mean...

Only he found that he wanted it to mean something.

He was familiar with grayscale. He *liked* it. It made his life easier. He had more than enough on his plate with Tula and his business and the daily effort of remaining undetected. But he wanted this to be something more. Not something grasping or controlling or trying to make him into something he wasn't, but *this*. This easy banter on park benches with a handsome man who occasionally forgot to let go of his hand.

Adrian studied him curiously. "Have I gotten food on my face? Spinach in my teeth?"

"Hmm." Lucas touched Adrian's chin by impulse, tilting his face to play at an inspection... and there it was. Stillness in Adrian's easy smile. Tension in his perfect jaw. No. Not yet. Lucas let go, returning to his meal. "Just checking for cavities."

"Ah," Adrian exhaled, breathing again now that the danger had passed; he touched Lucas' hand atop the table lightly. "Did you find anything I should get examined?"

"I didn't find anything that would impede an emergency fairy extraction. Beyond that, I couldn't say."

"I'll make sure to give you a call if I ever have pain in my incisors, then."

"That's all I ask." Lucas smiled to himself, stirring his curry into his rice. "I don't suppose you need a new suit for your conference? The last one I made for you was more formal..."

Adrian brightened. "Something I won't roast in, perhaps?"

"I'm not making you shorts."

"Not *shorts*. Just something lighter. Linen?"

"Linen." Lucas squinted at him. "Are you going to make sure it's pressed? I don't want someone thinking I intentionally sent you out in wrinkles."

Adrian rolled his eyes with a laugh. "I would never besmirch your good name with *wrinkles*, darling."

Again with the epithet. Lucas tried not to take it too personally, even as his pulse sped. "Then I'll consider it."

"Will you?" Adrian rested his chin on his fist. "I'd be much obliged."

Posing. Always posing, as though he'd stepped off the pages of some magazine. "Did you ever model?"

"They liked to put me in alumni magazines when I was in college. Stanford Swim and perfect grades. They loved to show those sorts of things to donors." Adrian shrugged, returning to his meal. "More than that, no. It's kind of you to ask."

"Stanford Swim... was in uniform?" Lucas asked, peering at his takeaway and attempting to sound casual.

"...some, yes. There are team photos somewhere."

"Interesting." Lucas smiled fleetingly, peering across the park. "I abhor swimming pools; I can't stand the smell of the chlorine."

"I didn't know." Adrian studied him curiously. "The uniforms are nice, though, wouldn't you say?"

"Well, I haven't seen. I'll have to do some due diligence before I can offer an opinion. Unless you mind?"

"Mind what?"

"My... seeing the uniforms. For professional purposes."

"Mine, specifically, or more generally?"

He gritted his back teeth, then forced himself to relax, meeting Adrian's gaze. He didn't *seem* offended. Usually, he puffed up like an angry squirrel when he was. "Do you have a preference?"

"I'm not sure I still *have* it," Adrian chuckled, "nor whether it would fit. I was leaner in college. I could probably dig up a picture..." He pulled out his phone, amused. "It might take me a moment if you'd like to dig up your ancient history."

"I wasn't in a swim team."

"You were in the Navy, though." Adrian glanced up from his phone. "An interesting choice for someone who doesn't like to swim."

"There are lots of ways to be in the Navy. Mine only took me onto a couple of aircraft carriers and those were more like traveling cities."

"But wasn't it a part of your basic?"

Lucas hummed under his breath. "Not entirely. Classified. No pictures to show for the little swimming they required."

"...classified," Adrian repeated, handing him his phone to show him a photo of a younger version of himself beaming next to a diving board. Planes of perfectly sculpted muscles. A swim cap tightly circled his head without a stray hair escaping. Adrian's silver eyes were hidden behind goggles. A time before the glorious, perfectly trimmed mustache, his face clean-shaven and sharp-angled. "There are some of me in considerably more clothes, but I imagined these were more entertaining."

"Very entertaining," Lucas mused quietly. Flirting, then. Definitely flirting; showing off like a preening peacock. No reason not to, with a body like that. "You look happy here. Proud. It's a good look for you."

"I'm well aware of my finer qualities." A pleased quirk of his mustache, a glint in his eyes. "Still, it's very nice to hear you say so."

He was going to need to do something about the images now burning into his mind's eye sooner or later. Probably sooner. "Any time."

"Do you still have my measurements, or should I return to your lair?"

"My *lair*." Lucas rolled his eyes, handing the phone back. "How dramatic. Have you gained some extra padding since your last fitting? Too many soirées with tiny cakes?"

"I *hope* not, but I don't walk around with a tape measure." Adrian huffed quietly. "Perhaps we should schedule another, just in case. Do you have time?"

"I can manage it Friday morning. Do you have a class?"

"Not Friday, no." Adrian tapped out a note on his phone. "Time?"

"Nine-thirty? I have to swing by my parents', but after." He touched Adrian's elbow. "Off-white, I think. Nothing too stark."

"I could join you in the morning. Zinnias and sunflowers." Adrian placed his hand over the top of Lucas', resting it there for a breath. "I'll pick up breakfast on my way over."

"As you like." He glanced at Adrian as he drew his hand away yet again. "Should we walk the blossoms before we return to normal life?"

"I'd like to, yes. The roses were almost fully out last time." Adrian bagged up the rest of his meal, rising from the little table under the Japanese maple that had become theirs, at least once a week from twelve to one. He held out his hand, flashing a warm, easy smile.

This time, the touch would remain, at least until the end of the walk. Lucas took the offered hand and squeezed it gently. "On-ward."

CHAPTER NINE

LUCAS

"You look like you're trying to solve the Millennium Prize," Adrian chuckled over his cafe menu, reaching across the space between them to touch Lucas' hand. Adrian's hair was wind-blown, sunglasses hiding the shimmering silver of his eyes, the corners of which crinkled to match a wide, warm smile. "I can't begin to say how nice it is to see you. The conference in Spain was lovely, but I did miss your company. You'd have enjoyed the beaches. Less, some of the clothing optional areas, though."

"So you do like the nude beaches or you don't?" Lucas set the menu down. "And what is the Millennium Prize?"

"A set of very difficult math problems," Adrian hummed, lifting his brows. "And it depends entirely on the inhabitants of the beach, not the concept itself."

"Have you tried?" Lucas turned his glass of water with his free hand. "Either?"

"Yes and yes." Adrian smiled, setting his menu aside. "I'll let you imagine which I had more success in."

"Is that why you live in a very nice condo overlooking the beach on a professor's salary? Here, I thought you had inherited wealth."

"That's very kind of you." Adrian shook his head. "I toyed with the Navier-Stokes problem in graduate school but lost interest rather quickly. My skills tend to lie on the more practical end of the spectrum. Your suit was very well received, though—" He waved their waitress over. "I'll have the *poulet basquaise, s'il vous plaît,* and a glass of Merlot."

"Same," Lucas nodded as the young woman jotted their orders down with a cheerful smile. As she left, Lucas glanced down, waiting for Adrian's hand to slip away like the tide again. Only it didn't. Lucas ran his tongue behind his teeth.

"A month ago I thought about canceling the trip entirely." Adrian's hand was a steady, warm pressure on Lucas' that didn't stray until wine arrived at the table. "I hope you realize how much I appreciate your support."

Support. Lucas bowed his head. "Happy to be of service."

"I mean it," Adrian continued, swirling the wine in his glass. "I know everyone says these things, but I mean it."

"I know that you do." Lucas summoned a smile and sipped his water, leaning back from the table. "It's no trouble."

"Ah." Adrian breathed in deeply, taking a sip of his wine. "I'm glad." He opened his mouth and closed it again before speaking. "I've been meaning to ask you... Has she mentioned anything about him?"

Seron. They were back to Seron. Lucas glanced across the street as a car idled in front of a shop. "Some things."

"He was a good man," Adrian said quietly. "Brave and kind and selfless, almost to a fault. You would have liked him. I never met a person who didn't. Even people hell-bent on not liking him were slowly won over; it was impossible not to be drawn into his orbit."

"You love him very much." Lucas forced his gaze to leave the car before it pulled away. Old habits from a childhood on the run. Memorizing plates to see if the same one showed up too often. Watching idling cars and trying to see through the dark windows for any sign of who might be inside, wondering if they would emerge to take him away. To take his parents away. Lucas shook it off. "She likes his stories; I imagine you miss them."

"I do," Adrian admitted. "More than I thought possible. He had this way of seeing the world: looking past the humdrum surface to find beauty and warmth underneath. It didn't take much to make him happy. An odd fit for the military, one might imagine, but he loved that, too. Felt like he was doing something important, making a difference. He wanted to change the system from the inside out. I imagine he would have if he'd... Well." He cleared his throat, quaffing the remainder of his glass. "I worry he's lonely, cooped up with my crusty old relatives. I hope they aren't giving him too much trouble. Though, given time, perhaps he could even win my father's approval. That would be a truly impressive feat. Millennium Prize-worthy, for a certainty."

"If anyone could." Lucas curled his fingers around his cup. "I haven't heard that he's complaining about his appointments. If that helps."

"It does." Adrian dipped his head. "I'm glad she can know him. It's a comfort."

"Good." He wasn't entirely sure how he felt about that or any of the other dead his daughter chatted with outside of their own family, but there wasn't anything he could do about it except to support her and try his best to protect her. Support and protect. It was what he'd been made for. Keeping secrets. Defending his own and others'. Lucas exhaled carefully. "I'm very sorry, Adrian."

"I know you are." Adrian's wine glass was abandoned and he rose to his feet, picking up his chair and shifting his place just to Lucas' side, taking his hand and squeezing it lightly. "He'd have liked you, too. Does, I think. I can almost feel him there again when I speak of you. Like sunlight on a winter morning."

"I'm sure he's glad you're out doing things again. That's a part of the process, too." What was he supposed to say? There was often a sense of elevating the dead when they were gone, polishing away their imperfections, but from all he'd heard, Seron Sharp didn't seem to have had imperfections. Nothing more than tiny blemishes easily erased by his own sunlight.

Adrian touched the inside of his wrist lightly. "What I'm trying to say is: thank you. From both of us."

"I understand." Lucas smiled fleetingly. "It's been a pleasure getting to know you."

"...is everything alright?" Adrian's silver gaze studied him, flicking between his eyes with concern. "If you'd prefer I didn't bring him up—"

"No, of course not. I'm honored you would choose to share."

"I find it easy to speak with you." Adrian squeezed his hand lightly once more before letting go and returning to his wine. "My confessor. You know, if you have any confessions of your own to make, I'm a very adept listener."

"What? And ruin my polished air of mystery?" Lucas lifted his water, drained it, and set the condensation-dampened glass aside. "I wouldn't be a very good confessor if I did that."

"The option is open, darling." Adrian studied him with a slight frown. "Should you ever wish to capitalize on it."

There it was again. That word that made his heart skip beats foolishly. Foolishly because Adrian was in love with his entombed sunlight and it was cruel to wish for or fixate on the thought, even if Adrian's touches sometimes lingered a little longer than usual. Grayscale. Friendship. Support. He nodded. "I appreciate the offer."

"You've not taken your communion," Adrian smiled, nudging Lucas' glass of wine back towards him. "Tell me what I've missed since I've been away. Any new belts or art projects? Have you gotten any new commissions?"

"Ah, no. Vivant made some noises about wanting a line for next spring, but they wanted more of that frilly nonsense I did for your friend; not my real work." He shrugged. "Belts take time, so I doubt Tula will take another any time soon, but she did make a lovely macramé plant holder in her crafts class. So now we have to find a plant for that."

"Do you have a picture? I can pick something up the next time I'm at the florist's—"

"Lucas?" A familiar voice called from the nearby sidewalk and Anara swept through the gate with a grin. "Lucas Halpern, as I live and breathe. Look at you acting positively human! Who is your very handsome friend? Oh!" She held out her hand. "Hello, there. I've seen you around my flower shop!"

"Adrian," he introduced himself as he reached across the table to clasp her hand. "It's lovely to see you in a more social setting. Do you know each other?"

"Ah. Yes." Lucas cleared his throat. "Anara and I are PTA allies against the sea of nonsense." He met her gaze steadily. "Adrian and I are cemetery neighbors."

"Neighbors, hm?" She lifted a brow, glancing at Lucas. "The one you were telling me about? The professor?"

"Indeed," Adrian hummed. "Are you telling tales about me, Luke?"

Lucas stared Anara down, not meeting his gaze. "I attempted to cajole Anara into educating her youngsters at your demonstration. She declined. Perhaps next time." He lifted his brows meaningfully. "Another spin class?"

"No, Reggie and the kids bought me a massage last year for Mother's Day and I'm finally cashing it in!" She beamed, glancing between the two of them. "I'll let you get back to your date, hm?"

"It's not a date," Lucas said quietly, wishing she would stop smiling quite so brightly. He felt his chest tighten. "We're just..."

Out of the corner of his eye, Adrian's expression fell slightly. "I do hope you enjoy your well-deserved pampering."

"Hm." Her lips pressed together as she lifted her other brow to match the first. "I suppose we'll need to catch up later, then. It was good to see you both."

"Hi to Reggie and the littles. Tula's been wanting to come by to try out that haunted mansion you all have." Lucas collected his glass, nursing it close to his heart. "Maybe on the weekend?"

"Yes. Let's try for that." She waved, tucking her braid over her shoulder. "I'll see you later!"

"Later," Lucas agreed, watching her go, and looked down at the glass. "Sorry about that," he murmured as she continued down the block. "We've been friends a long time. She means well. That is—She didn't mean anything by—I'm sorry."

"Sorry for what?" Adrian watched him curiously. "That we're not on a date?"

"That isn't what I—" Lucas grimaced. "That you had to—That it's awkward. That's all. She just—Some people are so insufferably *happy*, they expect everyone to tint their glasses rose to match."

"Are you not happy?"

"I'm fine," Lucas huffed. "I'm a reasonable amount of content." He could feel his pulse beating in his ears. He sipped the wine—pepper and cherry, but not too heavy. "I have nothing to complain about."

"Are you *blushing*?" Adrian chuckled, shaking his head. "Is it such a terrible thought to be on a date with me?"

"It is when that isn't what you want." Lucas gritted his back teeth, wishing he could reel the words back in and away. "Why haven't they brought those crinkly breadsticks?"

"I don't know." Adrian frowned. "I didn't realize you didn't want—I suppose I misread—" He cleared his throat. "I apologize if I've been forward."

"*You*. What *you* want—" Lucas shook his head. "It doesn't matter. It's fine. Grayscale. I promised you grayscale and you shall have it."

"What *is* it that you think I want?" Adrian lifted his brows. "Exactly?"

"I don't know," Lucas said quietly, watching the sheen on the side of his glass slip slowly. Lucas knew what *he* wanted. To touch Adrian. To taste him. To learn if he laughed when he was writhing. To make his damnably beautiful gray eyes cross in pleasure. "I'm not entirely certain that you do either, and that's—I'm content. I don't want you to feel pressured by the idle chatter of kind, well-meaning women."

"But you're not entirely averse to the notion."

"It does not matter whether I am averse or acute. I'm saying you don't need to worry about it one way or the other."

"It matters to me." Adrian glanced between his eyes. "Are you?"

Lucas swallowed a mouthful of the wine, barely tasting it this time. "I have a pulse, eyes, and an above-average intellect. And you're my friend. And I respect your wishes. So we'll just—"

"*Luke*." Adrian rested his palm atop Lucas', chuckling. "I'm not averse and I don't feel pressured. If that changes anything."

Lucas blinked down at his hand, somehow surprised by the contact, even after all the there and not there, fleeting and lingering touches. He swallowed past a lump that suddenly lodged itself in his throat. "You're not?"

"No. Of course not." His lips curved up at the corners. "To quote you, 'I have a pulse, eyes, and an above-average intellect.'"

Of course not, Adrian said as though it were obvious when it certainly wasn't. Still, Lucas found himself fighting the smile that threatened to spill sloppily across his lips. "I see."

"Polished air of mystery, *indeed*," Adrian chuckled, shaking his head. "I won't ask you how you feel, as I'm almost certain I won't get a real answer."

"I'm very fond of you," Lucas whispered, surprising them both.

"And I you." Adrian lifted his hand to his lips, barely brushing Lucas' knuckles.

Lucas pressed his heels to the pavement as the touch of lips to skin made him want to collapse into Adrian's arms. "I can't imagine you *needed* to ask."

Adrian laughed outright. "I'm *barely* beginning to understand your expressions; I didn't have the slightest idea what was going on behind them. When I'm ready... When you are..." Adrian leaned over to press a kiss to his temple. "I'd like to see what we have."

I'm ready, Lucas nearly said but he held his tongue. "As you will." He allowed himself to lean, taking the warmth and strength of Adrian's arms while they were offered.

"Ah," Adrian beamed, keeping an arm around his shoulder as the waiter returned with a tray of twisted breadsticks. "*There* we are. You were right. Can I order you another glass?"

"I haven't finished the first. Is it your intention to get me drunk now that you've pried some of my mystery asunder?"

"Ah! No." Adrian shook his head with a laugh. "No. Sorry, that's my glass, isn't it? I've become distracted, haven't I?"

He nudged his glass towards Adrian gently. "You can assist me. I won't complain."

"Gladly." Adrian lifted the glass to his lips, brushing his fingers past Lucas'. "I'm glad to be home."

"I'm glad, too," Lucas murmured, daring to rest his cheek on Adrian's shoulder. "Very glad."

When they'd parted, Lucas sat in his car, the sunlight through the window warming him in such a way that he could close his eyes and imagine it was the same feeling as when Adrian had wrapped his arm around him. *Around* him. Close. And he hadn't let go.

He rested his forehead on the wheel and breathed slowly.

Maybe.

Maybe there was some reason to hope after all.

Even though it was still foolish.

He texted Anara a white flag and exhaled slowly. He needed to get his heart rate under control, and his thoughts, among other things, before he picked Tula up from school and—

He answered on the first ring. "It was a date, after all."

"*Obviously*," Anara cheered from the other end of the line. "*Luke*. He called you 'Luke'. And didn't you see how he was looking at you?"

"No." Lucas curved over the wheel, clutching the phone to his ear. "...How was he looking at me?"

"Heart in his eyes like a cartoon character."

"I'm positive I would have noticed *that*."

Anara tutted and he heard someone cackling in the background. "Do you need glasses? Reggie knows a great optometrist."

"I already have reading glasses. Can you imagine a man like that hanging about if I had coke bottles attached to my face regularly?" He sighed low. "I didn't... I couldn't let myself think that there might be anything..."

"Why not?"

"Do you know what he's coming to you for all those flowers for?" Lucas wondered quietly.

"For you, I'd hoped. No... Oh." A quiet pause. "Neighbors. Right. What happened, exactly?"

"His husband was killed in action a little less than a year ago." Lucas squeezed his eyes shut hard. "The most perfect, decent person to ever walk the earth, to hear him tell it. So. Even if he does have cartoon eyes—which I haven't noticed—but even if he *does*, it doesn't mean anything. It isn't *about* me. It's grief. I *know* that. I don't know why I'm allowing myself to get caught up—"

"Because you've got a kinder heart than you like to admit," she responded over the sound of a sliding glass door opening and closing to mute the ruckus from inside. "Are you thinking you're some sort of rebound for him?"

"No. Certainly not. But I do think he's... processing what it means to still be alive. And there are a lot of layers to that. He's... experimenting. And that's good. That's healthy. I just..." Lucas sighed shakily, hating the sting of threatening tears and grateful that he was alone where no one could see him. "I *like* him. It would be a great deal easier to be a guinea pig if he weren't so very lovely."

"You really do like him," Anara realized. "Really, really. But, Lucas, have you considered this: what if you're wrong? For once," she added, teasing him gently. "Hypothetically. What if you're wrong? What will you do if you aren't a guinea pig? What if it's more than that for him?"

"It can't be," Lucas reminded himself, wrapping layers of gauze around his heart. "You haven't heard him talk about this—I'm not anything like his husband, Anara. Both of them were a different level of personhood. Heroes. Benefactors. Outgoing. I can barely stand a PTA mixer."

"You *are* a hero," she disagreed fervently. "You're a hero to a five-year-old girl who would be who knows where if not for you. You're selling yourself far too short. And PTA mixers are *dreadful*."

"You make them a damn sight better."

"I know I do!" She laughed, bright and full of life. "Listen. Bring your handsome, grieving date to the next fundraiser and he'll give you a medal himself."

"I don't want a medal," he admitted quietly. "I just want him to kiss me. I don't even care why. I'm pathetic."

"You're not pathetic. If I was sitting across from Professor Dream-boat all evening, I'd think the same thing. That's only natural. Does he know about Tula, yet?"

"They've met. They're... friends, of a sort." He sighed. "I don't want her to get attached to him, only for him to finish healing and skitter away."

"You're a good man. You don't like to let people see that, but it sounds as though your cemetery friend already has." Anara sighed a little romantic sound that Lucas would normally have teased her for. "He might be less likely to skitter than you think."

"I told him I needed them to remain more distant, for Tula, and he understood that. The trouble is she likes him. And they have... similar interests. I usually feel so clear about what is best for her, what she needs, and I don't—I worry that my own feelings might put hers at risk."

"You're doing what you can. You always put her first. I'm really glad you're seeing someone real, who can see how great you are. Try not to be so hard on yourself."

"I will attempt to take your advice." Lucas pressed his forehead to the wheel and swallowed. "Even if it's only a stepping stone, even if nothing... It's nice. I'd forgotten how nice it was to simply *sit* with someone. You know?"

"It is. It is very, very nice." He could hear the smile in her voice. "I'm proud of you. I hope it works out, Lucas. You deserve someone who makes you smile like you were today."

Maybe he *did* deserve it. Adrian could if anyone could, but Lucas wasn't Seron. He rubbed his palm over his face. He would never be Seron or anything like him. And he had a feeling that that was still who Adrian wanted, would always want. But for now. For now, without colors, he could enjoy what was, until it wasn't.

CHAPTER TEN

ADRIAN

When someone passed through one of his protection wards, Adrian felt a kind of tingling up his arms and neck. They were supposed to deter as well as dampen the energies within. For a moment, he stared around his ritual space wondering how the hell he was going to conceal any of this if someone came down, but the moment passed with relief when he heard Tula's laughter just before the creak of the iron gate. He smiled, resting his hand on the marble shelf. Five minutes early. He should have known.

"Good morning!" Tula sang as she skipped down the stairs. "We brought sunflower seeds!"

"And coffee," Lucas added as he followed her into view and held out a steaming cup. "You're sure we didn't need to bring anything else?"

"No, you're a saint." Adrian accepted his latte graciously, resting it on the shelf and taking inky black candles from his bag. "I have everything we need. Would you mind resetting the wards, though?"

Lucas nodded once. "I locked the gate on the way down. With my bolt as well as yours. Just in case." He looked grim relative to Tula's light as he drew his runes in the air, his movements were swift and sure, and the symbols he'd summoned shimmered like crystalline dust in the air for a moment before they dissipated.

"Papa taught me how to ward a bird cage and I kept floating marbles in it for a little while." Tula tugged on Adrian's sleeve, beaming up at him. "Now they're on strings, but they still float."

"That's amazing." Adrian smiled, touching her thick braid. "So you know your wards and telekinesis. What else have you learned?"

Tula glanced back at her father with a questioning look.

"Those are the necessities for survival." Lucas dusted his hands off, returning to them. "And Tula knows she could stand to have stronger wards and less of a penchant to show off her floating marbles to her friends before she learns anything else."

Adrian paused, his fingers hovering over a wick. "...are you sure you want to do this? We could practice what you've already taught her if you'd be more comfortable."

"I can't teach her how to close out the spirits. You can." Lucas sighed, leaning back against the marble wall. "Hopefully with a little more subtlety."

Adrian lifted a brow. "You know me well enough now to understand that subtlety isn't my strongest suit."

"I didn't always know how to make popcorn necklaces," Lucas told him archly. "Life is about learning new skills."

Adrian huffed a quiet laugh. "Fair enough. Now. I believe it's easiest to begin with someone *summoned* from the other side, rather than simply observed. Besides... they'll be able to help us get to somewhere special where we can practice other, more... noticeable types of magic safely."

Tula gazed up at him, wide and blue and full of curiosity. "You can bring them *here*? All the way?" she asked in wonder. "Doesn't it hurt?"

"We're guides," Adrian murmured, lighting the series of candles with a flick of his fingers and focusing his will to illuminate the chalk sigils he'd drawn on the floor before his guests arrived. "We can only lead them as far as they're willing to go. Likewise, they can show us the boundaries between this world and the next, where no Seekers can find us. But if we were to *force* them..." he clarified, "then yes, it would hurt them. It would hurt us, too, over time. Let me ask you this: do you know why some spirits choose to stay in this world?"

"They still have lessons to teach," Tula said, looking at the runes on the floor. "Or they're sad. Or lonely. Or really mad." She wrinkled her nose. "I try to remember they're not mad at me."

"No, I couldn't imagine anyone could be mad at you." Adrian sat on the floor, extending his hand to her and offering his other to Lucas. "Some of them have people among the living they're still looking out for, too. Like your grandparents, I imagine."

"Grandpop and Mada love us very much. They tell silly stories and Mada says when I can reach the stove, she'll teach me to make curry."

"It's a very special gift that you can learn from them." Adrian wiggled his fingers. "Here, please."

Her fingers were warm, resting like the summer sun on his palm, as Lucas joined their circle. Her shadow. And while Tula was alight with wonder and enthusiasm, her father was studying the runes. "Can you bring anyone back?" Tula asked. "Could we ask Mada and Grandpop to—"

Lucas ceased his inspection of the sigils to meet Adrian's gaze. "No."

"No," Adrian agreed quietly. "Their presence here is stable, should they wish to stay. There is no magic that I know of that can bring someone back from the dead as they were in life."

"Nor any guarantee of how long they might linger after they've left this plane," Lucas added, taking his daughter's other hand. "Like Mrs. Dimitri and Ms. Pennows."

"They turned into light," Tula whispered.

Lucas nodded. "Everyone turns into light eventually."

"Just so." Adrian patted her hand gently. "Think of your happiest memory. That should draw a gentler spirit to answer our call."

Tula wrinkled her nose, screwing her eyes shut tight.

"You're certain you want to—" Lucas began, glancing at Tula. "This is safe?"

"With supervision, yes." Adrian had warded the place strongly enough that only the most benevolent spirits could pass through and even so, the amulet that glowed faintly under Tula's tee shirt would provide its own protective aura. "Do you trust me?"

"Some," Lucas hedged, worry between his brows.

Adrian took Lucas' other hand, smoothing his thumb across his knuckles. "I won't let anything bad happen. I promise."

He nodded, frowning. "Happy memories, then."

"As happy as you can manage," Adrian agreed. "Words are a tool to help focus one's power. The most important aspect is not the words, but the *intent*. That being said, I can teach you the phrases I use, when you're ready." He began to chant in Latin, slow and deliberate, lest his aim be misunderstood by wandering spirits.

Tula wiggled, a smile growing across her face. "So many bubbles," she laughed, bouncing where she sat.

"*That's* your happy memory?" Lucas squinted, his frown twitching.

The little girl's giggles continued. "They were all over the floor. The kitchen was a puddle!"

"And now we know the difference between dish soap and dishwasher soap," Lucas sighed, his tension melting as he watched her. Her sunlight was infectious.

"Puddle floor!"

Effortless. She made him so happy, effortlessly, while Adrian had been working at earning that smile and the trust it suggested for months. Adrian focused on the warmth of Lucas' hand, the sound of laughter that bubbled around them, as he finished chanting the ritual; the candlelight bloomed and faded away, leaving a bobbing light dancing in the center of the circle.

The spirit's laugh matched Tula's, but its shape was ever-changing and ephemeral, transparent and opaque by turns, roaring colors fading to pale light and then returning. "Did you come to play with me?" the spirit asked hopefully, rolling a little red ball between Adrian and Tula. "I can show you my secret path through the mists."

"Oh! You're so pretty!" Tula gasped in delight.

"What?" Lucas asked, glancing around. His gifts were firmly of the world of the living, then. There was no hint of awareness even of the creature with them. What must it be like for him to sit with Tula while she spoke with entities he could neither hear nor see nor vaguely feel?

"The rainbow light." Tula beamed, glancing down at the ball. "*Can we play?*"

Adrian flexed his senses towards the spirit, examining its aura before nodding. "Yes. Do you feel the energy in the room? Touch the construct and let it flood through you. Hold onto that memory and float like a bubble."

"Construct?" Lucas' hand tightened on his, searching in vain for what was plainly there to both Adrian and Tula. "What—"

But Tula was already leaning in without fear and the spirit answered in kind, fluttering in place and making the room around them flutter in turn.

The walls bent like fabric. The air grew brisk and light.

"Welcome to the Aether," Adrian murmured, squeezing Lucas' hand. The void formed shapes around them, turning from swirling silver mists into a solid treehouse overlooking a forest pond. "The cemetery is on a ley line and imbued with the residual power of the mages interred within the mausoleum's depths; we wouldn't be able to travel here from just anywhere."

Lucas touched one of the low-hanging leaves, watching as it turned to ice and then water on his fingers. "I always called it the Liminal. You're sure that it's safe for her?"

"With supervision," Adrian repeated. "There are unsafe places here, ones where even I wouldn't go, but this one is... peaceful, I've found. Illuminating."

"I can see that." Lucas tilted his head curiously as Tula tossed the red ball back and forth with a dark-haired boy. "That's the spirit from before? The rainbow light?"

"Ah. Yes. If a spirit is truly of the Aether and has never had a form in the living world, it's difficult for them to maintain a shape outside of it. Here, they can be anything they wish." The spirit had wide silver eyes and looked almost exactly like Adrian when he'd been about Tula's age. Adrian wondered which of his memories the spirit had taken its shape from. A look in the mirror? A photograph?

"It's clever," Lucas mused quietly as Tula and the spirit began to play tag around the base of the tree. "I wouldn't have thought to take her to the Liminal. No satellites. No sensors."

"I'll graciously accept your compliment." Adrian dipped his head, smiling to himself. "Tula, there's a different version of hide-and-seek I'd like you to try your hand at." He motioned towards the spirit, whispering instructions in its ear. "Do you want to give it a go?"

"I like new games!" Tula cheered, hopping patterns in the ever-changing grass.

"Okay. The first round is just like normal hide-and-seek. You'll close your eyes and try to find our friend here. You'll need to follow your senses, not just what you see before you. He'll stay in this glade." Adrian lifted his brows. "Right?"

The spirit nodded, silver eyes glinting merrily.

"Good," Adrian continued. "He'll show himself again as soon as you find him."

Tula hugged herself in excitement, dutifully closing her eyes and counting aloud. The spirit boy ran, picking up speed until he was barely visible, and then he was gone. Lucas watched him even after he'd disappeared from view, eyes narrowed in curiosity.

Even as Tula ran around, peering behind the tree and under bushes and wiggling her fingers in the glowing water, Lucas seemed aware of the spirit's location. Keen senses within the Aether, then, allowing him to follow what he couldn't see in their world by the magical trail the spirit left in its wake.

"Close your eyes," Lucas told his daughter. "Remember how we talked about feeling the edges of the wards?"

"Uh-huh. Fuzzy sparky feelings."

"It doesn't feel like wards. But it does feel different than everything else. Feel for what's different."

"Like in the magazine at the dentist?"

"Exactly, sunbeam. Find the bow tie."

"The magazine?" Adrian asked.

"Hm?" Lucas glanced over at him, then smiled. "I suppose your dentist makes house calls and offers you champagne before your cleaning?" he mused, lacing his fingers behind him. "There are children's magazines in the waiting room that have pictures. They look the same but for small elements. Usually, there's a bow tie or a butterfly somewhere hidden."

"...no champagne." Adrian frowned, his gaze darting away. He couldn't recall any magazines in his dentist's office, for children or otherwise, and he'd certainly never played any games there. He turned his attention to Tula, watching her reach out blindly, her nose scrunched in concentration. She took two steps to the left, then two more. "Do you feel anything yet?"

"Mm... Maybe..." Tula tilted her head to the side, then to the other one. "I think it tastes like lemonade. Over..." She opened her eyes. "In that low branch? No..." Tula wandered towards the little pond and placed her palm over the surface. "*Under* it."

A laugh bubbled from under the water and ripples appeared, splashing her fingertips.

"Good! Very, very good." Adrian nodded, glancing at Lucas. "She's talented at finding them."

"Recognizing resonance—our own and that of others—is imperative to navigating this world safely." Lucas watched Tula splashing with the spirit. "I'd have known yours, had it not been for the talisman. I can feel it now."

"Can you?" Adrian tilted his head. "And what do you feel?"

Lucas blinked slowly, catlike, his lips curving. "If cardamom and starlight merged to become velvet," he murmured. "And then that velvet cloaked a volcano."

Adrian exhaled a little sigh, a familiar rush of heat gathering in his core. His feet began to rise off the strange, malleable ground, his pleasure becoming reality in this not-world, but he forced his toes back down. "Flatterer," he whispered. He might have kissed him right there and then. He nearly did. "The things you say."

"Most do not find the truth nearly so appealing." Lucas' smile was fleeting as he returned his attention to where the girl and spirit had begun to climb the branches of the tree. "I've dipped into the Liminal many times, but I've never found anything here. Maybe because I never chose to linger."

"Those who have passed on and travel between help give it shape. The spirits that reside here seem to long for the vestiges of our world and recreate it through our memories." Adrian nodded towards the boy. "He's taken his shape from mine."

"I'd wondered," Lucas admitted. "Was that what you were like as a boy?"

"What I looked like, anyway." Adrian glanced at him. "Is the tree-house yours or hers?"

"Hers, I should think." His lips curved, wry. "Perhaps that's why I've never seen anything here. I learned a long time ago how not to let anyone pilfer about in my memories."

"It's not *pilfering*. It's *reflecting*." Adrian chuckled, shaking his head. "Perhaps you might try it sometime, if only for the novelty."

"Reflecting," Lucas echoed suspiciously. "You want me to hand my thoughts over to be perused at will by—"

Adrian lifted his brows as Lucas seemed to realize that was exactly what he'd asked Adrian to do the night he'd revealed his gifts.

"I see what you did there," Lucas muttered.

Adrian couldn't help but smile. "Thank you very much for taking care of my memories then and trusting me with her now."

Lucas pursed his lips. "I understand you somewhat better now than I did then."

"And I you." Adrian stepped closer, bumping his shoulder against Lucas'. "I'm glad I do."

"Papa, look at me!" Tula shouted, swinging upside-down from a branch, her braids dangling in the air.

"I see you, sunbeam," he answered, softening at Adrian's side. "Careful or you'll become a monkey."

"No!" she laughed.

"Oh no, you're starting to grow a tail!"

Tula twisted to check, apparently enthusiastic about the possibility. "No, I'm not!"

Lucas glanced at Adrian with a little smile. "Aren't her ears looking a little rounder?"

"I think they might be." Adrian widened his eyes. "Are you craving bananas?"

"*No!*" Tula cackled and Lucas crossed to help her down to her feet again. The little boy watched curiously, disappearing from the branch above and appearing on the ground beside them.

"There's another game I'd like you to try and then you're free to play for a little while." Adrian tucked his hands into his pockets. "What do you say?"

"Okay!"

Adrian nodded once. "This time I'd like you to take that feeling from earlier—where you went looking for the spirit—and simply let it float right by you. You can think of it as music playing in a different room."

"Let the... the feeling? The bow tie?"

"Yes. The lemonade bow tie."

Tula looked up at him, wrinkling her nose. "But he's right there." She pointed at the silver-eyed boy. "He's not in another room."

"He's not going anywhere and you can play again when you're done." Adrian rested his hand on her shoulder. "There may be times you don't want to see people who have passed on or hear the spirits that whisper at the edges of the Aether. The hardest skill to develop is the ability to turn our gifts *off*."

"But I don't want him to go away!" Tula hurried to the boy's side, hugging him. "He's my friend."

"He won't go anywhere," Adrian assured softly. "He'll stay right here."

"And we can play tag and catch fish with our fingers and I can show you the catapult I built." The boy grinned, the little gap between his two front teeth visible. It must have been from a memory of looking in a mirror; Adrian could clearly remember that his mother had decreed no photographs would be been taken until he'd had that gap corrected by the orthodontist.

"It's important to know they'll still be there when you choose to look, too." Adrian tugged on her braid gently. "Will you try?"

Tula looked like she was about to cry, her eyes wide and damp. "But... won't I hurt your feelings?" she asked, looking at the spirit worriedly. "If I pretend you're not here?"

The little spirit shook his head. "Most people don't know I'm here, so I've been playing by myself. I know you won't forget me."

"Okay." She sniffled, pulling at her earlobes as she stepped back. She squeezed her eyes shut again, puffing out her cheeks with effort. "Are you still there when you go in the walls, Papa?"

"It's very similar," Lucas murmured, kneeling next to her. "I don't go away, just like he doesn't. It's a shift of perception like those seeing eye puzzles."

"Or the one that's a rabbit if you look at it one way or a duck if you look at it another way?" Tula asked.

"Mmhmm." Lucas held her gaze solemnly. "Think about the feeling of the tree. Or the feeling of the wards around your marbles."

The spirit stared at the father and daughter with hauntingly familiar silver eyes. Adrian wondered if he'd looked like that—wishful and awestruck—when he'd seen his classmates with parents who seemed to care for them. He wondered if the spirit was as lonely as Adrian had been as a child. He wondered what might happen when they left. Memories to hold, he supposed. Entire worlds for the spirit to draw on, from his mind and Tula's.

The girl concentrated, her brow furrowing. She sighed when she opened her eyes, scuffing her shoe against the grass. "This is *hard*."

"I know." Lucas rubbed her back, glancing up at Adrian. "See?"

"Just a couple more times," Adrian murmured, hoping he didn't sound too much like his own father. "Twice more and then you can play and we'll work on it another day."

Tula puffed out her cheeks. "I want ice cream."

"*Bribery*." Adrian lifted his brows. "Lucas?"

"It's a bit early."

"I want ice cream for me and my friend."

Lucas tugged on her pigtail. "Try again. For fun. Okay?"

"It's not fun. Playing is fun."

"Would pancakes be a decent compromise?" Adrian offered. "Pancakes with strawberries and chocolate for another go?"

"Strawberries, no chocolate, no whipped cream," Lucas lifted his brows. "Final offer."

"Sprinkles?"

"Coconut flakes."

"Okay." Tula huffed. "But I don't want him to go away."

"He'll be right here."

She hugged herself, rocking from side to side. "I don't like this game. I want to play the hide-and-seek game again instead."

Adrian sighed, looking to Lucas for guidance. It wouldn't work if she didn't want it. "Maybe you could—"

The boy transformed before their eyes, growing tall and stern.

"After you try again," the spirit resembling Adrian's father intoned, gentler than he'd been in life. "Once more, Tula. Make me disappear and your friend will return."

Tula stared up at him. "Why can't you both be here? He wants you to."

"What?" Adrian blinked at her.

"My friend told me he wants his father to play, but he never does." Tula looked up at the vision of Adrian's father. "If I pretend you're not here, will you go play with him? No one will watch. He wants you to see the catapult."

The spirit frowned, glancing at Adrian. He couldn't very well when he was both father and son, and there were no memories from which to draw where the spirit could see that old dream come to life.

"How about this: we will all go see the catapult," Lucas told her softly when Adrian looked away. "After."

Tula closed her eyes tight, jogging in place as though that might assist her in running away from the difficulty. "I can't feel the man in the tie," Tula grimaced, heels beating soundlessly at the grass. "I can't—"

"One thing at a time, sunbeam." Lucas rested his hand gently on Adrian's shoulder, watching her. "Focus."

Tula panted, opening one eye and then the other. "Oh. Oh! Where did they go? Did I send the man away? He said he was going to stay!"

Lucas glanced between her and the spirit. "Can't you see him, love?"

"No! And I can't feel him. Oh no! Did I do something wrong? Did I send him all the way away?"

Lucas shook his head, exhaling a relieved breath. "You didn't do anything wrong. He's right there."

"But the man in the tie—"

"Tula," Lucas murmured. "This is their world, not ours. The spirits here will find each other if they're meant to. I'm very proud of you for letting them go, even for a minute."

Tula looked up at them, rubbing her nose. "I don't like leaving my friends alone."

"They're not alone. Just as you're never alone. They have everyone who loves them right in their pockets, the same as you." Lucas touched her chin. "Now play the hide-and-seek game again and you'll find him, okay?"

Tula nodded, wrapping her arms around his leg and closing her eyes. "Ten. Nine. Eight..."

The little boy reappeared and tapped her on the nose, hugging her tightly. "You *did* it. Good job! I always knew you could! I'm so proud of you."

Adrian frowned, his heart aching as the spirit spoke. And now he knew where the spirit had seen this shape; Adrian had whispered just those words to himself in the mirror after his second-grade science fair, wishing he could hear them from his parents.

"Are you alright?" Lucas asked softly as the children took off at a run around the tree.

"No." Adrian pressed his lips together. "They usually take familiar shapes, but they don't understand the context of the memories. This one gleaned more than usual. I... am beginning to see your aversion to letting others in your mind."

Lucas touched his arm gently. "If it hadn't been for him—and you—I don't think she'd have managed it. Not today, certainly."

"No?" Adrian dipped his chin, comforted by the weight of Lucas' hand. "I'm glad it was a helpful exercise."

"If only there was always a reason for her not to pay them mind," Lucas sighed. "At least she knows that she can now." He tilted his head, peering at Adrian. "Are you alright?"

"No, not entirely." Adrian sighed, patting Lucas' hand. "I will be, though. Thank you for asking."

"*Did* you build a catapult? Or was that him?"

"Of course I did." Adrian snorted. "Several. Trebuchets and mangonels, too. I had a brief fascination."

"*Mangonels*." Lucas chuckled, the length of his arm leaning just barely against Adrian's. "What did you use for ammunition?"

"Tomatoes, mostly. Once I managed with some relatively large gourds. Covered my mother's rose bushes in pumpkin guts."

"Like a true gourmand."

Tula cackled as she and the spirit climbed up through the branches to the treehouse.

Lucas hummed quietly. "Shall we build one, then? I've limited experience with war machines, but you are a teacher."

Adrian blinked. "...right now?"

"One assumes that whatever tomatoes and gourds we generate here won't follow us home. Better here than where I have to clean squash out of wool." Lucas nodded towards the tree. "They'll enjoy it."

Adrian nodded, taking his hand and squeezing it. "I'd like that very much. Let's see what my little doppelgänger has built and go from there, shall we?"

"Is there a ladder, do you think? It's been quite some time since I climbed branches."

"I imagine if we go looking for one, we'll find it." Adrian led him towards the treehouse, skirting around the tree. "Ah." He rested his hand on a carved wooden ladder. "There we are. After you."

Lucas moved with precision, stepping up the rungs carefully. "We're quite sure it isn't about to turn into a waterfall or a kaleidoscope?"

"We can't be sure." Adrian watched him go, admiring the shape of Lucas' legs as he climbed. Only inches away from his lips, but it felt as though there were still miles between them. What was behind all of the walls Lucas had constructed for himself? Something fragile? A reason he approached all the minutiae of his life with deliberation?

He followed Lucas up the ladder, leaning against him when he arrived at the top of the platform in the little shelter mostly hidden by the tree's canopy. If Adrian were braver, he might have kissed him right there, but he wasn't willing to risk losing the trust he'd built brick by brick.

Better to kiss him in their world, in any case. Not in this place between places.

"We heard there was a catapult," Lucas was saying, leaning down to look through the door into the treehouse. "Might we see?"

"*Really?*" the spirit asked, with all the excitement one would expect from a lonely child. "I've got marbles! We can try and shoot down an apple! I did it once, but nobody believed me."

"Now there are witnesses. Adrian mentioned we might be able to fire tomatoes after the marbles. Why don't you show us how it works?"

It felt like hours. Strangely silly hours laden with Tula's giggles and the spirit's glad laughter and the thud and splat of invented fruits and vegetables to the various surfaces of the Aether. Dreams absorbed by the space in between. Adrian had often enjoyed his time there; the Aether was electric and full of the sizzle of possibilities, but it had never before felt as warm as it did when they were all there together, catapulting diamonds at prismatic apples.

After they returned to their world, Tula exhaled a surprisingly loud snuffling snore that echoed around them in the mausoleum as Lucas gathered her up into his arms.

It had felt like hours but was in reality only a matter of moments. The little girl was fast asleep despite the movement as Lucas tucked her to his shoulder. "Thank you," he murmured, meeting Adrian's gaze in the relative shadows. "That was... Well. I wouldn't have thought of it."

"Thank you for trusting me with her." Adrian felt pinned in place, hypnotized by the glint of candlelight reflected in Lucas' eyes: living flames inside of emeralds.

"You receive the trust that you've earned," Lucas told him quietly. "You don't need to prove yourself, Adrian. Just don't prove me wrong," he added with a quirk of his lips. "Alright?"

"I think I can manage that," Adrian agreed, cheeks warming. "Do you need help getting her back to your car?"

He shook his head. "Can I help you cleanse the space?"

"I wouldn't want you to disturb her." Adrian smiled slightly. "Go have your celebratory pancakes. I'll be fine finishing up here."

"That isn't what we agreed to." Lucas tilted his head curiously. "What's the matter? I've never known you to pass on pancakes."

"You're sure I won't be interrupting?"

"What on earth are you talking about?" Lucas wondered, stepping closer. "It was your idea."

"I—Right." Adrian nodded, glancing away from those eyes that saw too much. "Yes. I'd... Yes. I can have chocolate and sprinkles if I'd like, can't I?"

Lucas uttered a peculiar little snort, shifting the girl more firmly to one arm. "I doubt that I could stop you. Now that I've seen your throwing arm, especially."

"Pancakes, then." Adrian snapped his fingers, making the candles wink out as one. He captured the magical resonance like smoke in the palm of his hand, turning it into a silver marble. He laced his fingers with Lucas', gathering his keys. "Lead the way."

"That's a tidy little trick. What do you do with the marble?" Lucas asked as they climbed the few stairs to the gate.

"Shoot it into the harbor with a catapult." Adrian lifted his brows, chuckling to himself. "I'll show you sometime if you ever find yourself at my apartment."

"Have you noticed any boats clustering there?" Lucas frowned as they stepped outside. "Divers? There's still enough of a magical signal it could be picked up by the Seekers at close range—"

"Can you still feel the resonance?" Adrian blinked. Lucas must be even more sensitive to the arcane than he realized. "Most of the energy is consumed through the transmutation."

Lucas shook his head. "There's enough to trace—" He grimaced, glancing at him. "Probably not enough for the sensors, though; you may be right."

"Hm." Adrian squeezed his hand again, pausing at the gate. "I'll run some more tests. I don't want you to worry about it."

"Thank you. I know..." Lucas winced. "Her mother never agreed with me. Called me a worry-wart and less favorable names. But then Teresa was sent to a tower, so..." He shrugged helplessly. "It's different, I think, knowing that if they caught me, they would never let me go. Perhaps it's unfair to Tula that she has to live so carefully because of me."

"Let me ask you this: do you think she'd do particularly well if she were registered?" Adrian studied him. "I've heard that the towers are cold. Utilitarian. You're putting yourself at others' mercy."

"I don't know. The way Teresa described it..." Lucas shook his head. "My parents worked with a kid for a while who'd been in since he was four. He traveled with us for two years. Talked to birds. Couldn't light a candle. He was so nervous, he'd startle if you closed a door too loudly. I don't want that for her."

Adrian held Lucas' hand, tracing the muscle at the pad of his thumb. "I don't think you're making the wrong choice, for whatever my opinion is worth."

"It's a relief to hear you don't think that I'm an anxiety-ridden monster."

Adrian smiled, shaking his head. "I don't think it's possible to think of you as a monster, Luke. I think you're an amazing father and that you have a very lucky little girl."

Lucas glanced down at their hands, humming softly under his breath. "See. *That* was flattery."

"Flattery or a statement of fact?"

"Immense flattery," Lucas chuckled with a roll of his eyes. "'Amazing'. Someone might get ideas."

"One can only hope," Adrian murmured. So close. So close to crossing that boundary between friendship and something more. Adrian touched his cheek gently, his heart racing.

"Papa?" Tula stretched in his arms, yawning. "I want blueberries *in* the pancakes, too."

"Oh yes?" Lucas asked, dropping his gaze to hers. "No harm in some extra fruit, is there?"

"Uh-huh." Tula wiggled. "Down now."

"Yes, of course."

Lucas set her on her feet with a quiet sigh and tucked his thumbs into his pockets. "It was a magnificent catapult, Adrian," he murmured as she skipped ahead of them down the pass.

"It was a magnificent day all around," Adrian murmured, locking the gate behind them.

Next time.

Soon.

Whenever he managed to get Lucas alone again.

Pancakes and patience. That was all he needed.

Caught up in his thoughts, he bumped straight into Lucas' back as he turned from the gate. His spine was ramrod straight. Lucas' hand extended towards the gravel walkway.

"Tula," Lucas rasped, and as Adrian looked past Lucas' shoulder, he understood why.

Figures in dark suits were walking around the willow tree across the cemetery, some sort of measuring equipment in their hands. The bench where Adrian had cast and wept and Lucas had molded a tangerine out of starlight.

Seekers.

"Tula," Lucas repeated quietly and firmly, and the little girl finally turned around to look at him. Waning sunlight in her bright yellow hair. A smiling bear emblazoned on her blue tee shirt. "*Huc*," he said, growing calm and distant as he flexed his fingers and Tula blinked. At the Latin, maybe. Or the seriousness in her father's demeanor.

She hurried back to them, taking Lucas' hand. "Are those bad guys?" she whispered, a thread of fear Adrian never thought he would hear in her voice.

Lucas palmed the top of her head, drawing her to his side as though he could nestle her—safe and hidden—under his wing. "Let's play the animal game. I'll start. Tiger."

"Robin?" Tula asked, taking Adrian's hand. Her hand was shaking. "Papa, are we—?"

"Newt," Adrian murmured as they took the wider path back to the entrance, falling into step alongside them. Slow and easy.

Lucas glanced at him over the top of Tula's head. "Tomcat." Two figures in white hazmat suits were scraping the concrete of the bench.

The air.

They'd cleared the air.

They hadn't cleansed the surface in their wake.

Tula exhaled shakily as more figures stepped from the side lot, walking towards the tree in their lab protection gear. Preserving evidence. Which meant there was evidence to be preserved. "Turkey."

"Yak," Adrian added, squeezing her fingers gently.

"Kangaroo." Lucas kept his face forward, but Adrian could see the hummingbird flicks of his gaze to the gathering. "I bet Adrian will let you have some of his chocolate pancakes if you ask him nicely."

A hundred feet to the large iron arch that led to the main parking lot. Ninety.

"Owl?" So many birds. Tula pressed her cheek to Lucas' side, gazing up between them with wide eyes. As though she might wish to take flight.

"Leopard," Adrian suggested. Because Lucas was moving like one, steady and concentrated, relaxed and sharp at the same time. "Would you like some of my pancakes, Tula?"

"O—okay," she nodded, biting her lip. "Yes, please. Thank you." Meek. Shrinking already. She wouldn't do well in the registry at all.

"We can trade," Adrian offered in a conspiratorial whisper. "One of my chocolate chips for one of your strawberries." He squeezed Tula's hand as they neared the arch, only a few strides away. "It's your turn, Luke."

"Papa?" Tula swallowed nervously.

"Dolphin." Lucas transferred a kiss from his lips to the top of her head with his fingers. "What are the kinds of dolphins?"

"Bottlenose," Tula chirped against the pocket of his jacket. "Striped. Spinner. Orinoco."

Lucas glanced down at her as they passed a small gathering of men with meters, smiling reassuringly. "Orinoco," he ruffled her hair gently. "There's my little genius."

"Hourglass. Spotted. Snubfin," Tula continued, growing more confident under his study.

They reached the car.

Lucas opened the passenger door for her, waving her inside. "Princess or marine biologist," he said as he kissed the top of her head and buckled her in. "That's going to be a tough career choice." He glanced up over the top of the door, meeting Adrian's gaze steadily. "Let's get out of here, okay? It's a little too crowded, even for a weekend."

"Name the place." Adrian clenched his hands tightly in his jacket pockets. "I'll see you there."

CHAPTER ELEVEN

ADRIAN

Each day was a little cooler than the last; the ragweed made Adrian's eyes itch as the leaves changed from vibrant greens to rich yellows and oranges, growing heavy and blanketing the sidewalks of San Francisco. Adrian gazed out the wide window in Cymbeline's tastefully decorated living room. His friend, the talk show starlet, was hosting her monthly book club, which he'd been skipping since Seron's funeral.

Adrian sat, idly swirling honey into his tea long after it had dissolved. The steam soothed his poor sinuses while he listened to the others discuss the novel he hadn't quite managed to finish, nodding along at intervals so that they might not discover his ruse.

He'd been distracted, taking on extra outreach work to keep busy. Adrian had never expected to enjoy working with children, but their bright-eyed enthusiasm never ceased to warm him and watching them clap and exclaim made him believe his efforts were worthy.

The Seekers had remained in and around the cemetery for about a week, and when he'd thought they had finally gone on their merry way, Lucas had texted him pictures of nondescript cars lingering in the lot for the next two months.

Clever, discerning, careful Lucas. Exciting and beautiful in his own way, taking Adrian's hand as they walked through parks near campus between his lectures, getting brunch or coffee while Tula was at judo, coming over to his apartment on the weekends to watch movies or talk...

Three times, Adrian had nearly kissed him. When those delightfully full lips curved into a smirk or in the moments where Lucas gazed at him with such a distinct fondness Adrian thought he might weep. When they were so close that Adrian could smell the ink Lucas used to sketch designs and the spiced citrus in his shampoo.

It had been five months since the spellbinding week that they'd met in the moonlight and he'd discovered their shared secret, and longer since he'd been allotted three questions and wasted two.

He'd learned more about Lucas in that time than he knew about nearly anyone else and had shared parts of himself, in turn, that he'd only ever offered to the man who had been his husband. But when the moments arose where they might cross the boundary between friendship into something more, Adrian hesitated until they were gone. He couldn't bring himself to ruin what they'd built. Not until he was certain he wasn't just reaching for Lucas out of something more than loneliness and heartache. Adrian couldn't do that to him, not after the kindness he'd been shown.

"So, what do you think?" Cymbeline settled into the armchair at his side as her guests milled towards the counter laden with snacks. She was objectively stunning, with caramel skin and thick dark curls falling in a riotous waterfall over the shoulder of her trim white jumpsuit. Her beauty alone would have skyrocketed her to fame. Her empathy made her unstoppable. "Would it be a good book for my show? You were quiet."

"Oh, um..." Adrian cleared his throat, sipping from his cup. "The premise was certainly intriguing, though it did... lose my attention about halfway through." True enough, though that was only partially the author's fault. "Don't mind me; everyone else seemed to enjoy it."

"You didn't find the shark attacks too gruesome?" she asked.

Shark attacks? Perhaps he'd only made it a quarter of the way through. "I'm not the best judge on what the line is for 'gruesome', I'm afraid."

"No, perhaps not." She patted his knee. "Come with me. I want you to tell me what you think of my new painting. I have one of those dreadful reality shows coming for a tour next week."

"Not again." Adrian rolled his eyes, chuckling as he rose to his feet from the ottoman. "Haven't they tortured you quite enough?"

"Not quite enough. No." Cymbeline tucked her arm through his. "Though I do wonder how often they imagine I redecorate. The last one was only two years ago. Here." She led him down a long hall away from the living room—and her other guests—and into her front parlor. "You didn't read the book."

"...that's not *entirely* true," Adrian muttered under his breath bashfully. "I did *start* it."

She laughed, hugging his arm. "You're too busy to read." She touched his cheek. "Yes? I want to hear all about it."

"It?" Adrian raised a brow. *Him*, his mind supplied unhelpfully. How could he explain the man who had lifted him out of his doldrums so that he might walk again? Who had gotten him through the last months of his life with just the comfort of his presence? He couldn't even use the line that he'd started seeing someone because... *Had* he? They certainly *saw* each other, that was true, and they'd established that they were in the vicinity of dating, but even so... "I'm not sure where to begin."

"Start now and work backward." She beamed, tucking her hair behind her ear. "You're smiling again. You're smiling and working. What had you so busy this past week that you couldn't read one measly little best-seller?"

"Well, midterms are coming up," he began, running his fingers along the edge of a bookshelf, fingers coming away perfectly clean.

"Mmhmm." Cymbeline perched on a smooth velvet settee, still smiling at him. "What else?"

"I... accompanied a friend to his daughter's judo tournament." Adrian couldn't help the flush that seemed determined to immolate him from the inside out. "That took up most of last weekend."

"Oh? A new friend?" She looked like she was posing for a portrait: white silk on white velvet. He thought of the way Lucas sometimes pondered him, smirking, asking if he ought to get his camera out to take a picture. Posing. It was something he and Cymbeline had always had in common. A lifetime of never being sure when someone would snap a candid left its impression. Cymbeline leaned forward, and he realized he hadn't answered her when she asked, "Your friend with the beard or another?"

"...it's more scruff than beard." Adrian raised a brow, studying her curiously. "How did you know?"

"Kriss told me she thought she'd seen you having a tête-à-tête with a bearded romantic at the Trattoria Limone." Cymbeline folded her hands in her lap. Her film crew could easily have stepped inside and begun filming as a part of her daytime talk show and it wouldn't have felt at all out of place. "And I told her: 'he would have told us. Why wouldn't he have told us?'"

"*Romantic*," Adrian sniffed, rolling his eyes. "We're *friends*. I would've told you if there was anything *to* tell."

"You have a new friend who has a daughter who... fights? And this is not news worthy of sharing?"

"I'm certain I don't tell you about every friend I've made—"

"Adrian Sharp." She lifted her brows imperiously. "I demand details. I was told: handsome and romantic and *longing*. If I am being fed lies by the Admiral, I am going to be very irked."

"Kriss exaggerates," Adrian sighed, taking a seat on a nearby sofa covered with extravagantly embroidered pillows. "You know this. I know this. Everyone who has ever *met* her knows this. If anything, *Kriss* is the romantic. When she gets it in her head that any manner of affection might possibly, *possibly* be involved, suddenly it's rose-colored goggles."

"So your friend is not handsome."

The accusation was too shocking not to demand a response. "On the contrary, he is *exceedingly* handsome."

"Oh. He's not romantic, then?" she asked. "He's an unromantic, exceedingly handsome friend?"

"I don't..." He waved a hand negligently. "How am I to know if he's romantic? We're *friends*. It hardly comes up." Holding his hand. Getting lost in the myriad shades of green in his eyes. Teasing those pleasant little chuckles from the man's lips. "Barely," he amended. "Perhaps in some small ways. It's difficult to define." Because he couldn't get comfortable defining it, Adrian told himself. Because Lucas was allowing him not to. Because putting a name to what was simmering between them always came with the stark realization that Seron was well and truly gone.

"I want to meet him," Cymbeline insisted. "I know all your other friends. I want to know this one."

"...you've already met him, as it happens," Adrian admitted. No way past it, now that they'd sussed him out. Once Cymbeline had her mind set on something, it was hardly worth the effort of denying her. "He made the gown you wore at the arts gala last fall. The yellow one with the ruffles?"

"*Halpern?*" Cymbeline gasped, delighted, hands clasped at her heart. "The grumpy fellow with the eyes?"

"The eyes," Adrian chuckled. He'd spent god only knew how long staring into them: vibrant, grassy fields that darted away far too quickly. Bruised by a dot of ruby red, like poppy blossoms. "That's him, yes. He's not always so grumpy."

"I *liked* him. It was refreshing to have a stranger disagree with me. That hasn't happened in years." She clapped. "I shall have to pay another visit."

"I'm certain he'd appreciate it," Adrian agreed, not *entirely* sure that was true. "He doesn't skirt around his opinions."

"He does not," she agreed. "And I do have that daytime awards show at the end of the year. Here's an idea! Why don't you come along with me? We could both wear Halpern and make a night of it. You know Leopold abhors the pomp and circumstance."

Her husband was much happier in a lab surrounded by bacteria than in a ballroom surrounded by people, that was true. "I'd be happy to," Adrian agreed. "I'm sure he'd be delighted if you wore one of his creations to such a prominent event." It would probably give him a conniption, especially if she insisted on more ruffles. "Should I warn him or would you rather ask yourself?"

"Are you seeing him again soon?" she asked, her heart dancing in her dark eyes. Kriss wasn't the only romantic.

Adrian called him most nights now after Tula had gone to sleep, continuing the habit they'd developed while he was in Spain. It was nice to hear his voice, even if only for a few minutes, talking about work, the weather, or Tula's grades. "I'm sure I'll run into him."

"Well then, we'll see who gets to him first." She squeezed his hand. "I'm glad you're socializing. With me. With him. Even if Kriss is wrong about him looking at you like a lost puppy."

"A lost—Is *that* what she said?" Adrian snorted, rolling his eyes again. If that were true, it was only out of some sort of pity. However, he'd never felt that stifling concern from Lucas. "I'll need to speak with her."

"She said that, too." Cymbeline lifted a brow. "Do you think her gossip was only an elaborate scheme to get you to call her? That's far more underhanded than I've come to expect from her."

"I've *been* texting her. I don't understand why she would—" He shook his head, shrugging helplessly. "I don't think there are any puppy eyes. We're both still trying to figure out what we want from each other—I suppose I could be wrong."

"Even if there are—because you are adorable—you needn't do anything about them. Have your friend. It needn't be anything more than that."

"...and if..." Adrian glanced down at their hands, feeling a lump settle in his throat. "Never mind."

"No, tell me."

"I don't know," Adrian exhaled sharply. There *hadn't* been puppy eyes. He'd have noticed if there were. He'd been *looking* for them—for some *hint* of what Lucas was feeling beyond those smirks and quips. "It's nothing."

"Is it?"

When it seemed like she was determined to wait him out, piercing him with that knowing, gentle stare, Adrian gave in with a frustrated, "How am I supposed to *know?*"

"How are you supposed to know what?" she asked.

Adrian wrinkled his nose. "Say he did want to be more than friends. I like what we have and I'm hesitant to muddle that. It's good, as it is. It's more than good. It isn't that I don't want more; I do. I feel... things. Things I never thought I would feel again. But—"

"Knowing if you want more is more important than anything else, just at this moment, don't you think?" Cymbeline brushed her hair back over her shoulder, watching him as though he might break. "There's no rush. There's no 'right time.'"

He closed his eyes, rubbing his brow. "It doesn't seem wrong to you?"

"Adrian..." Cymbeline sighed his name. "I've seen so many marriages and divorces and friends lost to time. There's no one way to love. It's complex and strange and demanding and so frustrating sometimes but, in the end, it's worth it because love heals. That's the only thing that I'm sure of." It was the tagline to her show, but he knew she meant it. "Do you feel like you're ready?"

"I don't know," Adrian admitted. He was on his feet and moving again, spending more time out in the world than in his lonely apartment or the quiet walks to and from the mausoleum. Though, sometimes he'd catch a snippet of a voice that sounded like Seron's and he'd need to collect himself. The song they'd danced to at their wedding played in a coffee shop the other day and he'd managed to keep it together, nudging Lucas' boot under the table and maintaining the contact until it ended. Would he ever stop being transported by the mundane, back to the life he'd had before? Unlikely, if his time in the military had taught him anything. Wounds didn't entirely go away, even if they became less raw and agonizing over time. "I don't want to hurt him if I realize I'm not."

She squeezed his hand again. "Do you want to be?"

"...it's not outside the realm of possibility."

Cymbeline flung her arms around him, hugging him hard. "I love you. I love you no matter what. You are one of my dearest friends."

"You seem incredibly pleased with yourself," Adrian gasped as his ribs were being crushed. "Over gossip and rumors and things that haven't happened."

"I don't care at all about that. I care about you." She leaned back, eyes shining. "I can see your heart again."

"That x-ray vision of yours," he sniffed, watching her smile. "It's going to get you into trouble one of these days."

"More times than I can count already, yet here I remain. As do you." She kissed his cheek. "Put yourself first for once, will you?"

Adrian gave her a small, wry smirk, slipping his hand back into his lap. "I'm terrific. Of course I come first."

"You've never fooled me with that nonsense, Adrian." Cymbeline patted his arm lightly, rising to her feet. "My x-ray vision, you know. Come and try these mini scones; I'm thinking of showing how to make them in the next cooking segment."

Adrian shook his head, clicking his tongue, grateful for the change in conversation. "Alright, ply me with pastries and we'll see if they're worthy of prime time."

CHAPTER TWELVE

ADRIAN

H is fingers still tingled as he and Lucas left the opera house; Adrian wrapped his scarf more tightly around his shoulders. For three hours, Lucas had held his hand in the darkened theater as dancers twirled across the stage, the orchestra in the pit below playing triumphantly as the heroine was rescued and the evildoers were brought to swift justice. A simple story, conveyed in immaculate color, motion, and sound.

Adrian had spent most of the evening thinking of Lucas' eyes, the way his fingers flexed in Adrian's hand, the sound of his laughter masked by the applause.

"A bit contrived," Adrian murmured when they'd descended the steps, following the rest of the patrons through a crowded crosswalk. "But at least I'll be able to give Cymbeline a thorough review. What did you think of the performance?"

"Hm?" Lucas glanced at him, apparently summoning himself out of his thoughts. "Yes. Very nice."

"What's on your mind?" Adrian raised a brow, peering at him out of the corner of his eyes. "Did something happen at work?"

"No. Not—No. I was—" Lucas laughed quietly. "I was trying to think of what the name of that color was. The one the mermaid was wearing. Not teal or periwinkle, but in between."

"Turquoise?" Adrian offered. The sound of that laughter was sparkling champagne bubbles, bursting just on the tip of his tongue. He wasn't ready to wish him goodnight, not when Lucas' hair was windblown and he was grinning like he'd been caught sneaking cookies. "Are you hungry at all? We could grab something before you need to relieve Mattia of her duties."

"Tapas?" Lucas smiled wickedly, brows winging. "I've been starving for those little *pincho* ribs since that dastardly villain Alphonso was burned at the stake."

"Mm, just what I was thinking." Adrian chuckled, falling into step with him as the sidewalks thinned. "Grilled meat. *Delicious.*"

"They do say that men taste of pork when they're cooked. That's what Tula told me the rumor is in kindergarten anyway. I wonder how that even came up among them." Lucas bumped his shoulder absently... On purpose? In passing? "Men taste of pork and cats will eat you if you lie still too long. The wisdom of her class."

"It's no wonder you're macabre." Adrian shifted closer, debating whether his fingers would be warmer in his pocket or in Lucas' hand. "You picked it up from a bunch of five-year-olds."

"Oh, I've been a terror since I was her age, at least. I used to make my mother read to me about spies and serial killers before bed. Entirely rotten to my core." Lucas shot him a dark, sharp grin. "Give me a year and I can make a little forensic psychologist out of Tula as well."

"Forensics seems a little unnecessary, hm?"

"One should always play to one's strengths, if one can be subtle."

"Should one?" Adrian took Lucas' in his own, swinging his arm lightly. "Tapas it is, then, and a pitcher of sangria. We must cherish the last throes of summer while we can."

"'When summer's end is nighing, and skies at evening cloud, I muse on change and fortune, and all the feats I vowed, when I was young and proud.'" Lucas tilted his head back, eyes falling closed as he was apt to do when they walked hand in hand in the park. Trust walks. The blind leading the blind. "I think it's called *soleil sombre*."

Adrian's heart fluttered, falling leaves and hummingbird wings. He squeezed Lucas' hand, pulling him closer. Innately himself, biting at the fabric of the sky and touching with tenderness, and switching between the two at a head-spinning clip. "What is, Luke?" Adrian asked softly, wanting to draw him into his arms and sip on his joy, nectar to a butterfly. "The poem?"

"The color. Turquoise has too much green. *Soleil sombre* has that touch of night swirling in it." Lucas smiled to himself. "I suppose I could ask their designer."

"Ah, but that would hardly be fun." That wonderful, creative mind, sweeping in and out of subjects like partners at a dance. "You're in good humor this evening."

"I love the opera. All the drama and the color and music and *fabrics*. You don't get to see fabrics like that very often, having life breathed into them." Lucas beamed, smooth-browed. "Thank you. It was a nice idea."

"Thank you for agreeing to attend with me." If he could bottle up the warmth that spread through his body every time Lucas smiled like that—really *smiled* like he was releasing stored sunlight—Adrian was sure he could solve all the world's energy problems in short order. "I'm glad you were able to get a sitter on such short notice."

"Your TA is very generous with her time." Lucas cracked an eye open to turn that spotlight on him. "I expect she is anticipating extra credit."

"Oh, she hardly needs it," Adrian laughed.

"As though need has anything to do with want."

"That sounds like a rather pointed statement." Adrian narrowed his eyes in feigned suspicion. "What are you on about, Halpern?"

"I am not on or about anything. I am a leaf on the wind." Lucas hummed a stretch of melody from one of the battle songs. "Do you think I could get away with bringing brocade back into daily fashion?"

"You could get away with almost anything," Adrian told him contentedly as they crossed another side street, hand in hand, street lamps bathing them in a warm glow.

"I think it would brighten up the streets. There's a shine to thick satin that you can't get from anything else. Translucence and reflection. And the drama of it: intention and longevity." Lucas sighed. "My apprentice told me someone came in and asked if we had tee shirts. *Tee shirts*. To go with my tailored wool and silk." He shook his head, idly flexing the fingers of his free hand in the yellow light from the streetlamps. "Branded tee shirts. I hate all the damned names everywhere. Labels on everything. Why do people want to be walking billboards?"

"Because they want to show what they can afford?" Adrian guessed. Lucas brightened up the streets simply by gracing them with his presence, even when he was speaking of the taste of human flesh and walking billboards. "It isn't about the artistry of it."

"I know." There was genuine sorrow in Lucas' voice. "Maybe I should find a new line of work."

"Absolutely not." Adrian tugged him close, touching his chin with his thumb. God, how Lucas always managed to smell so delightfully edible was beyond him. "Cymbeline hasn't called you yet?"

"So you *did* know." His gaze had gone hummingbird again, shimmering as it alighted on different parts of Adrian's face. "I suspected you might. You could have warned me."

"I could've," Adrian agreed, trying desperately not to drown in the glittering pools of his eyes. "Does that please you?"

"Which? That she wants another dress she's going to ask me to massacre with puffery or that you knew and didn't tell me?"

"Not just another dress." Gods, that crooked little line of his smile. "You get to throw something together for me as well. And if you decide to put me in brocade, so be it. Consider it my penance for not divulging sooner."

"*Penance?*" Lucas laughed. "You would be lucky if I put you in brocade. A soft silver suit with moonlight embroidery to match your eyes. You'd have the whole place eating out of your palm."

"You've thought about this already?" Adrian raised a brow, watching the corners of Lucas' eyes crinkle with mirth. That damned fluttering again. "Do you have an outfit in mind for everyone you meet?"

"No." Lucas brushed his hair back from his forehead gently, looking away. "Not everyone. Some." His smile flickered as he dropped his hand. "Sometimes. I've had a couple of days to think about it."

"Luke," Adrian murmured, reaching for his hand again under the vine-covered arch that stood solitary before the restaurant. "Come back."

"I'm right here." More breath than words. He lifted his gaze, wry forest glades. "Too hungry to stray far."

Adrian stared, his breath suddenly caught in his throat as he smoothed his thumb across the curve of Lucas' cheek. He'd wanted to before, half a hundred times already, but for some reason, tonight, he didn't stop himself. The scruff was softer than he'd expected. "I've been curious, for a while. I wonder if you might answer a question for me?"

"You had your questions, remember?" Lucas quipped, then rolled his eyes. "Yes. Alright. One more. What."

"Hypothetically..." Why did his vocabulary choose this particular moment to vanish? Adrian cleared his throat, frowning. "Hm. If..." A couple approached the doorway and he was forced to move aside, cursing under his breath and leaning against the archway. "Might you be interested in reconsidering the nature of our..." He rolled his eyes as his cheeks warmed. "Hmph... Theoretically... Of course."

"Our 'hmph'?" Lucas quirked a brow. "I wasn't aware we had a 'hmph'. Did you adopt one without telling me?"

"For fuck's sake." Adrian glanced up at the sky, hoping some dcity would be kind enough to smite him on the spot. "Our *relationship*. Luke, really, do you need to make everything difficult?"

"I do. I really do." Lucas' lips curled with an evil sort of pleasure. "This is a hypothetical question? Or a theoretical one? I suppose—Theoretically, I enjoy the 'hmph' as it is but wouldn't mind reconsidering its nature. And hypothetically, that would depend on what exactly you'd like for it to evolve into."

"And what, in this world entirely disparate from reality, would the options be?"

"Well. I don't like sunset horseback rides or, I should clarify, horseback rides in general." Lucas itched his beard absently. "And I don't do matching outfits. It's grotesque."

"I would never ask that of you." Adrian raised a brow. "Those are your primary stipulations? No horses or matching getups?"

"I'm attempting to narrow down the options. There are an infinite number of permutations, aren't there? I'm rather out of practice."

"I suppose you're right." Adrian rolled his eyes, laughing uncomfortably. "I was, in this thought exercise, mulling over an arrangement where it would be considered quite reasonable for me to kiss you. Would that be on your list of—"

Lucas leaned in to kiss him, feather-light. There was a hint of wine on his lips from the intermission. The scent of ink and spice on his skin. The soft scratch of his beard against Adrian's chin. "Sorry. You were talking too much." Lucas leaned back, lifting his brows with a small smile. "Was that... Was that alright?"

"Why did you stop?" Adrian whispered, his pulse quickening as he tugged him back, hands clenching in Lucas' jacket. He heard a whimper and wasn't entirely sure if it came from himself or Lucas. Tentative, but growing less so by the moment, Adrian wrapped his arms around Lucas' waist and the rest of the world disappeared, save for the points of warmth between their bodies. He only broke away to breathe, resting his forehead against Lucas', leaning on him for support. Ages since he'd been kissed. What felt like a lifetime ago. "I suppose I only meant it hypothetically if you happened to say 'no.'"

"Ah. I see." Lucas gently traced the curve of Adrian's jaw, meeting his gaze. "If it helps, I don't consider this a renegotiation. I did tell you I'm comfortable with grayscale."

"You did, indeed," Adrian murmured, a grin curling his lips. "I'm... comfortable with more black and white than when we met if you prefer."

"I will take that under consideration." Lucas kissed him again. Wine sweetened, soft, and supple. "Thank you for asking."

"I've been wanting to," Adrian admitted. "Thank you for shutting me up."

"My pleasure." Lucas laughed, his arms caught between them, busying his long nimble fingers with tracing Adrian's chin and his ear and the curve of his hairline. Tiny touches, as flighty as his gaze. "Just the once."

"Mmhmm." Adrian nudged him with his nose. Butterflies. An entire flock of them took flight in his chest. "Still hungry? We don't need to figure everything out before dinner."

"I would like my pound of flesh, yes." He lightly nipped at Adrian's lower lip, sighing as he leaned back. "And sangria."

"Let's get a table, then," Adrian took his hand, pressing a kiss to Lucas' knuckles. "A bench with a view, where I can sit as close to you as possible."

"As you will." Lucas' cheeks darkened with pleasure as they ducked beneath the awning. Perhaps Adrian was learning to read between the lines of his expressions after all.

The restaurant was decorated with sconces and candlelight. Dangling silver stars overhead with pinpricks for colored bulbs to shine through. They spoke of music and wine, dance and fabric, physics and flight until the crowd began to wane and the moon hung high over the spired city skyline. Lucas tilted his head back to watch the stars as they stood outside, waiting for cabs. "I always forget how tiny the portions are at these places. It's good, but there's so little of it."

"Do you need another snack before you head home?" Adrian leaned close, pressing a kiss to his temple. "A drink? Anything to keep you with me a little while longer?"

That laugh again. Softer and more free each time as though, over the course of the evening, he was practicing. His arms circled Adrian's waist. "I've already kept Mattia longer than I should."

"Another time, then," Adrian murmured. "Soon?"

"Soon. Yes." Lucas tilted his chin up, kissing Adrian warmly. "When?"

"...your schedule is rather more restrained than mine." Adrian skimmed his hands up Lucas' sides. "Fencing tomorrow, yes?"

"I don't suppose you'd like to meet me for an hour and a half at an unreasonably early time of day?"

"Luke." Adrian quirked a brow. "I will meet you whenever you can, as often as you like, for as long as you'll tolerate me."

"Tomorrow at four, then?" Lucas asked, leaning against him as the cab pulled over to the curb. "It isn't the opera, but they play punk rock out of the pho truck beside the fencing studio."

"...four in the *evening*, yes?"

Lucas chuckled, peeling away. "Yes, Adrian. In the afternoon. I wouldn't call it evening."

"Four." He caught Lucas' hand as he reached for the door, squeezing his fingers lightly. "I'll see you then."

"I look forward to it." Lucas smiled, ducking into the cab. "Call me when you're home, alright?"

"I always do." Adrian grinned, waving on the sidewalk like a fool, missing him as soon as the door shut.

Chapter Thirteen

LUCAS

"What about this one?" Adrian inquired, lifting a bottle of sloshing green liquor from the shelf.

Lucas narrowed his eyes at the bottle of crème de menthe. "You're hateful. You realize that, don't you?" But he was working very hard to conceal a smirk. His lips still tingled from the kiss they'd shared under the awning outside the liquor store. "The longer that we spend here with your shenanigans, the less time we're going to have at the park for the picnic."

"It's raining."

"So?" Lucas lifted his brows. "Do you melt in the rain? Is this something I'm going to need to worry about?"

"In a sense, yes." Adrian turned to him, humor shining in starlit silver eyes. "This here?" He pointed to the thin layer of dark liner curving around his eyelid; the dark shimmer had been teasing Lucas' senses since he'd picked the man up that afternoon, making

Adrian's eyes seem impossibly wider and more mysterious and drawing attention to his enthralling silver irises. "I'm afraid I'll look like a dripping raccoon if I'm caught out in a storm." He paused as Lucas' smile widened. "What?"

"Hm? Sorry, you lost me at 'dripping'."

"I'd rather not look like a drowned rat, thank you." Adrian plucked a plump, multifaceted bottle of dark amber whiskey, turning it under the lights as though he could tell the quality just by the refraction.

"Rats are very different from raccoons. Don't tell me I'm going to have to force you to watch Animal Planet. You're a teacher, for god's sake."

"I'm not an ecologist. Neither rats nor raccoons have yet developed a penchant for flight." He smiled slightly, passing the bottle to Lucas for inspection. "You did have a backup plan, didn't you?"

"A backup plan for my exceptionally romantic picnic? No. But I'll tell you what: we can find a spot where you won't transform into some kind of trash panda." Lucas patted the bottle once, glancing over the label. "This should do nicely. You can check out and I will bring the car around so as to preserve your fleeting beauty for a while longer."

"I appreciate that." Adrian squeezed his shoulder, lingering for a beat to watch him. Soft silver, eyes crinkling at the corners with mirth. "You're the only person who could make me even consider lingering outdoors in the rain."

Lucas wiggled his brows, swaggering towards the door, drunk on the promise of having Adrian close. "You'd be amazed at the things I could make you consider, if I wanted to abuse my influence."

"Would I?" Adrian asked, slowly shaking his head with a chuckle. "Hurry back around and I suppose we'll see."

Gods and monsters, maybe today would finally be the day. Adrian had dragged him close when Lucas had picked him up from the university. His hands had poured over Lucas' arms and chest in the car as they drove. Adrian was hungry, alright. He was showing it. Fleeting meetings and phone calls could only do so much and now they had an entire afternoon... Time. Precious time when they could ease into things, peel away the last layers, and Lucas might finally, *finally* get to see the finely honed muscles he'd become so fond of touching through clothing. Muscles. And other things.

He hadn't felt this deep of an ache, this much yearning, in ages. It had been easy to fall into a pattern alternating between Tula and work, and sating whatever base needs that had arisen with quick app-based tumbles in between meetings and the reliable pressure of his hand.

But Adrian... Adrian had reawakened something in him. The quick, easy sound of his laughter. The way he teased, sometimes shyly as if he were testing Lucas or himself or both of them. The quietness that sometimes snuck into his cadence and caught Lucas off guard. Adrian was so confident most of the time and those moments when he was vulnerable were reminders that Lucas had to take care of him, if only to ease him back into the world of the living.

"What about here?" Lucas asked, nodding to a dry patch of ground beneath a heavy bough of trees. He held out a hand to prove that no droplets were breaking through as Adrian peered at him from beneath an umbrella. "Safe?"

"As safe as can be expected, I imagine." Adrian glanced up skeptically at the sky as the sun peeked out from behind a pocket of clouds. "I'm not certain I've ever seen this park so empty before."

"That, my friend, is the glory of stormy days. You can turn all manner of public spaces private. Parks. Ferris wheels. Gardens." Lucas unrolled the blanket attached to his backpack and spread it out on the ground, settling the picnic basket atop it as he knelt. "Tula and I once had seven rollercoasters almost entirely to ourselves." He held a hand out. "Would you join me?"

Adrian clicked his umbrella closed and slipped under the boughs to sit on the red gingham. He pressed a kiss to Lucas' offered hand like a gallant knight from a novel. "You don't seem to mind the damp in the slightest. I'm surprised, actually; with your predilection for high fashion, I thought grass stains and mud puddles would be your greatest enemy."

"I save my silks and satins for balmy days," Lucas explained, carefully maintaining the measure of his voice. Had anyone ever kissed his hand before Adrian? He couldn't remember it, or any time that a mere kiss anywhere on his body had made him want to leap onto a man wholesale and damn the consequences. He took a breath. He mustn't spook the man. Adrian had asked for time to adjust and he'd damn well have it. "And I keep my velvets for dry nights. It's all about time and place. Today is a cotton and alpaca day." He squeezed Adrian's fingers, gazing at him warmly. "You don't look remotely like a raccoon."

"No?" Adrian lifted a single brow. "I thought I'd have started running by now."

"I'm glad you haven't. I like you here." Lucas ran his fingers along the man's strong, tantalizing jaw. "Right here where I can admire you as long as I wish."

"You can admire me anywhere, though." Adrian pressed his cheek into Lucas' palm, nuzzling against his hand. "I appreciate you taking all this time to plan something special for us, even if nature seems determined to foil your schemes."

"What's foiled? We've got a lovely picnic spot with no squealing toddlers or people playing volleyball nearby. Nature and I are very nicely coordinated today, I feel." He leaned in to press a gentle kiss on Adrian's chin. "The question becomes: how do you feel about capers?"

"*Capers*," Adrian repeated with a chuckle. "What exactly did you pack in there, my dear?"

Lucas took out a couple of wrapped sandwiches, little glass Tupperware containers of fruits and sliced vegetables, cheese and crackers, and a round bowl of salad. Adrian reacted to each dish like Lucas was doing magic tricks. "It's a picnic. You've been on a picnic before, I'm sure."

"The university hosts one annually in the summer and they serve wine chillers in plastic cups," Adrian told him. "It's dreadful. This seems very much in a different vein." He picked up one of the sandwiches, turning it over in his hands, somehow awed by butcher paper and a baguette. "Is this salmon?" A bemused smile blossomed across his lips. "And yes, I love capers. You *made* all of this?"

"I assembled it," Lucas corrected, warmth spreading through him at the sight of that smile, knowing that he'd pleased him. The curl of his lips. The sweet, surprised wonder of him. He shook a little jar of capers. "I love them, too."

"Yet another preference we share." Adrian set the bottle of whiskey between them, his fingers grazing Lucas' thigh as he sat back, and Lucas had to reign himself in from dragging him closer to touch him again. Adrian looked so very happy, already busily investigating all the little containers, exclaiming, "This is delightful. I don't remember the last time someone cooked or '*assembled*' for me."

"I flatter myself that I'm adept at assembling. Also cooking, but that is an effort you'll need to earn." Lucas leaned against Adrian's shoulder, lightly resting his fingers on the back of Adrian's hand. The contact soothed him, even if it didn't sate. "I like your fingers."

"Is that how I earn a taste of your cooking?" Adrian nudged him gently. "With my fingers?"

"It very well might be." Too much? Grayscale was one thing, but this... Adrian had said that he wanted more, but each time they seemed to be crossing the boundary into being lovers, Adrian balked. If Lucas had been a lesser man, he'd have taken it personally. As it was... Lucas' patience was growing threadbare. Grayscale had been easier. At least he'd been able to imagine that they would part ways, but this? Lucas tried teasing again; that always seemed to help Adrian loosen up a bit. "Have you any particular talents with them, beyond gesticulating at starscapes and smoothing your infernal mustache?"

"Hm... Those *are* their main functions, I'll admit." He turned his hand in Lucas', tracing the lines between his fingers. "As you've not accepted my offer to take you flying as of yet."

"When was the last time you went up?" Lucas asked as they broke into the gathered finger foods.

"*Ages*. Well over a year, maybe two." Adrian nibbled on the edge of his sandwich. "Gods, this is delicious. *Assembling*. If I could assemble half as well as you, I imagine my favorite takeout spots would go out of business."

His words made Lucas' toes curl with pleasure. "You're too kind." He chewed a plump cherry tomato. "Why haven't you? Flown, I mean."

"Ah, well, something always seems to come up and I haven't had a good excuse to go through the effort." Adrian shrugged, a little furrow appearing between his brows. "To tell the truth, I haven't felt the urge to go up alone."

"You used to fly alone, though, didn't you?"

"I did, but that was before I lost Seron." Adrian pressed his lips together, his gaze dropping to the blanket. "There's such a sharp line between before and after. So much of what I used to think, feel, and enjoy simply doesn't—or didn't—feel relevant anymore."

There was a wellspring of hope in those words, but it was a small one. Maybe Lucas was trying to rush things. Maybe it was too much, too soon. He could wait. He could. He had set that part of himself aside for months at a time. That was more challenging to do when this very sweet, unfairly handsome man was *wooing* him and winding him into knots, but Lucas knew all too well that grief wasn't a straight course. There were hitches and bumps along the way and moments of free fall. "You'll go back up when you're ready."

"I'd like for you to be with me when I do." Adrian lifted his chin, flashing a small smile. "If you don't think it'd be too much trouble."

"Too much trouble to take a free flight in a private plane. Definitely." Lucas touched Adrian's chin, enjoying the shape of him. "Getting the time for an adventure would be tricky. How long do you generally go up for?"

"A few hours, typically, but if you can swing an afternoon or a weekend, there's a little island not far off the coast that has a landing strip. Miles of pristine beaches that are quiet even during the best of weather." Adrian reached up a hand, brushing a curl back behind his ear. "I could take you if you'd like."

"So long as it isn't raining," Lucas teased, leaning closer. "Yes?"

"Mmhmm." Adrian brushed his lips against Lucas', sweet and gentle, tasting of salty capers and fresh berries. "You catch on quickly."

"I'd teach you to enjoy the inclement," Lucas promised, nudging Adrian's nose with his own. "If you were inclined to let me."

"Is that not what we're doing right now?"

"Are you enjoying yourself?" Lucas asked, pleased by the thought as the rain drizzled tiny drops through their leafy canopy.

"More than I thought possible." Adrian wrinkled his nose as a raindrop landed there. "Though that has more to do with the company than the conditions."

Lucas leaned up to kiss the droplet from Adrian's nose, watching him. "Maybe we can learn to like both." Lucas kissed him again, nudging Adrian back onto the blanket. "Just a little bit."

"Luke..." Adrian breathed his name like an incantation, hands smoothing up his back. "I've been looking forward to getting you alone all week."

Kissing him was incredible. Adrian seemed to melt under his hands in the same liquid way that his eyes melted—only his body was hard and warm and felt so *good*—Lucas smoothed his hair back from his brow, grinning down at him. "You have me now. What are you going to do with me?"

"Maybe find a more tangible use for the fingers you're so fond of." Adrian ran his palm down Lucas' side, his touch just barely enough to register through his jacket. "The shade of the trees makes your eyes look all the more brilliant from this angle. You were right about this place; I'm feeling very romanced." He tilted his chin, tangling their legs together where they lay on the blanket with a canopy of emerald overhead. "Was there something in particular you had in mind?"

"Capers," Lucas admitted softly, tracing Adrian's cheek as he watched. He'd made a healthy career for a time out of observing the smallest inflections of expression and vocalizations. Truth and lies. Friends and foes. Adrian wanted him. Wanted this. Lucas was sure. "They always make me... hungry," he whispered, kissing his cheek, the firm corner of his jaw. "I'd rather like it if you'd use your fingers in my hair, while I..." He lifted a brow suggestively. "I've thought of it."

"Have you?" Adrian shivered, leaning into his touch. "Of me in particular or just the act more generically?"

Lucas laughed, kissing down his neck, letting his hands finally—*finally*—wander just a bit further. Down Adrian's chest. Broad and toned. Down his sides. Angling in, taut, a swimmer's body. Biceps and pecs and shoulders for days and that abdomen that he wanted to trace with his fingertips in low light. "You. I think of you." He hummed at his collar, tracing the waist of Adrian's slacks. "I think of what you'll feel like on my tongue."

"I..." Adrian paused, gulping audibly. Lucas glanced up as something shifted in his expression, heat transitioning to something more fragile. "Darling, would you hold me a little while longer?"

Too far. Lucas cursed himself as he eased to the blanket beside him, tucking his chin over Adrian's shoulder. He'd built it up too much in his head, dreams and fantasies and planning for time. He kissed Adrian's shoulder. "Have you ever ridden a bicycle?"

"I used to get to my classes that way when I was in graduate school." Adrian softened, curling against him. "Why do you ask?"

"I never did. Tula's been asking for one." At least he wasn't pulling away. Still here. Still close. Lucas hadn't botched it too badly. He watched the rain drip from the leaves at the ends of the branches, away from them. "I'm wondering how long it will take me to learn it."

"I thought you were going to make a crass simile," Adrian said slowly, holding him tightly.

"To what." Lucas rested his hand over his heart, thumbing where the patter had sped and was still a bit skittish.

"About bikes. And riding."

"I know. That isn't what I meant," Lucas whispered, kissing his shoulder. "Don't worry about it."

"It's *embarrassing*," Adrian murmured. "Not being able to... Feeling something stopping you from... How are you not mortified by proxy?"

"I never had cause to ride a bike," Lucas shrugged, looking up at him with a bland expression as he returned to a safer topic. "No bikes on an aircraft carrier or a submarine. My parents preferred walking and roller skating. But it looks fun. You're very handsome in this light. Would you like a slice of pear?"

"I would, thank you." Adrian peeled away, staying close but ducking his head as his eyes turned fractal. "I'd be happy to teach you both if you'd like."

"Ever the professor," Lucas teased.

Adrian laughed, clearing his throat and lacing their fingers together again. "Nothing would make me happier than to teach you."

"Bikes, then." Lucas squeezed his hand gently. "I will look forward to it. Adrian..." He paused, searching for the right words. He'd never been particularly good at the right words in these kinds of situations. Cutting, he could do. Sometimes clever. But kindness... He tried anyway. "I enjoy our time together. All of it. Bikes or no. Do you understand?"

"I had hoped so." Adrian's lips curled into a slight, awkward little smile, the corners of his mustache quirking just so. "I adore you. Truly. I don't want you to think otherwise."

Adore. Fancy. Lucas could have lapped up the way Adrian spoke like ice cream on a warm day. "You demonstrate that admirably," he answered in kind and kissed Adrian's fingertips for good measure. It was enough. It was more than enough. More than he'd realized was possible. The *connection*. The gentleness of this man who leaned into his lightest touches and made his heart quake with the sound of his laughter. Sex came and went, Lucas could manage those needs himself, but this ephemeral thing between them, nascent and fragile... He had to protect this, and do so better than he had been. He guided Adrian's hand to the back of his head and nestled against him. "Would you touch me, just here? Is that alright?"

"More than." Adrian pressed his lips to the crown of Lucas' head, running his fingers through his curls. Soothing, gentle circles that still managed to send a thrill of heat to his core. "Thank you for inviting me here today. I'm glad we didn't opt for a backup."

"Backup plans are admitting defeat before the assault," Lucas mumbled, swallowing his sighs so as not to spook the man. "I'm honored you braved the weather with me."

"You *should* be. I could've gotten *smudged*." Fingertips massaging into his scalp, lips caressing the shell of his ear. "Is there anything else you've been longing to learn? We could try an exchange. Perhaps you might teach me how to assemble a delightful picnic so we're not quite so one-sided in culinary endeavors."

"If you can assemble a plane's engine, I imagine a picnic is not far outside your skillset."

"You should've seen when I tried to make spaghetti," Adrian chuckled, thumbing his cheek. "I burned the noodles. I didn't know you could *do* that."

"My mother used to burn water." Lucas pressed a kiss to Adrian's hand when it came close enough. "She'd put a pot on the stove and wander off, completely forgetting it was there. The whole bottom would turn black."

"Ah, well, she and I have a few things in common, then." Adrian cupped his cheek, kissing him gently. "Do you think she'd like me, if she were here? Your mother, I mean."

"She *is* here."

"You know what I mean."

"I think she would, but I wouldn't have invited her to our picnic," Lucas teased quietly against his lips.

"Well, no, I would imagine not if you'd hoped for bicycles." Adrian glanced between his eyes, studying him. "I hope you're not disappointed."

"I think we'd get wet if we tried to ride them today. Some other time." He met those sweet silver eyes steadily. "You'll know if I'm disappointed, Adrian."

"If you look at me like you looked at the tennis mothers, I'll know."

Lucas shook his head at Adrian's nervous laugh. "I promise I'm not."

Adrian smoothed his hands over Lucas' shoulders. "If it makes you feel any better, I've thought of it, too. Extensively."

"Have you?" It did make him feel better, in some ways. Worse in others. Uncomfortable, physically, for a certainty. How extensively? What details? What did he imagine? He couldn't ask. "How complimentary."

"I'm surprised you're surprised," Adrian mused, kissing his shoulder. "Has it been that long since you've seen yourself in a mirror?"

"Ages," Lucas assured him, lying with ease, gazing at his reflection in Adrian's eyes. "In any case, it doesn't matter what I see when I see myself. What do you see?"

"Your eyes," Adrian began, cupping Lucas' cheek with a wide smile, "are entrancing. Crushed emeralds and rubies under delightfully expressive brows. They haunt me long after we've parted." He kissed the tip of Lucas' nose. "I love the little wrinkle that shows up, just between them, when I shorten your name. And your *hands*. I could write a dissertation on your hands if you asked. How they look, how they move... All manner of things they might do to me."

"When you're ready." Lucas' voice sounded a little too low, a little too much, even to his own ears, so he held those hands very still. "This is good," he whispered as he pressed a kiss to Adrian's lips, lingering, tasting the warmth of his breath against the backdrop of rain as he held him.

"Very good," Adrian agreed softly, his hands slipping down to hold Lucas' waist. "We've hardly made a dent in your spread. I could feed you *sicut Romani*. Would you mind?"

He should have guessed from the inscriptions in the Sharp mausoleum that Adrian knew Latin, but it was still a pleasant surprise to hear him speak it. Lucas laughed, nuzzling his nose. "No. I wouldn't mind at all." He nibbled cherry tomatoes and capers and cream cheese from Adrian's fingers, soothed by the quiet patter of the rain through the leaves and the mist that blew beneath their shelter. He was so warm. So damned kind. And still hurting. Adrian would probably be hurting for a long, long time. There were still days when all Lucas wanted to do was sit in the mausoleum and try to feel the presence that Tula felt so strongly: the people who had loved him above everything else. It was a difficult thing to let go of, and he'd had time. Not only time, but he couldn't feel what Tula did. What Adrian expected to. His gifts lay elsewhere.

"Luke?" Adrian asked softly, nibbling on the edge of a slice of peach. "Do you think I'd fit well into your life if the time came?"

"You're not in my life now?" Lucas asked drowsily.

"I mean..." Adrian watched him. "More. Could you see me as... I'm very fond of the little family you've built. I wonder what we might be ambling towards. Do you think I would fit?"

Lucas stared at him, tucking away whatever bubbling, broiling emotions threatened to shift his expression. Fit? Adrian didn't want to touch him—didn't want Lucas to touch him—past his waist, but he wanted to... what? More? More what? Wasn't that what Lucas was trying to do? Wasn't that what Adrian very clearly wasn't ready for? "...Could you be more specific?" he asked carefully.

Adrian touched his cheek. "I'd like to see you more often. However that's possible. If it is."

"More often," Lucas repeated, searching his eyes. "We can look for more time if that's what you want."

"I do. Very much. Yes." Adrian's eyes lit like moonlight again, a smile curling his lips. "You don't need to make a picnic every time. I'd be happy to simply be with you."

"I know I don't have to make one every time. I look forward to what you assemble, too." Lucas winked. "No jet fuel."

"I'll assemble a very tasty selection of takeout options next time Tula has tennis lessons," Adrian assured him fondly. "Just in case my offerings are as wanting as I imagine they'll be."

"I'd like to try your cooking. It can't be that bad."

"Hm. Well. I'll try, yes?" Adrian huffed a quiet laugh. "Next time."

"Next time," Lucas agreed quietly.

Chapter Fourteen

LUCAS

Lucas promised himself he'd take his time. He did not want to put Adrian in the position of feeling as uncertain as he had in the park again. Adrian had been clear with where he was most comfortable: he had asked for closeness. Companionship. Maybe he dreamed of more, but he didn't want it. He didn't want Lucas, at least not the way Lucas wanted him.

Lucas could admit to himself and Anara that he wanted more than that. Much more. The first time Adrian had asked him over to his very well-decorated condo, he and Adrian had fallen upon each other on the sofa like horny teenagers, which was a clear sign that Adrian didn't find Lucas displeasing by any means. But Adrian still wasn't ready for what came next, even as he tried to convince them both that he was. He pushed himself too far again and again, then retreated in apologies and—Christ, Lucas was getting tired of hearing Adrian apologize. But then the man's patient hand-holding would slither beguilingly into touching his arms or his shoulders, and Lucas found himself drawn in like a fish on a hook once more.

He swallowed a moan as Adrian cupped the back of his neck, drawing him in closer. He hadn't spent this much time making out since he'd been a teenager. Hours of it. Conversation dissolving into breath and tongue and... Lucas swallowed again, struggling to keep himself from bucking against Adrian's leg as the man slid closer—

"Hey," Lucas managed to sum up the wherewithal to sound like a whole, decent human person. He ran his fingers over Adrian's cheek, leaning back to admire him. Flushed and decadently handsome, lips full and soft beneath his very askew mustache. "How was that symposium? You still haven't told me anything; all I know from that snapshot of a champagne bottle is that it was well-funded."

"Hm?" Adrian's eyes fluttered open, dark lashes brushing his cheekbones. "Oh, I got into a very heated debate about biofuels with a fellow from another university." He chuckled, nudging Lucas with his nose. "The champagne was fabulous. I had to take note of the brand in case we have an occasion for bubbles."

As though one needed an occasion. Lucas lightly stroked the line of Adrian's throat. He liked to feel when Adrian swallowed, liked the bob of his Adam's apple under his fingers and the tension in the muscles of his neck. "How very thoughtful." Now the question was: how to carefully avoid the man becoming aware of his unruly erection? Something. Anything. Because Adrian was very close to lying on top of him again and that would remove all doubt of where Lucas' literal and figurative head was. "Heated debates always make me tense. Maybe you'd like a massage?"

"That would be wonderful." Adrian brushed his lips to Lucas'. "Thank you, darling. How do you want me?"

There was a loaded question. "Just..." He carefully turned Adrian away. That was better. "You enjoy your view of the sea." He ran his hands lightly over Adrian's shoulders and down his back. "I like your place." He did. He liked the minimalism of it. Clean and sharp. Smelling of salt from the sea below and of Adrian, warm and spiced. He leaned his forehead to the back of Adrian's head, working his thumbs into his broad shoulders.

"Thank you. I was never much of one for clutter." Adrian rolled his neck, his muscles flexing under Lucas' fingers. "This is heavenly."

"Good." He smelled so good and he was warm under Lucas' hands, softening each time Lucas found a crinkle of tension and loosened it. Just to *touch* him without watching that wary, apologetic tension rising in Adrian's expression was a relief. "I like to be useful."

"Always moving. Keeping busy. Flitting from one place to the next or sketching out your masterpieces." Adrian tilted his head back, leaning into Lucas' arms. "I like to feel useful, too. I used to spend so much time sitting on my balcony, sipping coffee and watching the waves roll in, but these days, too much quiet and calm lets other things creep to the forefront of my mind."

Was that why he was so energetic these days? Avoidance? Lucas didn't think of himself as someone who hid. Protected, yes. Considering people and their motives before letting them in. But...

"Not that you *need* to be useful," Adrian continued. "I simply see the appeal."

"Right." Lucas trailed his fingers down either side of Adrian's back, then up his sides before wrapping his arms around him. "So no more sipping coffee watching the waves for you?"

"Not recently, no." Adrian nuzzled his cheek, smooth skin against his scruff. "Perhaps when the weather warms, I'll try again."

He'd felt Adrian's chest a few times now, sneaking his hands up under sweaters and tee shirts when Adrian was feeling particularly brave. His arms. Gods, Lucas loved Adrian's arms. The bulk of them. Soft and muscular. And the way Adrian pressed back into his hold. No matter how uncertain Adrian seemed about taking the physical side of their relationship to another level, he obviously *cared*. Caring was more than Lucas had expected for a long time.

"Mm, right there," Adrian groaned gratefully as Lucas worked his thumbs into a particularly tight knot in his lower back. The words and the tone and the lean of the man made Lucas sweat. "How was Tula's diorama received?"

And they were back out of it again. Lucas stretched his jaw from the emotional whiplash. "'Gruesome' was the rave review from her friend Fatib. I have the rare and exciting honor of getting to go and speak with her teacher about it." He pressed his thumb into the offending knot and felt it crumple. "I don't know what they expected. There are three dead dogs in that book. She takes things like that very seriously."

"Of course she does, your budding necromancer," Adrian chuckled. "I'd expect nothing less."

"She's too smart for that class anyway. I warned them. But they won't test her into another grade until the spring." He paused. "It doesn't bother you to talk about her?"

"Why would it bother me?" Adrian glanced over his shoulder at him. "She's your daughter."

"I'm well aware." He pressed his hand over Adrian's heart. Was that why? Why he wouldn't... Yes, he was grieving, moving through the stages of loss. And Lucas wasn't—could never be—a replacement for Adrian's husband. But Adrian did want him, at least until he didn't. Was it Tula? Did he think of her and get turned off? A family. Adrian wanted a family, but wanting a family wasn't the same as wanting a lover. Lucas shook his head, squeezing Adrian's shoulders. "Bother was perhaps the wrong choice of word. I appreciate that you..." He could have kicked himself; the mood was gone again. He might as well give up on attempting to resurrect it. "Do you remember the first time you could hear them?"

"The departed?" Adrian asked thoughtfully. "I was probably three or four? My parents' cook passed on: a kind, lovely woman who always snuck me a dollop off of whatever spoons she was using to cook with when I passed by. One day she apologized and said she couldn't give me treats anymore. It took my parents three weeks to realize I was still seeing her after she'd passed. Greta always said our house was much too cold for a child without sweets; she was right, even if it took me a bit longer to realize it."

Adrian hadn't spoken much about his family; it was difficult to imagine a man so warm coming from somewhere icy. "That lightning you showed me... Was that a natural part of your gift or did you study it somewhere?"

"I discovered it by accident. I had a fight with my father and called a thunderstorm from the sky. I'm not sure I'd seen him so happy before or since."

Lucas lifted a brow, studying Adrian's profile. "He was happy that you created a storm?"

"My family has long prided themselves on the strength of our lineage." Adrian shrugged, sighing. "He was pleased that I would be able to continue that tradition."

"Yes, but weather is so... public."

"It is. It takes a careful touch to make it subtle." Adrian winked, cocksure and valiant. "Very useful when I'm up in the air. I'll show you." He turned in Lucas' arms, cupping Lucas' hands in his own. He exhaled, closing his eyes, and a puff of cloud formed between their hands, floating up into the air. After a moment, snowflakes began to fall, dusting their fingertips with a miniature blizzard. "I can teach her that, too, when she's a bit older; it wouldn't do to have a preteen summon lightning in a fit of pique."

Lucas stared at the little storm system; the clouds disappeared as the snowflakes melted on their skin. "No. No, it wouldn't."

"The whole place is warded, Luke, just like before. No blips on anyone's scanners, I promise, even if I made it snow in every room." Adrian watched him warily. "...Was that too much?"

"No. It's—I suppose it's interesting. You're not afraid of the power. Of using it. Of talking about it."

Adrian sighed, "I could be more circumspect, I know."

"That's not what I mean." Lucas wiggled his fingers as the rest of the snow melted. "Your family must not have worried about what might happen if the Seekers found out."

"Not terribly, no. They had enough connections to keep us out of trouble if we were discovered."

"Ah." Lucas nodded slowly. "That's what I've tried to do. What my parents tried to do. But it was always... My father liked to say: 'Be careful who you tell because once they know, they know'. That was before we discovered that I could make someone un-know." He grimaced. He tried not to think of the times that he'd needed to—the drunk man whose car his mother had pulled back to the road when it had gone through a barrier into a ditch, and the Seeker who'd come to investigate one of his parents' projects—a little girl so quiet Lucas had felt a need to whisper when he was around her. The emptiness in their eyes when he'd worked. The confusion when they couldn't touch the memories he'd taken. The strange pleasure he'd felt in the taking, like a drug that could have become far too addictive if he'd allowed himself to indulge it. "I don't ever want to do that again," he asserted, grim. "I will if I have to, but I don't want to. I won't go to one of those holding facilities, to be tagged and studied like the others. I won't let them take Tula either."

Adrian cupped his cheek. "She won't. *You* won't." He brushed their lips together, gentle and tender. "Not if I have anything to say about it."

"I can protect us," Lucas murmured, studying Adrian's eyes. "I've taught her everything I can to control herself, and if that fails, I've accepted that her freedom may come at the cost of my wish not to touch that part of my power again."

"I'd rather you didn't need to resort to altering minds. I'll help you keep her safe," Adrian promised. "Because it's the right thing to do and because I'm very, very fond of you."

"Are you?" Lucas held Adrian's hand against his cheek. "I'm very glad." He smirked. "It's because of the massage, isn't it?"

"Oh, *entirely*. You see, that was my plan all along." Adrian made a poor attempt to hide the grin that blossomed across his lips. "Meet a handsome stranger among the headstones, then spend the better part of a year getting to know him in hopes that one day he'd turn my legs to jelly with his hands." He laughed, bright as the sunlight on the waves outside the window. "Though, actually, that is one of the main purposes of dating."

Dating. He supposed they were. Lucas felt a rush of warmth spread through his core. Gods, but he wanted a chance to turn the man's legs to jelly. He'd been able to think of little else for the weeks since Adrian had kissed him in the wake of mermaids and brocade. *He trusts you*, he reminded himself sternly. He tried to match his smile to Adrian's. Light and easy. Nothing to worry about. He was definitely not imagining Adrian spread-eagled and groaning 'just like that' again. Just a perfectly innocent massage. He could do that. "Let's see about getting rid of the rest of these knots then,"

Lucas said firmly as he turned Adrian away, settling behind him again to refocus on his back.

The sounds Adrian made as he inched towards his lower back did little to dissipate the heat: low grunts and groans and pleased sighs that could've just as easily been elicited from an entirely different activity. Lucas studied Adrian's cheek; it was warm and smooth compared to Lucas' perennial stubble. Was there a trail of dark fur leading down to his groin, the same raven as his hair? Did he trim? He was so fastidious with his mustache and the hair on his head, Lucas could only imagine what he might do down—*Stop thinking about it*, he chastised himself, shutting his eyes.

Lucas was going to need a cold shower. A long one. It took actual effort not to rock his hips like a teenager in rut. He wanted to peel Adrian's clothes off, slide his hands over his bare skin, coax him into sighs inside and out and—Stop. He had to stop.

Lucas kissed the back of Adrian's head and stood, retreating from the man and the couch. Sweat on his spine. "Just going to use your bathroom before I head out," he announced over his shoulder as he fled, ducking into the powder room and leaning against the wall inside. He was hard and hot to the touch, with a firm obvious line tenting his trousers. He peeled himself free and gripped, stroking himself hard and fast to clear the gates and get back to being a good friend. A good date. No pressure.

Such good pressure.

Lucas swallowed a moan, tripping quickly towards ecstasy, remembering the soft little sounds Adrian had made in answer to his massage. He wiped himself clean when he'd finished and washed his hands, staring daggers at his reflection. *Unruly, untrustworthy cur*, he thought, straightening himself and running clean, damp hands back through his hair.

Back in the living room, he forced an easy smile. "Tacos tomorrow?"

"Yes, thank you." Adrian's voice had deepened, the flush on his cheeks and the parts of his chest exposed by his deep v-neck making his skin glow. He snatched up a discarded tissue from the upholstery, blinking slowly. "I'll meet you at the plaza at one-thirty."

"Alright." Had he been upset? He searched Adrian's face. Lucas had always had a knack for reading faces and guessing intentions, and the Navy had honed that knack into a skill. But what he wanted had never gotten in the way of those questions when he'd been in the service. He hadn't wanted anything but the truth. And the truth here... The truth here was confusing. Here and gone. Want and away. "If you're late, I'm not going to save chips for you."

"I wouldn't expect you to." Adrian cleared his throat. "Shall I walk you out?"

"If you'd like." Lucas hadn't figured out how to leave without this awkwardness. He didn't *want* to leave. But he had to. He had to limit the time they spent together because his life was full of Tula and work and errands... and because too much time made it impossibly difficult to contain wanting to just *touch* him. And more. "Thank you for the visit."

Adrian stood, wrapping his arm around Lucas' waist and kissing him fondly at the base of the stairs. "I'll see you tomorrow, one-thirty sharp."

"I'll look forward to it." He always did. Lucas traced the curve of Adrian's mustache and kissed him. "Very much."

CHAPTER FIFTEEN
ADRIAN

Cool winter light filtered through the mausoleum window, brightening the pictures Adrian had arrayed on the little altar in the center. Framed prints of their wedding and of their first military ball, when they were still getting over the rush of being able to kiss and hold hands in public without worry. A scrap of leaf-embroidered brocade Lucas had had laying about that reminded Adrian of Seron. The hideous stuffed horse Seron had won him at that carnival after Adrian had nearly gotten sick on the Ferris wheel.

Adrian traced the smooth edge of the framed, folded flag, peering at the image of his grinning husband. Sharp-toothed and exultant, beaming at the sky.

"I had something I meant to tell you," Adrian murmured, waving a hand to light all of the scented candles at once, making the runes he'd drawn glint. "To ask your advice, maybe, or..." He chuckled, shaking his head. "I suppose just to let someone know, in case everything ends up topsy-turvy."

No answer, but that didn't make Adrian's eyes grow misty any longer. Luke was working overtime, trying to perfect Cymbeline's dress to a point he wouldn't be embarrassed when she wore it to the gala at the end of the month. He'd already made the final adjustments on Adrian's suit. Moonlit brocade, just like he'd promised, as soft as a dream. When Lucas had taken all the pins out, Adrian had pressed him back against the nearest wall and kissed him until they were both breathless.

Two months of kissing and snuggling and rambling through the city. He'd been surprised Lucas didn't push him further, not even when they were red-cheeked and cuddled up under a blanket in Adrian's apartment with a forgotten movie playing in the background. Instead, Lucas watched Adrian with those too-perceptive eyes, waiting for Adrian to make the next move.

Gods, Adrian *wanted* to. But it wasn't just that; he was growing weary of bidding Lucas goodbye at the end of every evening and falling back into his bed alone.

Not that there was anything to be done about that. They were what they were, which was... in between, in an emotional manifestation of the Aether, lingering in a space full of possibility that never quite touched reality, to Adrian's increasing frustration. And Lucas was still keeping Tula at a distance from him, their lives as separate as possible from Adrian's. To protect her. To keep her from being disappointed when Adrian decided to leave.

But what if Adrian didn't wish to end things? What if that was the point? What if Adrian *wanted* to intertwine their lives, to be a part of Luke's world, to wake up next to him in the mornings and give Tula, the miracle of a girl, a hug before she shuttled off to school?

"I'm going to ask him if he would mind..." Adrian wrinkled his nose, frowning. *What* exactly? If he could stay over? If they could be more serious, again? "For more, I suppose. I haven't been able to—"

The candles flickered and an unseasonably warm breeze brushed across Adrian's skin like butterfly kisses. He blinked, staring at the portrait.

A steady pressure heated his shoulder and a familiar voice sounded behind him, muddled as though through spoken underwater. "Haven't been able to what, Adrian?"

"Seron?" Adrian whispered, more breath than sound. He was rewarded by more of that sun-kissed warmth wrapping around him like his husband's arms used to, then pressure against the nape of his neck, almost like a nose nudging him gently. "You're—" Adrian swallowed, fighting against his traitorous eyes, the burning in his throat.

Seron's spirit crossed in front of Adrian, kneeling before him and cupping his cheek, his fingers more warmth than weight. His hair was cropped short and he stood in uniform, just as handsome and strong as the day Adrian had driven him to the airport for the last time. He was smiling. After all this time and distance and *death*, Seron was still smiling. "Hello, love."

Adrian choked, reaching for him. His hand slowed as it touched Seron's cheek, just for a moment, then passed through him like mist. Words, too many and not enough, firmly lodged in his throat.

"I like him," Seron said softly, his dimples shadowed in the candlelight, blue eyes shining. "I think he's good for you, and you for him, in case you were wondering."

Adrian exhaled a shaky breath, closing his eyes. "I love him," he admitted softly.

"I know you do," Seron murmured, his voice faraway and ethereal. "I see you blooming again. Do you remember the first time you told me you loved me?"

"In the sunflower field," Adrian whispered, cheeks damp. "It took me months longer than it took you to say it."

"I think Lucas will take even longer than you did," Seron told him with a chuckle. "If my conversations with his parents have been anything to go by. You'll need to nudge him, love."

"Nudge..." Adrian peered up at him, trying to memorize the gilded shape of him, haloed in light like an angel from a painting. "You want me to tell him?"

"I want you to live," Seron murmured, pressing his incorporeal forehead against Adrian's. "Loving is the most important part of that."

"I still love you," Adrian said, more breath than sound.

"I know that, too." Seron didn't smell like himself, but instead like tallow candles and the sharp, magical scent of ozone. *He isn't here anymore*, Adrian reminded himself. *Not fully.* But he was kind and warm and smiling. "I hope you always do. I hope that, over time, it hurts less to remember me. I love you, you know that?"

Adrian nodded, lungs burning. After all this time? Had he been here all along? Had Lucas been right about why Seron had been silent?

"I'll be here for a while longer, love," Seron continued. "Go. Go live. Love. For both of us, okay?"

"Anything." Adrian bit his lip, nodding slowly. "I'll see what he says."

"Good man." Seron stood slowly, still smiling, and winked.

The candles fluttered again and Seron's spectral form faded from view.

"I love you, too," Adrian whispered, bowing his head and slipping out of the mausoleum, the warm trickle of tears chilled by the winter breeze.

CHAPTER SIXTEEN

LUCAS

The drive to the studio was always quick; that was one of the reasons Lucas had chosen the location, despite its proximity to some less-than-savory warehouses. It was an easy hop on and off the freeway between work and home, which meant it was close to Tula should anything happen. Lucas found a parking spot a block away, stuffing his hands in his pockets and inhaling the bitter wind, letting it burn his lungs. The smells of cold asphalt and ice were in the air. Lucas had always loved winter.

His studio—and even after four years, it still pleased him to linger on those words—was a low, flat-topped little warehouse with windows covered by dark shades and bars. One word—Philomela—in stark wrought iron beside the door was the only clue to what lay inside. And what lay inside was... well-earned chaos. Lucas eyed the scraps of fabric and mostly empty racks and hangers. He loved his studio just after a show: used up and glorious, waiting to catch wind again and sail to the next. For now, though, it was quiet and dark and smelled of the coffee that had probably burned to the bottom of the pot after the last frazzled week.

He needed a little quiet to gather his thoughts. He needed to figure out the next port of call for his business. For his life, he thought ruefully, which was somehow less sure than his fledgling studio.

Lucas picked up the scraps from a gray velvet suit he'd been working on for weeks and laid them out, gathering strips of satin and turning on the overhead lights. It hadn't made the cut. He'd negotiated four suits into the showcase. Four arias to the human form. It was only a sliver of what he could do, but being part of a larger line's catwalk had gained more eyes on his work. And why were the lights making his gray look blue? Lucas held up the velvet alongside a strip of green satin and then glanced up. One of the lights had burned out. He would have to replace it and do his work in the back closet in the meantime.

He could make this suit work, for next time. It was perfect in his mind; he only needed to find its path into dazzling reality. Reality was what he was best at, after all.

Or he'd thought he'd been. Before Adrian. He'd thought he could read people, too. He'd thought a number of things, all of which Adrian had turned upside down. Because Lucas was in love for the first time in his life—sparkling, shimmering, midnight brocade love that he could have worn to any opera—and it was killing him.

The knock at the front door made Lucas check and double-check his watch. He wasn't supposed to have so much as an assistant in for another few hours yet. They'd earned their rest. A second knock. Lucas rubbed his brow, abandoning the dream of gray velvet for the door, praying silently that it wasn't one of his model's managers coming to negotiate for a better deal. And then he felt it. That subtle shift in the air that he'd begun to associate with Adrian. The spicy scent of his cologne. The energy that moved ahead of Adrian—not magic, just him.

Lucas paused to check his hair in the mirror, fussing with his curls uselessly until he gave up and nudged the door open. "Good morning?" He tried to keep the concern out of his voice as he met Adrian's eyes. "Did you want to come in?"

"Yes, thank you." Adrian had visited his studio so many times that he breezed past Lucas, navigating to the little waiting room; Lucas couldn't look at the long, low couches now without remembering how they'd lain together on them after Adrian's last fitting, laughing and kissing like teenagers.

Lucas locked the front door and followed him, tucking his untrustworthy hands into his pockets. "Is everything alright? Did I forget something? Your final fitting isn't until next week."

Adrian dropped to the couch, fidgeting uncharacteristically, his fingers flexing over his knees. He was disheveled, which was also entirely out of character, as was the fact that he was out of his apartment before eight. "I had to see you."

"Oh." Lucas glanced back towards the work that was waiting, then shut the door and crossed towards him. "I'm just... in the middle of some things." He raked his hand back through his hair. "It's very early and you're askew." He adjusted the neck of Adrian's coat. "You've seen me. Now what."

Adrian touched his cheek, a self-deprecating smile blossoming across his lips. "I know it's not a good time."

"It's a fine time; it's only that I was given to understand you and dawn had a bit of a feud going."

"We do," Adrian admitted. "Typically."

Not just askew, Lucas thought, noting Adrian's unsteady breaths. *Arrhythmic*. "Did you run here?" He smoothed Adrian's lapels.

"I'm trying very hard not to leap to terrible conclusions. Can you tell me what's going on?"

Adrian pressed his forehead to Lucas'. "You're very important to me. You know that, yes?"

"...what's the matter?" Dread worked its way beneath Lucas' collarbone. "If you think someone is onto you—"

Adrian hissed, "No, no. Nothing like—" He reached for Lucas' hands, taking them in his and holding them to his chest. "I went to visit Seron this morning," Adrian began, the words tumbling in a rush. "To ask for his advice... Anyway, he spoke to me." Adrian exhaled slowly. "He was *there*. For the first time since he died, I *felt* him again. Saw him again."

"Ah." There it was. His sinking intuition had been correct, only it hadn't been warning of danger. Just heartbreak. Lucas bowed his head, looking between their hands and the couch and the covered window for something to focus on that wasn't that awful feeling. "That's what you've wanted."

"It is. Was. It was good to see him again, to know he hadn't gone entirely." Adrian pressed his lips to Lucas' knuckles, the barest of touches. Lucas was going to miss those kisses on his hands, as though they were precious. As though he were. "I think you were right," Adrian whispered.

Sometimes Lucas hated being right.

"I keep telling you: I usually am. And I'm glad for you." Lucas smiled, a fleeting thing. "Thank you for telling me."

Adrian held Lucas' gaze. "That wasn't all I came here to say." His eyes were extraordinary starlit pools of molten mercury. Lucas would miss those, too.

"That's alright. There's no need; I can deduce the rest." He patted Adrian's shoulder once—all that he could trust himself to do—and made to leave.

"Stay." Adrian caught his hand. "Please."

"You don't have to do this," Lucas murmured, hating the scratch in his throat. "I'm in the middle of—I said that already." Gods, redundancies were boring. Being broken up with was worse than boring. "Listen: I understand, and I'm glad for you. I really am."

"I don't think you *do* understand," Adrian insisted with a laugh; the sound was too sharp and bright for the darkness gathering around Lucas. "Stay with me for a moment and I'll—"

"I told you I'm used to grayscale. I don't expect anything from you. I haven't. I only wanted to see you at peace and it sounds as though you are. So. Good." Lucas couldn't look at him. Looking at Adrian would break him, melt him, make him want more than he'd agreed to. He studied the door handle. The light reflected on the bars on the window. The shadows threw patterns on the rug. "Unless—did you not want the suit anymore? I'm not in the habit of issuing refunds."

"I love you." Adrian stayed where he was, smiling and sure and looking silly with his hair askew and his shirt rumpled. "I came here to tell you that I love you. Luke." He held out his hand. "Come back. No refunds, no grayscale."

Lucas pressed his lips together, a suspicious sting behind his eyes. "You..." He blinked rapidly, staring. "What?"

"I'm in love with you," Adrian clarified, reaching for him.

The curves on the rug began to move on their own. Lucas crossed the room and sank to the cushion beside him. "Are you?"

"Desperately." Adrian's voice cracked, but the hands that smoothed down Lucas' shoulders were steady. "Are you—I suppose I should've led with that."

"With what?"

"That I want to be with you. Do you... Is it too soon? Not what you want?"

Lucas fought a shiver, caught between his hands. "Not—" he began, then laughed, shaking his head. "No. It's... No. I..." He swallowed, leaning to press his forehead to Adrian's. "I love you, too," he whispered, the words tasting like sweet, stinging curry on his tongue. He hadn't dared to say them aloud before. He could barely think of them without losing his composure. "I didn't know what it would feel like and then I *did*, but I didn't know if I should tell you."

"You can tell me as much as you like," Adrian murmured, cupping his cheeks. "I'd like to hear you say it again."

"I love you." Lucas lifted his gaze, searching those endless star-touched eyes. "I didn't know it would hurt this much. To be in love for the first time and not be able to say so, not..." He grimaced, biting his lip when it trembled. "Gods and monsters, I thought you were leaving."

Adrian shook his head. "That's the last thing I want to do."

Lucas could taste his own heartbeat, ripe on his tongue like lychee; he could feel it dancing under his skin. "Alright," he said, sure he would float out of his skin.

"Are you?" Adrian murmured, touching his chin.

"Hm?"

"Alright?"

He'd been sure he couldn't fall in love, then that surety had cracked into pieces. He'd told himself again and again that Adrian would heal and move on... Lucas nodded slowly. If he moved too quickly, he was worried he would fall apart. "I—yes. Thank you for asking." *Breathe*, he reminded himself. "You were saying—go on."

"Less grayscale." Adrian replaced his fingers with his lips, kissing along Lucas' jawline. "I've always had trouble with the terminology: 'partner' sounds too sterile and 'boyfriend' juvenile."

"Terminology only matters if you're in a hurry to tell people." Why couldn't he stop trembling?

"That's fair enough." Adrian nudged him. "Although, I would like to when you do. You know the important part: I love you and I want to be a part of your life."

Lucas couldn't help but laugh. "You *are* a part of my life, rather inextricably."

"And I'd like to stay that way." Adrian spoke slowly, sweet and earnest, and gods help him, but Lucas believed him. "What do you think?"

Lucas glanced between those otherworldly eyes. "I think I like my life with you in it, whatever you want to call yourself."

"The feeling is mutual," Adrian assured him. "Do you think you might be able to swing an overnight sitter soon, once everything calms down here? I'd like to have you over for an entire evening."

Lucas dropped his gaze to their twined fingers, fighting an inane giggle that was brewing somewhere in his chest. "It can be arranged." He glanced up, wondering if Adrian could tell how very unwieldy he felt. "Why? Did you want to watch both Top Guns this time?"

Adrian laughed, rolling his eyes. "Something like that."

He wanted to push Adrian back on the cushions and kiss him until neither of them could breathe. He wanted to run from the room and find somewhere dark and quiet to wheeze and shake without anyone seeing him. Lucas took a small, quick breath, turned his head, and kissed him. He wondered if it had been inevitable that he would. Kiss Adrian. Ache for him. Learn to love him. Some path that had been set the moment they'd first spoken. Or before, in the months of passing glances along the gravel paths between the mausoleums. Or before that, even. When their families had made their marks in marble and granite.

Then Adrian was hard against his hip, bending over him, and Lucas thought of how he'd wanted those hands on him in the park and the way they'd felt—just the other day—sliding over the silk of his vest... He shivered as Adrian plucked open the buttons of his shirt, then sighed gratefully when Adrian's kisses traveled down his neck.

"...maybe I should let you get back to your work?" Adrian whispered, teasing.

Steady. Lucas knew he was meant to remain steady; clear and present and reliable. Adrian loved him. The words made him want to spin in a circle. He held onto Adrian to keep himself from floating. He tried and failed to form words.

Adrian tilted his head to the side. "Shouldn't I? You said you were in the middle of something."

"Oh." Lucas looked to the door. "Yes. I am." Adrian loved him. Adrian wanted more. How much more and how... That could wait. It was enough to be free, for the moment, to love him without trying to pretend otherwise. He sent a flurry of will across the room, shutting the waiting room door. The rituals and warding marks hidden throughout the studio would conceal his art, Lucas knew, and he took some indecent pleasure at the sudden widening of Adrian's eyes. The heat that pooled in them.

"And you call me brash," Adrian chuckled, smoothing his palms down Lucas' sides. "Is it safe?"

"Protection wards." Lucas pointed to the corners of the room where he'd painted the slips of embroidered cloth against the ceiling in a bland white to match the surface. They were imperceivable unless someone knew where to look. "I like to be able to focus on my work. It's easier to do so without worrying someone might come bursting through the door. Did you want to discuss works and wonders?" he asked, slipping his hand beneath Adrian's sweater to smooth up his back.

"Not at this exact moment, no," Adrian murmured slyly, unbuttoning the last of the line of buttons along Lucas' shirt to fan it out and touch the skin beneath.

Lucas had always enjoyed this part. The reveal. The revel. Hands and fingers, friends and strangers. But he'd never been touched like this by someone he loved. He'd never had each breath cataloged by clever, curious eyes that he could gaze into until he forgot to breathe. Adrian could have unwound him without any skill at all—except he did have skills. Strong hands. Deft fingertips. Coarse, warm palms. Lucas heard himself exhaling breathy sighs; he'd never made those sounds before and wasn't sure he could have on purpose, but he couldn't seem to stop. He needed air. He needed to be bare, kisses trailing down his chest and belly, with the bristles of Adrian's mustache tickling his skin.

Each article removed brought more of those sighs, sending heat shuttling to his core. Adrian unzipped Lucas' boots and kissed Lucas' ankles, whispering words of affection over the tender skin there. The words were unnecessary; Lucas could feel Adrian's ardor in even the most glancing of touches, each one making colors float—lovely and perfect—behind Lucas' eyelids.

For months, Lucas had wanted this. Waiting and not daring to let himself hope too much. And now... "I love you." Words he'd heard before that usually meant nothing. Words he'd never spoken to a lover before today. All of Adrian's hesitations seemed to have melted away and he was hot: a roiling storm that made Lucas sweat as they tangled together. "I want you," Lucas moaned again, pressing his heel to the arm of the sofa as Adrian stretched him, trailing kisses over his skin until Lucas thought he might come unseamed.

Adrian's mustache was askew, his perfect hair more disheveled than when he'd arrived, and Lucas was sure he'd never seen him more handsome than in those minutes when he lifted his flushed face and grinned, confident and eager and a little wild.

Lucas pulled him up, tasting himself on Adrian's tongue as they kissed and Adrian stroked him. "I'd wondered if you were a top," he gasped. Hard muscle. Strong arms. He felt Adrian grin against his neck.

"I'm versatile," Adrian chuckled, breathless. "I need—"

"Right. Right pocket." Lucas tugged his pants towards them and fumbled.

"You just carry it around?" Adrian asked, amused.

"I like to be prepared," Lucas murmured, narrowing his eyes as Adrian took the small tube of lubricant and grinned over it. "There's a condom in my wallet. Don't simper. You'll ruin the mood."

Adrian laughed outright, working some of the lubricant over his fingers while Lucas coated him. The logistics that were so second nature to him, Lucas had never considered how much tenderness could be present in the exchange. The careful, loving way that Adrian prepared him and held him. No rush to get to the next step. The goal. They were the goal. This connection that they'd somehow, miraculously, found and built.

Lucas tried his best to control himself, but months of wanting and waiting had left him more wanton than usual. He ran his hands over Adrian's body as though he were made of clay to be shaped and admired. Every curve. Every plane. Every sharp angle. "We all have to be—versatile—sometimes," Lucas gasped, then groaned as Adrian added another finger.

"I am all the time," Adrian insisted, kissing him back onto the cushion. "For example, I would very much," he murmured, working a very human kind of magic over Lucas' mind and body, "like to switch if you're open to it."

The words went through him like fire. "Soon," Lucas agreed, catching himself on a moan. He squeezed the thick base of Adrian's member, licking his lips. "Next time. Now, I need you." It was more begging than asking and this time Adrian didn't laugh or tease. He was there. He was warm and joyous. And he was Lucas'.

CHAPTER SEVENTEEN

ADRIAN

As it happened, that weekend's slumber party plans fell through, leaving Adrian relieved he hadn't ended up purchasing the entire stock of camellias in the city. He waited until the next weekend for the flowers but proceeded to stock up on scented candles and ice cream and...

What was he supposed to *do* now that he *knew*?

He couldn't stop laughing. He was in love again, but even better, he was *loved*.

Time passed agonizingly slowly. Lucas was so busy with work that Adrian had begun bringing him coffee and takeout just as an excuse to see him. To talk to him. To kiss him, even if only for ten minutes before they needed to part again. He was impossibly beautiful when he was blissfully happy. And now that they'd finally tangled, there was a *hunger* in Lucas' eyes, in his touch, that Adrian hadn't felt before. Delightful. *Delectable*. It was nearly impossible not to lock him in a storage closet and attempt to satisfy those honey-sweet smirks, but somehow they managed to make it to Friday night without pouncing on each other again.

There was a knock at his door and Adrian ceased his pacing, filling the apartment with candlelight with a flick of his wrist, suffusing the hallway with a soft amber glow.

He opened the door to find Lucas leaning out over the railing to peer down towards the beach. "I still can't believe the view from this place," he muttered as he turned, offering a small ceramic pot full of violets. "Hello, Adrian."

"Luke." He grinned, taking the planter and dipping his head to breathe in the scent of fresh flowers. "You shouldn't have." He set them on a side table and wrapped his arms around Lucas' waist. "It's lovely, isn't it? I'm sorry it's too cold to keep the windows open."

"Summer will come again. Sooner than we expect." Lucas laced his fingers at Adrian's back, humming low as he nudged the door closed with his heel.

"As long as you're with me when it does," Adrian murmured, brushing his lips against Lucas' and locking the rest of the world out of their haven.

Lucas smiled into the kiss, answering with touch and tenderness rather than words.

Adrian had had a plan. The candles. Some wine. Some music.

Lucas kissed him back against the wall, skimming his palm up Adrian's shirt under his blazer. "I dreamt of you again last night."

Adrian shivered under his hands; they were hot and sure, brushing his nipples through the soft fabric. His kisses were hot and sure, too. Every moment he'd been with Lucas—the whole of their acquaintance—the man had been tentative when they'd touched. Testing. Querying silently.

He wasn't asking questions now. "Oh, yes?" Adrian wondered, head falling back to the wall as Lucas kissed down his neck, unbuttoning his shirt swiftly and unerringly.

"You were running through the woods," Lucas whispered, licking the words to Adrian's collarbone. "You kept looking over your shoulder at me, begging me to catch you." He raked his teeth where his lips had traveled and Adrian gasped.

This.

Seron had wanted him. They'd made love languorously for years. Love like the ocean on calm days, deep and slow and beautiful. Sunset painted and so tender it still made Adrian ache to remember it. And when he'd stripped Lucas down and finally *finally* tasted him and had him whole cloth, Lucas had been gentle there, too. Wonder-filled and beaming and melting under Adrian's hands.

But *this*. Adrian had never been on the receiving end of this. Never mind melting; he was being set ablaze and, with the way Lucas was grappling him, it was probably so that he could be cooked and eaten alive.

"Fuck, you're gorgeous," Lucas panted. "Do you still want me to catch you, Adrian?" He'd peeled Adrian's shirt apart and kissed up his throat to meet his lips again, warm palms heating Adrian's skin.

Adrian opened his eyes to find Lucas watching him, gleaming verdant forest-green eyes holding his own as he kissed the breath from Adrian's lungs.

"Do you still want me to take you?" Lucas asked, demanded, beckoned, dragging his thumb down Adrian's belly, nails skimming his skin.

"Please," Adrian rasped.

Lucas grinned, sharp and hungry, and Adrian felt himself start to sweat. He shook, biting his lip with a groan, as Lucas held him in place. Delicious power. Surprising strength. Adrian's shoulders and wrists pressed against the wall. Lucas' leaned forward, massaging Adrian's swelling cock with his thigh.

Adrian had planned for tonight. Romance. Soft pillows. Warm lights.

Lucas, it seemed, had a plan of his own.

And teeth.

Sweet gods. Lucas gnawed on his shoulder, nipping a path down his bicep. His short nails skimmed up Adrian's back and down his sides.

"Please," Adrian found himself begging, shivering despite the heat, as Lucas made his way down. He tugged Adrian's pants down and moaned as he freed his cock, lapping at Adrian's slick head.

"You taste so good," Lucas panted. Palming Adrian's thighs. Spreading them wider. His tongue curled and flexed and Adrian's toes responded in kind.

Not like this. Never like this. This was... Adrian rapped the back of his head against the wall as Lucas swallowed him whole. "Oh, gods," he whispered. Wet, hot suction making his eyes cross. Wet, hot breaths warming the base of his cock. He staggered to a wider stance, failing to stifle another groan as Lucas bobbed over him. As he cupped his sack, fingers seeking past it.

"I've been wanting to be inside you all day." Lucas kissed the admission down Adrian's length. "Wards?"

"Hnnn... what?"

"Are you warded?" Lucas asked, tapping Adrian's ass sharply enough to draw him back from the edge of ecstasy.

"Yes. Of course. Yes." Adrian blinked down at him, trying to fumble his way back to sentience. "Why...?"

Lucas could have made the devil weep. His teeth looked sharp and white as he grinned, green eyes sparkling. And that was when Adrian felt the pull of power in the air, the flex of Lucas' will. Lucas gathered a honeyed trail of wax-warm liquid from the Aether, drizzling it over Adrian's length before he swallowed him whole again. His knees were shaking before Lucas carried the continual drip of living mana between Adrian's thighs.

Power. Pure power ricocheted against his skin.

Adrian panted, planting his palms firmly against the wall as Lucas brushed his entrance. Careful. Gods, careful, but so certain. Willful.

"Do you want it?" Lucas asked as heat rushed to Adrian's core and his whole body felt as though he were about to combust.

"Yes," Adrian answered. Then "Yes," he begged as Lucas lavished feverish attention over him, stretching him, exploring him, devouring him. Then "Yes," he groaned when Lucas turned him towards the wall to do it all over again, delving with a talented tongue inside of him to make Adrian croon and hug the painted plaster for support. His knees threatened to give way and he couldn't catch his breath to do more than moan that word against the gray wall.

Lucas folded around him, wrapping his arms around Adrian and kissing the side of his neck. "I'm going to fuck you until you melt for me," he promised, lips to Adrian's ear. "Alright?"

Adrian was fairly sure he said "Yes" again.

Whatever the precious otherworldly elixir Lucas had summoned was, it was going to break him. Especially when Lucas pressed his lips to Adrian's shoulder and began to hum a lingering, lilting tune. The lubricant warmed at the song, flexing around Adrian and inside of him, quaking and forcing quick gasping swears from Adrian's lips. It only stopped when Lucas did, after they'd stumbled down the hall and Lucas paused to take in the candles and the light and the plan that Adrian had prepared for.

He was beautiful by candlelight, all shadows and edges and sweat at his temples, his lips full from his efforts thus far. He studied the deep red blossoms and petals scattered around the room, then met Adrian's gaze in the doorway. "Camellias?"

"They symbolize ardent affection." Adrian's skin was still buzzing. "I—"

"Take off your shirt and jacket," Lucas interrupted him softly, cupping his cheek. He leaned close, humming that wonderful little song against Adrian's ear again and the liquid shimmered again, thrumming and loosening and making Adrian roll his hips helplessly. "Now, please."

Adrian's knees felt unwieldy as he stripped the rest of his clothes off and let Lucas continue his sonorous manipulations. *Let* him. Begged him. Longed for him. And then begged again when he was on his hands and knees on the bed with Lucas behind him making him tremble all over again.

He was sure he was going to come before Lucas even had a chance to take him, but then Lucas eased inside of him, and Adrian could have wept at the feel of him. Lucas was rock-hard and the sensation of his cock sliding deep inside of him, joining the sultry dance of Lucas' summoning, was unlike anything Adrian had felt before. He ached for more. He begged for it, and Lucas gave him exactly what he asked for. Deeper. Harder. Lucas pulled him flush, nearly sending Adrian to the rafters between his hands and his lips and his increasingly, gloriously vigorous thrusts.

He couldn't hear the low music anymore. He couldn't hear the waves. There was only the two of them, skin slapping as they met again and again and again. Breaths ragged and catching as they traded hungry half kisses. "I love you," panted as a mantra, passed back and forth between them, as Adrian took and took and took.

This.

Adrian shuddered, caught in the eye of Lucas' storm, and let the winds take him.

The familiar burn in his muscles shifted to the foreground of his mind as Adrian stretched awake the next morning. A chill breeze blew through his bedroom, accompanied by the rushing sounds of waves in the quiet.

He groaned, recalling *why* his body ached, *why* he was lying in a wet spot, and a brief moment of panic had him clutching the sheets when he realized he was alone in the bed. Had Lucas left him after...

Adrian sat up quickly, glancing at the open door to the balcony, and the sharp pang of fear dissipated as quickly as it had come. There he was: Lucas' curls hopelessly mussed, a steaming cup in his hands, and a blanket from the foot of Adrian's bed wrapped around his shoulders. Beautiful, peaceful, gazing out over the water with a slight upward curve of his lips.

Relief poured through him like a wave and he dragged the comforter around his shoulders without waiting for his racing heart to slow again, crossing the chilly wooden floor to join Lucas and lean against his shoulder.

Lucas opened his blanket to gather Adrian closer. "Good morning."

"I thought for a moment you'd gone," Adrian mumbled, curling into the warmth of his body heat.

"I like watching sunrises. You were sleeping so soundly, I didn't want to wake you." Lucas kissed his forehead gently, lips warm and a little damp from the coffee he was drinking. "I didn't mean to worry you."

Adrian squeezed his bicep. He smelled so damned *edible* between the coffee and camellias and sweat. "How was the sunrise?"

"Gossamer," Lucas murmured. "Cirrocumulus nimbus and a very nice example of a corona as the sun crested the horizon." He sounded drowsy still, relaxed, resting his cheek atop Adrian's head. "How was sleep?"

"Unimaginably deep," Adrian hummed, tracing the muscles of his arm. *Gossamer*. The miracle of a man, with his clever, beautiful mind. "I love you."

"Still?" Lucas smirked, amusement plucking stray threads from the hush of his voice. "How long do you imagine those symptoms might persist?"

"For as long as you'll have me, I think," Adrian sighed, nestling closer.

"I suppose I'll need to feed you, then. Keep your strength up." Lucas rested his coffee on his knee, the rich aroma caught in the steam melding with the salt air to caress them. "I worried I may have overused the phrase."

"Which?"

"'I love you'," Lucas murmured, gaze darting between his eyes. "You don't think so?"

Adrian chuckled, lifting his chin to kiss Lucas'. "I don't think it's a sentiment that can become cliché. Do you?"

"Not the sentiment, no. The phrasing, though. I'd hate to become predictable or redundant."

"Predictable can be wonderful, sometimes." Adrian nudged him, teasing. "Though I still can't understand why you insist upon mixing eggs in your coffee. We have *time*."

"I spent several years not having any. One grows accustomed to certain comforts." Lucas drew him closer still, his arm strong around Adrian's shoulders. "I could grow accustomed to this, I think, and you should know I find it very difficult to shake free of habits once I develop them."

"You're going to need weekly sleepovers, then."

Lucas huffed a laugh, brushing a kiss across Adrian's cheek. "Fortunately, my daughter is as much a social butterfly as you are. I could probably manage two months without a repeat."

Two months. Two months of this? Of tangling together without any barriers between them? "And what will you do when repeats become necessary?"

"Hopefully, by that point, it will have been two months already and the first set might be willing to revisit the idea," Lucas chuckled. "They dressed up as mermaids last night and fell asleep on the floor. Meredith sent pictures." He glanced down at Adrian, gently stroking the back of his neck. "I was worried, you know, that you and I might not fit. That everything that was in my heart might—I don't know. Get in the way. I've never felt so much at once, not about this." He exhaled, nuzzling Adrian's nose. "But you're intoxicating and I'm—I find I am reluctant to untangle."

"Yes?" Adrian whispered, chest tight as he bit his lip. So was he. More and more so each time they met. "That's a coincidence, as I'm reluctant to let you go." He pressed his lips to Lucas' cheek, tucking himself as close to Lucas as their separate chairs would allow. "You're a good father; I understand the desire to proceed cautiously, even if it means we have to work around Tula's sleepovers to stay in the same bed."

Lucas pressed a kiss to Adrian's forehead, settling against him. "You're used to your freedom and flexibility. I'm as concerned about rushing you as I am about rushing her."

"And yourself?"

"Yes," Lucas admitted quietly. "And myself."

"So long as you know how much I adore you, I'll be content waiting." Adrian touched Lucas' cheek, smiling slightly. "Do you?"

"I have an inkling." He leaned into Adrian's touch, shutting his eyes contentedly. "I may need a lot of reminders. The camellias help." He pressed a kiss to Adrian's palm. "Do you know that I adore you?"

Adrian made a vague attempt to conceal his smile. "I would never have guessed! Not nearly enough clichéd phrases for me to have noticed."

"I'm serious," Lucas insisted, even as he puffed a low laugh. "My wanting to take time with this doesn't mean I don't want you."

"You made that abundantly clear." Adrian kissed the corners of his smile. "And you're wrong, a little, about my freedoms and flexibilities. I'd never been with another mage, for instance."

Lucas' smile sharpened with pride, and he must have read something in Adrian's expression, because he preened as he laughed to himself. "I take it you found the experience pleasant enough."

Pleasant didn't begin to describe the sensation of being held aloft by both of their wills, their power tangling as surely as they did. Adrian knew, between the hazy throes of passion, he'd begged for it never to end. "Mildly acceptable," Adrian teased him.

Lucas kissed him in answer, slowly, and Adrian felt himself melt again from the memory, the touch, the simple act of being held. "Aside from my being spectacular, how are you doing?" he asked.

"It's strange," Adrian exhaled, watching the tide wind its way toward the shore. "I thought I would feel..." He scrubbed his hand across his morning scruff. "I don't know. I suppose it *is* an adjustment, having you here like this. The apartment always felt more mine than his; Seron was overseas or on base as often as not. I—Gods, he seemed so *happy* for me. He was always one for enjoying life to its fullest." He chuckled, shaking his head. "I was worried that moving on might be... some kind of betrayal to his memory, but I'm not certain the man had a jealous bone in his body."

Lucas sipped from the mug. Adrian was beginning to understand that those moments of pause were the man's way of giving himself time to put his thoughts in order. "There's no hurry." He glanced out over the sea. "I'm not going anywhere unless you want me to."

"I don't feel rushed," Adrian murmured. "You've *never* made me feel rushed." Not even when Adrian had thought that was what he'd needed. He'd been wrong. He needed this. Calm and patient acceptance. Love. He rested his chin on Lucas' shoulder. "Thank you."

"You don't need to thank me. Only to be honest with yourself and sure of what you want. You're not alone. You don't need to barrel ahead to feel like you aren't."

"Is that what I do?" Adrian wondered, lacing their fingers together. "Barrel? It sounds so indelicate."

"You are many things, Adrian. Dashing and kind and brilliant and funny and excruciatingly handsome and devastating in bed, but you aren't delicate." Lucas paused, his brow furrowing. "I don't think. Are you?"

"Not in the slightest." Adrian smoothed the concern from his forehead. "Or I try not to be."

"Then, yes. Barrel." Lucas leaned into his touch. Every time. Subtle tilts of his head, little touches of pressure. He abandoned his coffee cup on the little metal side table and pulled Adrian to his lap, wrapping his arms around him. "I want to share my world, my life, with you, but not because you want to be less alone. I want you to come to us because we give you more, once you feel whole."

"I'm *trying* to be whole," Adrian whispered, swallowing. "I *am*. I'm doing what I can manage right now. You do give me more." He drew the blanket more snugly around them to ward off the chill. "Both of you."

"When you're ready," Lucas repeated. "When you're sure that it's *us* that you want. I'd let you break my heart a hundred thousand times, but I have to protect hers."

"I don't want to break either of your hearts," Adrian told him earnestly. "Are you afraid I would?"

"Not on purpose. I don't think you have that in you." Lucas pressed his cheek to Adrian's shoulder and swore softly. "I know that you *could*, and that's as new as knowing what this feeling is. I've never been in love before. It's... amazing and... frenetic and it changes things. It's a new kind of vulnerability, as much as it's incredible. And I think... Knowing what this is, I can imagine what you've been going through a little more clearly. I don't mean to say that I can understand what you've lost; I don't think that I can. I just wanted to tell you that I'm here for you."

"You're a thoroughly decent sort of man when you wish to be," Adrian chuckled, peering up at him. "Should I keep that knowledge to myself? Unless you'd like to be approached by all manner of unwanted prospective friends."

"*Friends*." Lucas rolled his eyes. "When would I have the time, between my sunbeam and my sunrise?"

"Cymbeline has wanted me to invite you to her book club for ages." Adrian nipped at the scruff on his chin, beaming. Luke's sunrise. The warmth he woke up to, every morning. The gilded glow of morning, banishing the silvery-blue moonlight and burning away mist. Was that how Lucas thought of him? What a phenomenal thing to be. "If we're going to be seeing each other, I'm afraid you'll need to make an appearance or Admiral Zielinski might just show up at your doorstep one day."

"I don't want that." Adrian regretted the joke as Luke sobered, his expression grim. "If I have to sit in a book club to avoid Seekers showing up at my door, then I will."

"They're nice little gatherings," Adrian assured him gently, trying to soften the shift of mood. "Cymbeline has a rather elevated taste in novels. Kriss' choices have been a touch questionable in the past."

Lucas cinched his arms around Adrian's waist, holding him close in the warm circle of blankets as the day brightened and warmed. "Questionable how?"

"Oh, lots of nonsense about swooning ladies and how love conquers all," Adrian chuckled low, kissing his cheek. "Silliness."

"Sounds like it." Lucas ran his fingertips down Adrian's throat. The touch made him shiver, points of warmth in the salted morning breeze, skimming past his collarbone. "But I like the way your lips form words. I like the taste of your voice on my tongue. And the swell of my heart when you laugh. Perhaps, if not all, love can conquer a few things."

Adrian nuzzled his cheek. "If anyone had told me the sullen man at the cemetery could be such a prolific poet, I'm not certain I would have believed them."

"It's a very good thing no one told you. I have to keep some of my mystery."

"At least a little," Adrian laughed, shaking his head. "You wouldn't mind getting to know my friends?"

Lucas rolled his eyes. "If you can argue feminism with judo fathers, I can read Lady Chatterley's Lover with your friends."

"I love you," Adrian murmured, kissing up his jawline. "Truly. *Desperately.*"

Lucas held him tighter. "Desperately! My, my, we can't have desperation. Do I need to take you back inside to sate you again?" he asked, tilting his head to give Adrian greater access to his neck.

"*Sate* me." Adrian rubbed his lips along the tight muscles of Lucas' shoulder. "You can certainly try, darling; I'd like to work up a hunger before you go."

"A vicious cycle," Lucas chuckled, sighing as he shifted Adrian's weight across his knees, his fingers tracing down his stomach. "If I only make you hungry the more I try to ease your ache." His hand dropped lower, palming Adrian through his boxers. "But I will try valiantly regardless."

CHAPTER EIGHTEEN

LUCAS

"Did anyone actually read the book?" Lucas asked under his breath, lingering next to Adrian at the kitchen counter. The women—and they were all women in the book club—were chatting about someone's divorce and someone else's upcoming honeymoon. People he didn't know in an eye-poppingly glamorous house.

"I did," Adrian promised as he nibbled on a lemon cookie. "Listened to it, anyway." He touched Lucas lightly. "How are you doing?"

"It's like a PTA meeting with no agenda and better food." Adrian's touch on the vulnerable skin at his wrist made him wish very much that they were back in Adrian's apartment. Lucas would have liked to drag that tender touch over his body until they were both shaking. "You tell me: how am I doing?" he asked. "Am I faking the socialization skills well enough?"

"Very well," Adrian assured him, "though I must admit that I spent much of the last hour considering your hands." Adrian lowered his voice even further, barely audible among the chatter. "So I may have missed something in the meantime."

Lucas couldn't fight the smile that curved his lips, the words and tone warming him from the inside out. "I'll fill you in on the details. You keep your attention on the important things." He glanced up, warmth transforming into heat as he met Adrian's eyes. Need and want warred inside of him these days, more and more, freed after years of being held back. "Adrian..."

"Hm?" Adrian winked, plucking a baby carrot from Lucas' plate and nibbling on the end. The Admiral clearing her throat loudly from the dining room worked just as well as a cold shower. Cymbeline chimed that there were mojitos in the parlor. "Ah, looks like we're being summoned again." He squeezed Lucas' hand gently. "A thought for later, then."

They abandoned their wine for the mojitos as the 'book club' spilled back into the parlor again. Would they talk about the book now? Or ever? Adrian had made a decent point that trying to avoid his old friend Kriss would draw more attention than it would avoid, but there seemed to be no end to the gossiping of these strangers; Lucas yearned fervently for doors that shut and locked and the bed that had filled his fantasies most of the last few weeks. He wanted to linger under Adrian's hands, in the study of those eyes, and *be*, exquisitely.

"I'm so glad you were able to make it," Cymbeline murmured, touching Lucas' elbow. The gesture surprised him; they'd only met on a handful of occasions. "What do you think?"

"Of the book?" Lucas asked. "Or..."

She grinned at him like they were old friends sharing a secret. "The book."

"His first was better, but I enjoyed how he took a different journey with this one. Sequels can sometimes be redundant."

"We wouldn't want that," Cymbeline agreed.

"It was unique and special in its own way," Adrian added, stepping closer to him. "I quite liked it. More mature, I think. Grounded. It's not always a bad thing to be grounded."

She lifted a meticulous brow, gazing at them both cheerfully. "Indeed, it is not. An often overlooked virtue."

"Without a doubt." Adrian squeezed Lucas' hand gently, watching Cymbeline. "How have you been lately? I'm glad our schedules finally aligned."

"Between your travel and mine and your mysteriously busy social life, you mean," Cymbeline teased fondly. "Now that we've sussed out precisely why you've been so difficult to get ahold of lately, it makes a great deal more sense."

Lucas ducked his head. Had he been taking too much of Adrian's time? He couldn't be. He barely felt like he was seeing him at all. Hours and minutes stolen here and there between those lovely weekend afternoons and the occasional skillfully scheduled evening.

"Spending time with my bearded romantic," Adrian chuckled, the corners of his mustache quirking in amusement. "Just so. Did you make bets with Kriss?"

Bearded romantic? Lucas glanced between them curiously. "Bets?"

"If I told you," Cymbeline chuckled, "that would negate the terms of said hypothetical wager."

What could they possibly bet on? Lucas wondered. Whether they would last? That seemed cruel.

"It's still *ongoing*." Adrian lifted his brows. "Hm. Perhaps the Admiral will be more forthcoming."

"Don't you dare." Cymbeline swatted his shoulder fondly. "I might actually win this one. Speaking of winning, I owe you a debt, Lucas. May I call you Lucas?"

"I wish you would," he murmured, sending a sideways glance at Adrian. "But you don't owe me any—"

"I was named Best Dressed in two separate magazines, and it's probably because you were so strict with me." She winked. "I'll need another for the awards in the spring. Maybe more brocade. That was fun."

"We did look stunning, didn't we?" Adrian hummed. He and Cymbeline had dominated the red carpet like they were born for awards shows and Lucas had been up to his ears in work ever since. "Let me know if you need a date again. I'd be delighted to oblige."

"And that saves me the effort of convincing you to do so," she winked. "You're quite sure you can be spared?"

"Send me the details and the dates and Luke and I will discuss it." Adrian was so cheerful, the proximity of his friends making him hum with energy. "Though if you keep outfitting stars, darling, soon enough you might find yourself among their number."

Lucas had done them both a disservice, not joining Adrian to watch him shine in public more often. There was an effervescence to him that had only grown over the hour they'd been in Cymbeline's house. Even the gossip seemed to charm him. Maybe Anara was right that Adrian would enjoy the PTA meetings, if only for the chance to wield his wit and winsomeness. "I will leave the gleaming to those more suited to it."

"Agree to disagree." Adrian shook his head with a laugh. "That's quite alright, though; I am more than happy to have you to myself."

"As am I," Lucas admitted quietly.

"I adore you." Adrian's eyes shone silver with flecks of gold, his gaze flitting between Lucas'. He glanced at Cymbeline apologetically. "I'm afraid we might need to duck out early if that's quite alright."

Cymbeline waved them off airily. "I doubt we're going to get to Hannibal's Surprise today anyway. Do enjoy the rest of the sunshine."

"We will. Undoubtedly." Adrian hugged her, then practically dragged Lucas to collect their coats on the way out the immaculate front door. "You," he murmured, backing Lucas up against a tree on their way to the car, "are so very tantalizing, you realize? How long before you need to pick up Tula from your friend's?"

"An hour..." Lucas checked his watch as he melted under the assault. "And a half. Adrian—" He swallowed a groan as Adrian snuck a hand beneath his vest. "You're sure you don't want to stay a little longer? You've been talking about this thing for a week."

Adrian nudged him with his nose. "That hour of socializing is more than enough for me when you're busy until *Thursday*. Which is closer: yours or mine?"

"Yours." Lucas swallowed, his heart racing. He touched the shell of Adrian's ear. "Thank you for bringing me to see your friends."

"Thank you for coming with me. They'd been asking about you for ages." Adrian winked, taking his hand. "Kriss saw us at a restaurant once and they've been calling you my 'bearded romantic' ever since."

A slither of discomfort twined around Lucas' stomach. "They asked you about me?"

"Endlessly." Adrian rolled his eyes, leading him down the street to where they'd parked.

"...What did you tell them?" Lucas asked, glancing up at the trees that dotted their path.

"That I met someone wonderful." Adrian unlocked the car door and kissed him, leaning against the chilled steel. "And that I wanted to let him speak for himself when the time came."

'Wonderful.' Lucas found himself smiling like a fool, searching Adrian's eyes. "Then I'm insulted they didn't interrogate me," he murmured, trying to keep the quiver of emotion from his voice.

"They probably didn't want to risk frightening you off," Adrian mused as he reluctantly crossed to the driver's side. "Interrogations are for second and third meetings. You had best prepare your notes; there's likely to be a quiz."

"On what, precisely?"

"Everything. How we met, what you like to do, how you wound up designing after leaving the Navy, oh, and *Tula*." Adrian chuckled. "You can probably be a bit cagey about the rest if you tell them about Tula."

"I would rather give them copies of my discharge papers." Lucas slipped into the passenger seat. "She's not for barter."

"You like talking about her, though." Adrian glanced over at him as he started the car. "You did with me."

"That's different. You're not in the military anymore. Or on television. And I trust you." Lucas wrinkled his nose. "I didn't like how your friend the Admiral looked at Tula at the library. It put me on edge."

Adrian reached across the console to take his hand. "We'll talk about us, then, or the book we were supposed to talk about today."

"Good." Lucas exhaled gratefully as Adrian pulled out of the space. "Thank you." He kissed the back of Adrian's thumb. "You think I'm overprotective."

"I'm not a father," Adrian murmured. "You should be as protective as you feel is prudent."

"I don't mean to suggest you would endanger Tula on purpose. I trust you. And I'm sure you trust your friends." Lucas sighed, looking out the windshield as they slid through the streets. "I just..."

"Luke, it's alright. Really." Adrian glanced at him as he pulled up to a red light. "You're cautious with her and perhaps you should be. She has a giving heart and the world isn't always kind. You're giving her time and a safe place for her to learn what she needs to protect herself. I don't judge you for that."

"Good. Because if you did, I'd have to kill you and steal all your teeth," Lucas murmured, tongue-in-cheek.

"And I'd *deserve* it," Adrian laughed, a bright, warm sound like bubbles drifting to the top of a freshly poured glass of champagne. "I would give them to you in my will if I weren't convinced that'd number my days the moment I signed the paperwork."

"You're crafty, I'll give you that." Gods, but Lucas loved the sound of Adrian's laugh. "Perhaps I'll just have the papers near at hand...

the next time..." He ran his hand down Adrian's chest and across his thigh. "...we find ourselves alone. Soon, very soon."

"I'll admit, I'm very suggestible after you're done with me." Adrian lifted a brow meaningfully. "You could have me lock, stock, and barrel if you wanted."

"I am dearly fond of your barrel, it's true." Adrian was hard beneath his palm. "Locking you in a stock would give me considerable access to it."

"Luke," Adrian groaned. "Are you going to make me pull over?"

"That depends." Lucas leaned close to brush his lips to Adrian's ear. "When was the last time you were fucked in a parking lot?"

The words had the desired effect: a quick inhale followed by a little whimper as Adrian rocked into his hand. "Not since I was a teenager."

"It's terrible," Lucas assured him. "Your bed is much better."

Adrian shook his head with a laugh. "I was worried we might not make it back to my apartment."

Lucas nipped his ear, leaning back. "Not that I wouldn't put up with a gear shift shoving into my hip for you, but only when necessary."

"Another time, then," Adrian chuckled, shaking his head as he shifted lanes. "I like being able to splay you out among the pillows in any case. Nothing comes close to the sight of you basking exquisitely in candlelight and camellias."

"I believe you. I believe a great deal when it comes to you." Lucas studied Adrian's profile as he drove: soft, eager smiles that he'd never entirely expected to have focused on him for even this long. Love. Love, and they were still getting to know each other's ups and downs, rhythms and syncopations. "You're an exquisite sight, yourself," he murmured, "as you well know."

"I do." Adrian glanced at him: a flash of silver over a pleased crescent smile. "It's nice to have the affirmation, though."

"It is," Lucas agreed softly. It had been one of many awakenings in the last weeks. How pleasant and downright good it felt just to be seen, exactly as he was, and adored for it. "You're exquisite in many ways," he continued, tracing the line of Adrian's triceps through his shirt. "I find you thoroughly enjoyable." He paused. "I already regret the day I will have to steal your teeth and organs. I hope it isn't soon."

"As do I, darling." Adrian caught his hand and held it, smoothing his thumb over the back of his wrist. "You'll make sure they're put to good use, won't you? And that I'm still pretty when they bury me."

"I can't imagine you are capable of being anything less than pretty in any circumstance. I've seen you with your mustache askew now and I must admit: it's nearly an improvement."

"How dare you."

"More tangible." Lucas walked his fingers across Adrian's shoulder and up the back of his neck. "More edible. The way just a button—" He slipped his own collar open. "—can make a world of difference between polished treasure and something you can really get your hands on."

"Luke," Adrian said his name as a warning. "*Darling*," he added the pet name for emphasis. "You're making it difficult to focus on the very important task at hand."

"Am I?" Lucas dabbed at his lower lip, humming low. "Are you thinking of my hands again? I've been able to think of little other than your hands, and the warmth of your breath on my skin, and the way you haunt my dreams between the times that I see you. Holding me down. Covering me. Should I tell you what I dreamed last night?"

Silver melting into mercury, pools of liquid stardust in Adrian's eyes as he stared resolutely at the road ahead. "Yes, please. I'd like to know."

"You were in a sunbaked room with sheer curtains the color of turmeric." Lucas stretched out in the seat. "And you were steaming the suit I made you with that look that you have when you're concentrating on something important. And the sweat and steam were gleaming on your spine." He touched himself, watching Adrian. "And you were *delightfully* askew. And bare. And mine."

"I *am* yours," Adrian assured him, a flush spreading up his neck and onto his cheeks. "I have been yours. Do you require another demonstration?"

"I require a hundred demonstrations," Lucas told him with a smirk. "I am greedy and deviant and utterly enamored."

"Thank the gods." Adrian hummed as he pulled into the parking garage. "Because I'd be in dire straits if you weren't."

"Would you?" Lucas leaned across the console as soon as they'd parked; he caught Adrian at the back of the neck, lapping hungrily at his lips as he tugged his shirt free of his trousers. He felt as though he might burst at the seams if he couldn't touch him, kiss him, and make him sweat. "How dire?"

"Dreadfully," Adrian murmured, fumbling with Lucas' vest. "I'm exceedingly ill-suited to unrequited affection."

"Unlikely you've had experience with that." He was hot to the touch and slick-tipped. Lucas moaned, tugging him free of his boxers and bending down. He tasted the way Lucas had always imagined gold should taste: smooth and salty, spice and mineral and musk. His skin was soft as velvet beneath Lucas' fingers, but hard and smooth as oak. Lucas moaned again, taking more into his mouth until he was lapping and bobbing feverishly, his eyes watering whenever Adrian brushed the back of his throat. Adrian's fingers laced into his hair. Wanted. Loved. Hungered for. He'd had the first more times than he could count, but the last two? That need and gentle adoration poured together into an intoxicating cocktail.

"I thought you didn't want to make love in my car." Adrian smoothed his thumb over the hollow in Lucas' cheek, his cock firm and full under his tongue. "Have you already changed your mind? How very capricious."

Lucas took a deep breath, lifting his head. "This part I don't mind," he panted helplessly. "It's the attempting to fit legs and arms into cramped spaces that's less fun."

"Far be it from me to deny you," Adrian breathed, fingers flexing in his hair. "You'll need to help me up the stairs when you're done, though."

Lucas laughed, kissing along his shaft. "Happily; I'll even—" The fluttering fairy song of Tula's emergency cell phone ringtone interrupted him and Lucas frowned, sitting up. He ran a hand through his hair, clearing his throat and glancing over at Adrian apologetically before answering on speakerphone. "Hey, sundrop, how's the—"

"Shannon pushed Samantha into the pool and now everyone has to go home," Tula reported excitedly. "Mrs. Greenbaum says you have to take me to a doctor because I'm bleeding but it doesn't hurt."

"What?" Lucas tightened his grip on the phone, fear and adrenaline racing. "Why are you—?"

"I lost my step on the diving board and cut my foot on a piece of plastic, but it's okay because I'll get a cool scar like a pirate and—"

"I'm coming to get you."

"That's what she said you'd say."

"Keep pressure on the wound. Where's Mrs. Greenbaum?"

"She's calling the other parents, but I said I could call you because I'm a big girl and it doesn't hurt and—" Tula took a deep breath. "Mr. Greenbaum had to jump in the pool in his clothes to save Samantha and Shannon was *laughing*. She's so *mean*."

"It sounds like it," Lucas muttered. "Just stay sitting down and keep a towel on—"

"I am, Papa. Don't worry."

Don't worry, she said. It was a damned fiasco was what it was. "I'm coming to get you."

"Okay! Bye!"

Lucas stared at the phone and then looked at Adrian.

"You have to go," Adrian said. So matter-of-fact, tucking his shirt back into his slacks.

"She says she's not in pain, but her interpretation of pain has been a little skewed since she came into her power... Anyway, they're calling off the party." Lucas cupped Adrian's cheek. "I'm sorry. Next weekend. We'll pick up where we left off. I have to go." He kissed him hard. "I love you. Forgive me."

"There's nothing that requires forgiveness." Adrian took his hand, squeezing it once. "What if I drive you, that way I can drop you off and get anything you need in the meantime? Just in case."

Lucas hesitated, glancing out the window and back to him. "...You're sure it's not an imposition?"

"Not at all." Adrian's eyebrows had drawn together in concern. "Besides, I'd like to know sooner rather than later that she's alright."

Lucas nodded slowly, biting his lower lip. "Yes. Alright. Thank you."

It was not a small cut. Lucas hissed under his breath as he knelt beside her by the pool and peeled the bloody towel back to reveal the long gash.

"It's okay, Papa. The lady by the pond had way worse cuts than this—"

"Shh. Alright." Lucas wrapped the towel back around her foot tightly. "Hold this nice and tight and I'll carry you to the car." Shannon was a menace was what she was and she absolutely was never coming to their house again, even if she hadn't been the direct cause of Tula's accident. He lifted her into his arms and held her close as he brought her out of the house and to the car.

"Hi, Mr. Adrian!" Tula waved. "I fell off the diving board!"

"I heard," Adrian said softly, glancing at Lucas for reassurance. "I've done that more than once. Are you quite alright?"

"I didn't even scream. And everyone was panicking about Samantha, but she knows how to swim, so I don't know why... And the lady who lives in their attic said I'd look just like a pirate when it heals, so—"

Lucas hushed her softly. "Mr. Adrian is going to help us get to Dr. Nangella's office and we're going to see about that foot, okay?"

"Uh huh. Can we get ice cream after?" She looked at Adrian with a cheerful smile. "I got ice cream after I had stitches last time," she told him excitedly. "With extra sprinkles *and* bananas."

"That's up to your father." Adrian typed in the address he'd been given and started the directions on his phone. "Maybe your ice cream can come to you, rather than the other way around." He lifted his brows, mouthing the word 'bad?', with a questioning tilt of his head.

Lucas widened his eyes and nodded, slipping into the backseat with her to buckle her in and keep her foot elevated. "You're very brave and I think brave girls deserve to get ice cream in bed."

"Like a *princess*?" Tula gasped.

"Exactly like a princess."

"And the evil toad monkeys won't come and eat the crumbs?"

"We'll make sure there are no crumbs." Lucas patted her knee as they took off. "Only princess sprinkles. You can wear your crown."

"This is the best day *ever*!"

Lucas puffed out his cheeks. "Yes. Absolutely wonderful."

"Sprinkles and ice cream?" Adrian asked, watching them occasionally in the rearview mirror. "Just so I'm prepared, what flavors of ice cream and types of sprinkles do princesses like?"

"Strawberry and chocolate and blueberry pie and rainbow sprinkles and mochi balls and banana slices and chocolate fudge!" Tula rattled off her list as though it were permanently prepared. "And I won't get any on my princess dress because that would be unladylike. Can I have an eyepatch to go with my pirate foot?"

Lucas sniffed, so proud of her and worried at the same time that he wanted to cry. "I'll make you an eyepatch to match your crown."

"Can I wear it to school on Monday?"

"We'll see."

"'We'll see' means no," she informed Adrian with an exasperated expression.

"'We'll see,'" Lucas squeezed her hand gently, "means we'll see how the situation progresses. You're sure it doesn't hurt?"

"Not as bad as it could." She lifted her chin. "Brave girls get lollipops from Dr. Nangella. I'm a brave girl."

"You are, indeed, but you can be brave and also ask for help."

"Okay." Her bright smile softened a little. "It doesn't feel very good right now, but it will get better. And if it doesn't, then I'll have a peg leg."

"Good lord," Lucas huffed instead of swearing in front of her.

"It sounds as though someone has been watching quite a few pirate movies," Adrian surmised. "You know, I have it on good authority that seafaring life is actually pretty dull. Much less swashbuckling than you'd imagine and considerably more scurvy."

"Inestimably more scurvy," Lucas agreed heartily.

"But that's why we drink our orange juice and eat our fruits and veggies!" Tula seemed entirely unconcerned with the injury and it was probably best to allow her that. The adrenaline was likely keeping the worst of the pain at bay. Then again, she'd never been particularly bothered by gore. He could feel his emotions ping-ponging uselessly in his chest and he was suddenly exceptionally grateful that he wasn't the one driving. That he could sit here and hold Tula's foot and worry silently in his head. What if she really couldn't feel any pain? Did that mean she'd severed a nerve? Or that the wound was worse than it looked?

"Papa was in the Navy and they taught him all about scurvy and he won an award for it," Tula announced. "Did you have to worry about scurvy in your planes?"

"No, I can't imagine I was up in the air as long as your father was at sea." Adrian pulled into the parking lot of the doctor's office, slipping from his seat to open the door for Lucas. "You're taking all of this in stride, aren't you? You definitely deserve a lollipop."

"Worse things happen to people all the time. Mr. Orlando two doors down slipped in the shower and broke his neck and he said it *really* hurt, but then it was okay."

"*Tula.*" Lucas lifted her into his arms, wondering if she would ever become more cautious about her friends beyond the veil of the living. "No more stories. I mean it."

"I'm sorry. Can I have an orange lollipop? Or a lemon one? I don't like the red ones; they make my tongue look funny."

Lucas exhaled slowly, holding her to his chest. "No funny tongues."

"Okay!"

Lucas negotiated a yellow lollipop before the visit to keep her mouth occupied while the doctor examined her and pronounced that she was indeed very brave and that she would need several stitches and to keep her weight entirely off her foot for at least a week.

Adrian waited for them near the front desk, his elbows resting on his thighs, rising to his feet as soon as Lucas stepped back through the door, wheeling a surprisingly pleased Tula back to the front of the clinic.

"How did it go?" Adrian murmured, touching Lucas' elbow as he held the door open. "Are we going to need to find a boat and a plumed hat?"

"No peg leg," Lucas announced. "Only ice cream and rest. And no judo for a little while."

"But I can still go watch, huh?" Tula reminded him. "And practice my punches?" Nothing slowed his girl down, not even stitches along the side of her foot. "Do you want to see, Mr. Adrian? It looks like I've grown caterpillars!"

"Ah... Perhaps not, Tula." Adrian winced. "I don't like thinking of you being hurt more than necessary."

"But they closed up my skin like a zipper! Papa even said they were good stitches and Mada says he's very *particular*."

"*Great*." Lucas ran a hand over his face.

Adrian watched them curiously, nodding to himself as they clambered back into the back of his car. "All is well and you're both safe and sound," Adrian said once the doors shut. "Perhaps once your foot heals, we can speak together about your friends, hm? The ones that others can't see?"

Tula blinked at him, then looked at Lucas.

"When you're feeling better," Lucas whispered, exhausted. "If you have to talk to someone about it, you can talk to Adrian. And me. You just—"

"Can't tell other people," she grumbled, frustrated. "I *know*, but Mr. Adrian already *knows* about it."

Lucas shook his head wearily. "It isn't only talking *to* people about it," he reminded her. "It's talking about it *around* other people. It..." He closed his eyes and took a deep breath. "I'm not trying to pester you."

"I didn't mean to make you sad, Papa."

"I know. I'm only trying to keep you safe." And what a terrible job he was doing at that. Lucas swallowed the panic and met Adrian's gaze in the rearview mirror gratefully. "Thank you," he murmured. "Would you like to stay for dinner? And ice cream? It's the least we can do."

"I would love to." The warmth in that silver-flecked gaze showed he meant it. "I'm glad that everyone is alright."

"Yes," Lucas whispered, cuddling Tula close to his side. "So am I."

CHAPTER NINETEEN

ADRIAN

Blueberry pie flavored ice cream was as difficult to find as Adrian expected, but at the third store, he found the last remaining carton wedged at the back of the supermarket freezer. By the time he returned to Lucas' cozy little brownstone with his haul, Tula was settled in bed and her father was less flustered now that they were all safely tucked behind wards.

Before Tula, Adrian had never considered what it might be like to be a father. After the stern upbringing in his household, he hadn't felt any sort of paternal inclination and, given his proclivities, he hadn't expected it would be something he would ever need to consider very seriously. He hadn't thought of what it might feel like to be responsible for another person's entire existence, with their safety and their future in his hands.

It was terrifying.

It was a wonder anyone survived past infancy.

Adrian left the spare key he'd borrowed on a side table near the entryway, stowing the groceries in Lucas' immaculate kitchen. Up the stairs, he could hear their voices: Lucas' low murmurs and Tula's giddy laughter.

This was what a home could be. Hand-painted clay sculptures made by tiny hands, holding air plants. Crayon drawings on the refrigerator door. A canvas with larger and larger handprints growing up from one corner in a variety of colors. Framed photographs of Tula and Lucas in silly costumes. Lived in. Loved. And somehow still sparse. Lucas hadn't filled the space in any room, leaving wide swaths of hardwood floor unoccupied between utilitarian furniture. A table that could be extended and shrunk. A couch that seemed built more for ease of cleaning than the aesthetics that occupied so much of Lucas' attention outside of his home.

The sound of footsteps down the stairs alerted Adrian moments before Lucas emerged into the kitchen, arms wrapped around himself in a show of vulnerability Adrian hadn't witnessed before. Proud, usually. Defensive, sometimes. But Lucas was softer here, in his own space, surrounded by trailing pothos and dangling tillandsia, barefoot and unwound.

"I'd wondered if you were coming back," Lucas admitted quietly.

Adrian slipped out of his jacket, hanging with the other pair of coats near the front of the door. "I said I would. I don't typically back out on promises."

"No," Lucas agreed. "You haven't. There's always a first time." He bowed his head. "I have an inherently suspicious disposition. I'm sorry."

"You've been apologizing a lot today for things that aren't your fault." Adrian crossed the space between them, wrapping his arms around Lucas' shoulders.

"I know I can't protect her from everything. I know that," Lucas whispered, leaning into Adrian's hold. "But I try. If anything happened to her... If she'd hit her head instead of her foot... If—"

"You'll drive yourself mad thinking of 'ifs'," Adrian murmured against the crown of his head, rubbing circles onto his back. "I'm sorry she scared you, darling. I'll admit, she had me worried as well. All that *blood*."

"I've seen a great deal of blood, but whenever it's hers, my own runs cold." Lucas pressed his forehead to Adrian's shoulder, shivering. "Thank you for being there today. It was... Thank you."

"Thank you for letting me." Adrian closed his eyes, breathing in the scent of antiseptic from the doctor's office mingled with the smell of ink and old library books that always clung to Lucas' skin. "This is what I want," he murmured, holding tightly to the man he'd fallen in love with, piece by piece, as he'd learned how to put himself together again. "In case you were wondering."

"I love you." Lucas' voice was fierce, muffled, warm where he spoke against his shoulder. "I really want that to be true."

"You do?" Adrian asked softly, touching his chin to lift it and meet his gaze. "Truly?"

Lucas laughed weakly, his gaze skittering away as it had in the beginning. "Have I fooled you?"

Adrian drew him back with a gentle touch. His fingers tingled; his heart felt light in his chest. "Tell me again."

"I hope that you will choose us," Lucas whispered, glancing cautiously at Adrian.

"So we'll make sure. I'll need more information, I think." Adrian studied the play of the light that drifted in through sheer curtains and the shimmering reflections they made in his eyes. "I'll need to know what I'm signing up for. Don't you think?"

"You will." Lucas bowed his head, exhaling shakily. "I need to put actual food into the gremlin; she'll never eat it after ice cream." He cleared his throat. "Into the lion's den. How up to speed are you on My Little Pony?"

"Oh, *not*." Adrian laughed, wrapping his arm around Lucas' waist. "Though, I imagine I will be soon."

They ate on the same gingham picnic blanket Lucas had brought for their afternoon in the park, spread over Tula's bed beneath gauzy purple curtains while the princess lectured on the names and histories of each of the ponies, sending her father to fetch their replicas from around her room for Adrian to admire and study. Four episodes later, tucked into her bed with her crown on the pillow beside her, Tula fell asleep mid-sentence and Lucas carefully collected the remains of the feast to bring downstairs.

"Ready to run yet?" Lucas whispered.

"Not before I find out what happens to... I've already forgotten the name of the one with the balloons on her hip."

"Pinkie Pie. I'll send you a chart." Lucas set the tray down on the counter. "Did you get enough to eat? Can I—Gods, I haven't even given you the tour, have I?"

"No, but you had other priorities." Adrian wrapped his arms around Lucas' waist. "I'll take it now if you don't mind."

"Welcome to my home," Lucas murmured belatedly, resting his hand over Adrian's heart. It was fascinating to see the way he changed from moment to moment, like a prism in light. He was so vigilant and composed when Tula was near him, but his concerns unraveled around him like stray threads when he didn't need to be her guide.

In addition to the kitchen and the living room, there was a dining room that looked to have largely been transformed into a crafting space for the both of them. A sewing machine and glitter and panels of fabric and organized cubicles full of pipe cleaners and crayons and popsicle sticks. Outside, a small yard housed a hanging porch swing and four fruit trees. Lucas leaned against him in the dim porch light.

"Those were my mother's." Lucas nodded to the trees. "She had a greener thumb than I do, but I try to keep them alive."

"It's beautiful," Adrian murmured, cupping his cheek.

"It is," Lucas agreed softly. "Thank you. My mother always wanted us to have a real home. A place to belong. I think... I think I made her feel guilty enough times over all the moving and running." He grimaced. "It mattered so much to me, that ideal. I never even saw this place until after they were gone. She'd asked me to visit. She'd wanted to show me she'd heard me and I turned them down."

They'd wanted their songbird to have the nest he'd always dreamed of. They'd found the place, planted the trees, but Lucas had been the one to make it a home. For himself and for Tula. It felt more like a home than anywhere Adrian had ever lived. Even the place he'd shared with Seron had been more of a way station than a destination. "Thank you for letting me come over."

"Thank you for coming." Lucas glanced between his eyes. "I wouldn't have asked, and you... you've been a blessing. I appreciate the support. It's *odd*," he admitted quietly, "but I appreciate it."

"Thank you, I do like to be odd," Adrian muttered, oddly ruffled by the comment.

"*You* aren't odd." Lucas shook his head. "Just... Having someone here... helping. Anara pitched in when Tula had the flu a couple years ago, but she has three of her own and..." He bowed his head. "Just. Thank you. You made Tula very happy, allowing her to play professor and pirate and princess. And the ice cream; I don't know where you found that."

"It took some sleuthing, I'll admit." Adrian nudged him with his nose, kissing him fondly. "I love you. Making things easier on you is a part of that."

"Is it? I don't think I've ever tried to make things easier on anyone," Lucas admitted wryly.

"Hm." Adrian rolled his eyes. "Some part of me believes that."

"Only *some* part? Which? Is it your teeth? They've been threatened enough to know the truth when they hear it."

"I can't tell you," Adrian murmured, leaning in close to whisper in his ear. "I don't want that part of me to become a particular target."

"So *not* your teeth. Your pinky toe?" Lucas arched a brow, wrapping his arms back around him in the cool night air. "Your spleen? Your third vertebrae?"

"I might require a thorough examination." Adrian nipped at his lips. "If that's on the table with Tula asleep and safe."

"Let's give her time to settle. I'm a little worried that the adrenaline is going to wear off in the middle of the night and she's finally going to start feeling the pain."

Adrian leaned back to study him. Too soon? Too much at once? "What do you normally do on Saturday nights when your tulip is drowsing and you're all alone?"

Lucas rolled his eyes, shaking his head with a laugh. "These days? Call you."

"I could go into an adjacent room and we can pretend we're apart, if you'd like."

"Don't you dare." Lucas grabbed hold of his arms and held him firm. "I like you here. I've just said."

"Good." Adrian leaned in to kiss him. "Then let's put on a movie and canoodle like teenagers."

"I left you in a raw spot earlier. You've been very patient and accommodating, but I don't want you to think I've forgotten." Lucas slid his arms around Adrian's waist. "We could try ignoring that new movie about time travelers."

"I'd love that." Adrian leaned against him, thrilling under his touch. "See? It's turning out to be an exhilarating evening."

"You're very kind. I'm sure the last thing you wanted to do today was visit a pediatrician and learn about a cartoon."

"I got to spend all day with you when I thought I'd only get a few hours," Adrian told him seriously. "I am more than content."

Hummingbird eyes and a nightingale voice. Caramel skin softened by the dim glow of the fairy porch lights. Lucas was so sure of himself so often, but his vulnerability—when he allowed himself to show it—was intoxicating. Adrian nudged him with his nose. "Shall I show you?"

"Adrian," he chided softly, his lips fluttering between a smile and something sweeter. "I think you'd better."

They settled together among the blankets on the couch, a travel show playing softly in the background after they'd finished the movie. Lucas' cheek lay pillowed against Adrian's chest, his breaths warm against the fabric of his tee shirt.

Adrian ran his fingers idly though Lucas' curls, watching the screen flicker. "How did you come to care for Tula?" Adrian asked finally, his voice low, the television a gentle undercurrent of sound underneath. "Is that a story you're willing to tell?"

"I told you about her mother, didn't I?" Lucas asked quietly.

"Not who she was to you." Adrian wondered if he'd crossed a line that would send the man's gaze and heart skittering away.

"Oh." Lucas frowned. "Teresa was one of my parents'... cases. They would take people in from time to time. People who were down on their luck. Mages who were not quite in *trouble*, but nearly. She was... I don't know. We didn't get on well, but my parents loved her. They helped her move half a dozen times; first between her relatives, then—when she was becoming more paranoid—to various safe houses they had set up. She was in and out of my life for years from the time I was ten. I hadn't heard from her since I went off on my own. And after they... well. She didn't come to their funeral; I didn't expect her to. I moved in here, when I learned about the place, and then one day she was just... here. On my porch. Very pregnant and panicking." He tensed under Adrian's hands just from the memory of it. "I took her to doctor's appointments. Paid for them. My parents would have wanted me to support her. I did what I could. She wouldn't go see anyone for her mental health and that was infuriating. She insisted they would turn her over to the Seekers. She needed more than I could give, but I tried. In the end, it wasn't enough. She was afraid that she would be caught because of Tula. She threatened to leave her at a fire station, for fuck's sake." He rested his chin on Adrian's chest. "So, before Tula was born, I promised Teresa I'd look after her daughter and keep her safe. For my parents. For the work they'd lost their lives to and the girl they'd tried to save for years. And then I met Tula," he whispered. "She was so tiny and bald and she wrapped her fingers around my thumb... I was done for. It wasn't about anyone but her after that."

"Does it change you?" Adrian wondered quietly. "Becoming a father?"

"Entirely," Lucas murmured, droll. "I used to be short and have red hair."

"I'm being serious."

"I know you are." Lucas smirked sweetly, touching his cheek. "*Life* changes us. Everything changes us, for better or for worse. I think loving her has changed me in a lot of good ways. It's given me a great deal of insight into my parents, for instance. More patience. More silliness." He rolled his eyes. "I don't know." He paused, dropping his gaze. "...does it worry you?"

"No, I'd just wondered." Adrian sighed, smoothing his hand over Lucas' shoulder. "My father and I never got along. He never interacted with me much more than to tell me I was wrong in some way or another... if *that* was what being a father meant, I decided quite a long time ago that I never wanted anything to do with it." He touched Lucas' cheek. "You don't seem to be that sort of father at all."

"I can't imagine... Well. That's not true. I *can* imagine. I had a number of COs who were hard as nails, but that's command and drill, not... I'm sorry your father didn't give you what you needed. What you deserved. You're a good man despite it."

Adrian exhaled slowly. "I'm glad you think so."

Green and poppy blossoms studied him steadily. Landing and nestling. "...I take it you worry that you might become like that? If you were to..." Lucas tilted his head. "To take on that sort of role?"

"I hope I'd have someone to tell me if they felt I was," Adrian murmured, shutting his eyes for a moment. "I wouldn't wish to make anyone feel the way my father did me."

"Nor would I; that sounds dreadful." His fingers traced Adrian's brow, soothing. "Tula seems fond enough of him."

"She's fond of everyone, though. Except perhaps Savannah, given today's excitement."

"Shannon," Lucas corrected him gently. "Shannon, Savannah, Samantha, and Sarah. That's all the S's. Then there's all the Brians; there's five of those."

"Do you have a chart for them, too?" Adrian murmured, breathing against his. "I'll study up on ponies and Tula's friends and you can study for book club. We can trade notes."

Lucas kissed him tenderly. "You're *sure* you don't want to run away? Because we can keep on as we have been," he murmured, smoothing Adrian's hair back from his brow. "You don't owe me anything more than yourself and your teeth."

"I don't want to run," Adrian whispered, holding his hands. "If I could stay here tonight and tomorrow and every day after, I would."

Lucas gazed at him, his Adam's apple bobbing. "That's quite a lot. Why don't we start with tonight, no pressure, and go from there?"

"Tonight," Adrian agreed softly. "We can start with tonight."

CHAPTER TWENTY

ADRIAN

'Tonight' had turned into the rest of the weekend, then the next, but they'd dialed it back to only having their sleepovers when Tula had hers when she'd very nearly caught them kissing in the kitchen. It was enough to be close to them, to see more of Lucas' soft side as they let Tula paint their faces with glitter and took turns trying to draw the scariest monsters.

It had been a month and her foot was mostly healed, though she still hadn't yet returned to either of her sports, a fact that had been driving both Tula and Lucas slowly up the wall. The sleepover had been a necessity for both their sanities, letting them get back to their regularly scheduled programs and let off steam in the way most appropriate to each of them. For Tula, that was a princess party with her best friend. For Lucas... Well. Their morning shower had gotten steamier than originally intended and they'd barely managed to drag themselves out of Adrian's apartment at half-past noon to amble over to pick up Tula from her friend's house.

Adrian couldn't help but study the subtle smile that curled Lucas' lips as he drove through the city, his hand entwined with Adrian's on the median. Lucas was striking, the sun streaming in through the windshield of his hatchback to turn the tips of his curls golden brown.

"I've been remiss," Lucas murmured as they stopped at a light, glancing towards Adrian.

"Hm?" Adrian asked, wondering if he'd missed something while he'd been sitting there enamored. "How?"

"It's been nearly half an hour and I haven't reminded you that I adore you," Lucas sighed with all the drama he could summon. "Can you ever forgive me?"

"Oh," Adrian chuckled. The damned delightful wonder of a man. "Maybe, after I've had another cup of coffee."

"As you will." Lucas bowed his head, adjusting his sunglasses as the light changed. "If you'd had an egg in your first cup, you might already be awake."

"Now, now, I wouldn't want to turn into you." Adrian rolled his eyes, gazing out the window. "I have my own assets; we wouldn't wish to overlap too much or we might start to confuse people."

"I very much doubt there's any danger of that." Lucas snorted softly, turning into a street with rows of townhouses on either side. "You're too pretty to be confused for me."

"I'm going to buy you an excessively large mirror." Adrian wiggled his brows. "Perhaps we can put it on the ceiling so you can see just how pretty you are."

Lucas tipped his glasses down to wink at him. "I am perfectly wonderful, yes. Handsome, even. But *you* have that jawline and the line of your neck and the..." He hummed a snatch of a merry, lilting tune, tapping his tongue to his upper lip. "—whole angle and curve of you that belongs on a pedestal in a hidden garden somewhere. Guarded by thorns and dragons. The kind of beauty that's found in moonlit sonatas and dim galleries."

"My beloved poet," Adrian admired him, exceedingly pleased. "*Moonlit sonatas*. You're right, of course, but it's not often I get to hear such truths. You really do love me, don't you?"

Lucas twisted, peering back over his shoulder as he parallel-parked. "After all my protestations, spoken and unspoken, I'm not sure what else I can do to convince you." He glanced at Adrian, a half-smile playing at his lips as he put the car in park; he leaned across to brush his lips across Adrian's cheek. "Perhaps arrange another sleepover for next weekend?"

"I didn't realize there was a question about that." Adrian squeezed his fingers with a grin. "Did you want me to come in with you?"

"I'll—No, I'll grab her. It should only be a few minutes." Lucas kissed Adrian's thumb. "Are you sure you want to tell her today?"

"I do." Adrian cupped his cheek to kiss him gently. "You?"

"We'll just tread carefully," Lucas answered, still sounding nervous about the prospect. "No false hope." He rested his cheek against Adrian's palm. "She'll be fine. She will, won't she?"

"I think so." Adrian's brow furrowed. He hadn't been so worried about Tula; she had always seemed to like him and take things in stride. "Right?"

Tula hadn't taken it well, Lucas had said, when people left. Her mother, the only semi-serious boyfriend Lucas had dated since he'd formally adopted her, then her friend Eloise going to the Presidio Tower. Lucas shook his head, summoning a smile that didn't quite fill his eyes; they were soft and somber when he studied Adrian again, kissed him, and slipped out of the car. "Two minutes."

"I'll be here," Adrian murmured, frowning as he watched him go. He fiddled with the radio and the heat absently as he waited, only to look up a few minutes later to the sound of a girlish squeal as Tula catapulted down the stairs in a glittery ball gown, closely followed by Lucas who was trying to watch her and finish a conversation with the dark-haired woman in the doorway. Anara, Adrian remembered: the florist and friend.

Tula dragged the car door open and threw her arms around Adrian, beaming. "Hi, Mr. Adrian! Papa said you're taking me to brunch!"

"That is the goal, yes!" Clad in mustard yellow, the girl was bright-eyed and giggling; Adrian always enjoyed her company, but Tula's joy at seeing him did wonders to ease the tension that had started brewing since Lucas had gone to retrieve her. "How were your friends?"

"We were sunflower mermaids!" Tula exclaimed excitedly. "It was so fun! And we had almond milk ice cream and Katie thought it was going to be gross but then she liked it and we watched a movie about dancing goldfish and it was so funny because goldfish don't have feet—"

"Backseat," Lucas reminded her, returning to the driver's seat.

Tula scurried into her booster seat and clicked her seat belt into the booster seat without missing a beat. "And I taught Malcolm how to do a shoulder roll and we knocked the lamp over, but it didn't break, so that was okay."

"Quite an adventure from the sound of it." Adrian watched her bop her head to some little tune she was humming from the rearview mirror. Like father like daughter. "Do you know where you want to go?"

"I get to choose?" she asked, wide-eyed. "*Really?*"

"Within reason, no?" Adrian glanced at Lucas, suddenly unsure. "I suppose it's up to your father."

"I want the cheesecake place! Have you been to the cheesecake place, Mr. Adrian? They have a *thousand* cakes. A thousand!"

Lucas puffed his cheeks out. "We can go, but you only get one slice of one cake."

"But there's a thousand!" Tula leaned forward, blinking innocently. "What if we all get different kinds? Then I can taste, right?"

"After actual food."

"Mr. Reggie made us waffles and eggs that were wobbly."

"Lovely." Lucas tucked his tongue in his cheek, looking at Adrian out of the corner of his eye. "Then you should be full."

"No! I want cheesecake! Mr. Adrian's taking me to brunch and Mr. Adrian said that I could pick!"

Lucas said, "So he did," with a slight smirk.

"You can go home if you're going to be grumpy," she told him sweetly. "Maybe you need a nap."

Adrian glanced between them helplessly. "I imagine after three slices of cheesecake we'll all need a nap."

The little girl giggled, hugging herself. "*No,*" she chided as though he'd just suggested that turtles could fly. "We *run*. Don't you know the rules at all?"

"I don't." Adrian tilted his head. It had been nearly a year and he'd seen no evidence of any running besides the kind the girl did every time she had a chance anywhere. "Evidently. What are they, if you don't mind me asking?"

"Whoever finishes their cake first has to win a foot race and if they can't win the foot race then they have to go to bed that night with only one story! But if they *can* win the foot race, then they get three stories and a song! So no naps! Cake and then running!" She clapped her hands. "Otherwise the sugar turns into fairies in your feet and makes you do silly things."

"...cake and then *running*." Adrian quirked a brow. "How often do you win the foot races, Tula?"

She grinned like a wicked little princess. "I used to lose all the time. Then I got faster."

"And you run?" Adrian peered at Lucas with a slight smile. "I'd like to see that."

"You'd like to see me run?" Lucas asked under his breath as Tula took off singing behind them. "I could have sworn you wanted the opposite."

"Just for the spectacle," Adrian murmured, "hopefully not permanently."

"If you eat cake, you might have to run, yourself," Lucas warned. "Those *are* the rules. They're quite well entrenched. You don't want to go to bed with only one story, do you?"

"Under no circumstances." Adrian raised his brows in mock horror. "What if you win, Lucas?"

"He makes you read the newspaper to him," Tula piped up, leaving off her song in the middle. "It's *so* boring. Not even the good news. The *weather*."

"It's soothing." Lucas looked just about as mischievous as his daughter.

"Mmhmm." Adrian tapped his fingers on the median. "And what if I'd like a reward other than stories?"

"Papa does really good stories," Tula beamed. "And songs. He knows all the songs. And he can play them on the harp! So they sound like fairy songs, even if they aren't."

"You didn't tell me you played."

Lucas shrugged. "I don't recall the subject being broached."

Adrian chuckled to himself, leaning back in his seat. *Philomela*. The name of his store. The name of his company. Latin for the evening songbird. "Nightingale, indeed. I think I'd like to hear you play, too. Perhaps we should start a list?"

"A list?" Lucas queried, squinting at the street names as they passed. "Of what?"

"All the lovely things I'd like to see you do, of course. Fairy songs and stories and foot races? A veritable panoply."

Lucas lifted his brows pointedly, glancing towards the backseat. "Adrian."

"She said you know *all* of the songs," Adrian teased warmly. "How am I to resist *all* of the songs?"

"Try." Lucas rolled his eyes, failing to control the pleased flicker of his lips. "Tula, you should tell Adrian about your judo class."

The next twenty minutes were a detailed play-by-play of her class and her expectations for her upcoming match against the older class, told with giddy joy and breathtaking violence until she was demonstrating punches and kicks for Adrian as Lucas found them a parking spot. "And then if they try to trip me—because they always try to trip me—then I'll jump away." She hopped as she walked between them towards the double glass doors of the restaurant. "And then I can circle behind them and use their feet against them!"

"A truly impressive strategy." Adrian held the door open for them, watching Tula skip towards the hostess. "Though wouldn't that be what they expect you to do? What if they see that particular maneuver coming?"

"Of course they do! We all know the same things! It's just who does it faster and better." Tula spun circles under his hand as they were led to a table and left with menus the size of novels. "And I'm the fastest and the bestest."

"Mmhmm, the bestest, indeed." Adrian glanced at Lucas, lifting a brow. Was it selfish, wanting to tell her now? They were certain of what they wanted to be, but there was still time to get there. Should they wait until they'd arrived at that impenetrable certainty, the point of no return? Only it didn't seem plausible to get there with things as they were now. She would figure it out on her own before they could explain things. Adrian swallowed, taking a seat in the booth across from them. "There certainly seem to be at least a thousand cakes on display. You weren't exaggerating."

"You see?" Tula was bouncing in her seat already, hugging herself, and she hadn't even had any sugar yet. "Which one do you want? Do you like strawberries? Or chocolate? Do you like cookies?"

"You can pick yours." Lucas rested his hand on her back. "Let him pick his own." He dropped a kiss on top of her head. "Coffee, you said?" he asked as he glanced at Adrian.

"Coffee, and not all of us had waffles and wiggly eggs." Adrian's palms suddenly felt clammy. "I think my cake will need to wait until I've eaten something more substantive."

"*Thank* you." Lucas smiled warmly. "Two votes for wisdom, at last. Alright." He flipped Tula's menu back toward the chapter on sandwiches. "Choose something for lunch. Then your cake." He waved their waiter down. "Waters, two coffees, and a steamed milk."

"Almond milk!" Tula chirped.

Lucas shot her an odd look but shrugged and nodded to the waiter. "Alright." He cleared his throat, turning his menu over and setting it aside. "Tula, I've been meaning to—"

"Can I have one of the vegetable sandwiches?" she interrupted him.

"Mmhmm." Lucas lifted his brows, glancing at Adrian. "Tula, would you feel alright if Adrian started spending more time with us?"

She nodded, poring over the options on the plastic-covered menu. "Yes, please."

Adrian tapped the top of Lucas' foot under the table, meeting his gaze. "I'd like that. And...?"

"And—" Lucas turned his menu on the table again. "And." He squinted. "The reason he would be spending more time with us would be that—that Adrian and I are... friends. Good friends."

"I know," Tula said, frowning in concentration at the menu.

"Yes. Well. Sometimes when adults are good friends, they like to do silly things like—" Lucas puffed out his cheeks. "Hold hands and give each other flowers."

"So you and Mr. Adrian are boyfriends now?" Tula peered up at him curiously.

"...yes. That is—yes," Lucas murmured. Flushed. Adjusted his silverware. Met Adrian's eyes. "That's a fair statement, I think. Right?"

"Boyfriends," Adrian agreed with a wink.

"Okay." She looked up from the menu and smiled at both of them. "You could get the Oreo cheesecake, Papa. It has a chocolate crust that's made of cookies."

Lucas took a deep breath. "Fine."

"Okay!" She patted his hand, clearly proud that he'd taken her suggestion. "You can also have a vegetable sandwich. Meat is murder."

"...is that what they say at your friend's house?" Adrian quirked a brow, peering back down at his menu. It hadn't even phased her in the slightest.

"Uh huh. Malcolm has a book about how cows scream when they get murdered for sandwiches."

Lucas rolled his eyes and rubbed his temple. "Well, that will be a nice conversation I get to have with Anara."

"I'm a vegetable person now."

"Vegetarian," Lucas told her gently.

"Oh." Tula widened her eyes. "Yes. That's what they said."

"Vegetable person." Lucas closed his eyes. "Christ."

"Quarter for the swear jar!"

"Remind me when we're home."

Tula peered over at Adrian. "So are you going to have sleepovers with us now? Like when I cut my foot?"

Adrian blinked, heat rushing to his cheeks; he looked helplessly towards Lucas. "That's up to your father."

"Okay." She poked at Lucas' shoulder. "Can we have Mr. Adrian over for sleepovers now, since you're boyfriends?" Before he had a chance to respond, she returned her attention to Adrian with a considering squint. "Do you tell good stories?"

"...not as good as your father. And I can't play the harp, I'm afraid. But I may know a few stories you haven't heard yet."

"You'll get better if you practice. Practice makes everything better." She smiled brightly. "Do you love my papa yet?"

Lucas swung his head to stare at her. "*Tula.*"

"Mada said it was going to take time, but it's been *forever.*" She rolled her eyes. "So do you?"

"Very much so," Adrian said, more breath than air. "I do. Your... Your grandmother said...?"

The little girl squealed, wrapping her arms around Lucas as he gaped. "See! You *do* get to be Prince Charming! I told you!"

"Excuse me?" Adrian's eyes widened as he watched her crowing. "What *exactly* did your grandmother tell you?"

"Mada told me that you can't hide your bushel in a basket and the smiling man said that you would probably really like my papa if you got to know him, but Grandpop said that was going to be tough because his cashew is a hard nut to crack."

"Christ," Lucas wheezed again.

"Fifty cents!" Tula cheered.

"You spoke to *Seron*," Adrian whispered, "about *us?*"

"Uh huh!" Tula blinked wide, soft blue eyes at him. "Oh. Was I not supposed to? He's so nice."

"He is." Adrian pressed his lips together, his breaths short. "He *is* very nice. I'm glad you're friends."

Lucas reached for him, resting his hand over Adrian's. "I'm—Do you—"

Tula snuggled against Lucas' side, the sound of her heels kicking against the booth beneath the table a steady thump like a heartbeat. "Did you finally realize that you love him, Papa? Mada said you're too stubborn."

Lucas held her close against his side, his hand shaking slightly where it rested on Adrian's. "That's—more than enough now, sunbeam. Remember what we said about talking about your... friends... outside of the house." His voice sounded like something that had been scraped off a plate.

Adrian squeezed his fingers tightly. "It seems we were part of a conspiracy," he said quietly, glancing between Lucas and Tula. "I'm not sure I know what to make of it."

The little girl stretched across the table to put her little fingers atop theirs. "It's okay to miss him, Mr. Adrian. He misses you, too. He said he hoped you'd be happy again. Are you?"

Adrian swallowed, the back of his throat burning. "I am happy." He reached across the table to touch Lucas' cheek. "I'm happy because of you and your papa."

"Good! So you can have cake and then play with my Legos. They're all different colors and some of them have names. And we can watch My Little Pony again!" She grinned. "Papa, you have to tell him you love him, too. That's the rule."

Lucas trembled under Adrian's fingers as he lifted his gaze, studying Adrian with concern. "I adore you," he whispered, raw, holding onto his little necromancer. "Whatever you need, love."

"I'm not delicate, remember?" Adrian murmured, exhaling slowly. It was true. He felt stronger than he had in months.

"And I love you, too," Tula chirped, bright and happy as a sparrow.

"Yes?" Adrian asked, unsure if he could smile any wider. "Is that so?"

"Uh huh! You made me fly!" She grinned. "I'm a sunflower mermaid princess and my papa is Prince Charming and you—you can be the Wizard King! Okay? And we can go on adventures and we can build a Lego spaceship and I can show you my books and all my drawings."

"Luke?" Adrian asked softly when he heard a suspicious sniff and noticed Lucas thumbing his eyes.

"Don't mind me," Lucas whispered, dabbing his cheek with a napkin and folding it neatly on the table. "They're good tears."

Was it possible to love him more? Adrian thought of that acerbic wit, a ward against vulnerability, that he'd been chipping away at for months. Here was the man behind it: crying in a chain restaurant because his daughter welcomed Adrian into their lives.

Adrian stroked the back of Lucas' hand with his thumb. "I'm in love with Prince Charming and I have a sunflower mermaid princess giving her blessing. I might cry, too."

Lucas blinked and the wet study spilled, slipping down his cheeks to catch in his scruff. "As you will," Lucas whispered, lifting his hand to kiss Adrian's knuckles gently. "My Wizard King. My sunrise."

Now he'd done it. "Tula." Adrian blinked as his vision blurred with tears. "You can order an entire cake for me, my dear, and we'll take the rest home." He cupped Lucas' cheek with a smile. "Right, darling?"

Lucas, as he always did, leaned into his touch, a slow smile curving his lips as more tears slipped from the dark forest glades of his eyes. "We're going to have to run for miles," he murmured.

"Then we will," Adrian chuckled, wiping his cheeks with the back of his hand. "Rules are rules."

"I love you." Lucas pressed a kiss into his palm. "So very much."

"And I you." Adrian caressed his cheek, touching his feet under the table as their waiter approached. "We'll figure out the rest as we go along."

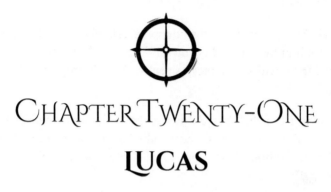

CHAPTER TWENTY-ONE

LUCAS

He'd always enjoyed the solitary quiet dark of the cemetery at night. A sky full of stars, untroubled by the lights and structures of the city. Usually, at this time, he'd have been here alone, nestled against the mausoleum where he would one day be interred, considering what had come before and what might come next, wishing he could speak to the people beneath the stones and ask their advice about one or a thousand items on either end of the temporal spectrum.

Tonight, he was not there to wish and wonder. Lucas had surveyed the area for weeks, checking the cemetery three times before he'd begun to set the wards of protection over the small area behind the mausoleums, just to be sure. He was a lookout, keeping them safe from the Seekers who had finally stopped patrolling this area. A tall, uncannily handsome ex-pilot and a little girl with sunflower hair who had become the center of Lucas' world the first time he'd met her. His lodestones. His anchors.

They whispered together by moonlight, their quiet giggles and low laughter ricocheting in Lucas' heart until he felt that it might burst. Tula had taken to Adrian's persistent presence as though he'd always been meant to be a part of their lives; trust and joy were her trademarks. And Adrian... Lucas had spent months carefully interrogating his behaviors for signs that Adrian was becoming weary or overwhelmed by the responsibilities he was gradually taking on, but he seemed energized if anything.

His last serious boyfriend, years before, had started enthusiastically as well, for a few weeks. Perhaps, if he'd only ever had to go to zoos or theme parks, he might have been there still, but the first temper tantrum had set him on edge. Negotiating schedules to make room for Tula's had worn him down. The work and wonder of actually guiding her into adulthood had been more than he'd wanted, more than any time with Lucas was worth. And Lucas hadn't loved him. Not yet. Maybe that had been a part of it, too. That had been then. Now, Adrian was teaching his little girl how to make room for herself in a world Lucas couldn't even touch, building boundaries and barriers to protect her, teaching her to use her amulet to hide her from prying eyes. Not that Adrian didn't enjoy the zoos and runs through the park, but he took the daily efforts and rescheduling and occasional battles of wills in stride, too.

Lucas scanned the cemetery again, glancing away from them to make sure that their work could proceed uninterrupted. Their work. That, too, was a blessing. Adrian could see the spirits that Tula did, could advocate for her, and be a reference and guide to her as she navigated her ability. It was destiny, as his mother would have said. And the night seemed made for magic, with the low stratocumulus clouds like shredded gauze between them and the sky, softening the night sounds and granting them mystery as they whispered to another world.

"The most important thing," Adrian murmured, sitting cross-legged on a patch of grass directly opposite Tula, "is to be able to discern the difference between those who have passed on and those still here. At first, they seem virtually indistinguishable by sight, but..." He took her hands and closed his eyes.

"Oh, warm!" she chirped, glancing excitedly around. "Wait—Mr. Dunnow is glowing now! Can you make him sparkle, too?"

"Perhaps, but that isn't *quite* the point—"

"Do they *all* sparkle if they come back?"

"If you learn to see it, yes. You have to..." Adrian paused, donning what Lucas had started thinking of as his 'professor face': a thoughtful, quizzical expression that wiggled his ears for some reason. "Do you know how you feel when you focus really hard on something?"

"Yeah! Like there's a bubble in the middle of my forehead, like a baby unicorn horn." She glanced at Lucas with a grin. "Papa can't see that either."

"Very good. We want the opposite feeling." Adrian smoothed his hand over her forehead, brushing back blonde bangs. "Like you're focusing on nothing at all; your mind just floats like you're laying in a swimming pool or drifting through the clouds."

"But how can I listen to them if I'm not focused on them?" Tula asked, worrying her lower lip with a little frown.

"You'll be able to listen to them and see their aura, eventually, if you practice." Adrian nodded towards something Lucas couldn't see. "Why don't you try it without my help and see if you can find that halo? Closing your eyes might help, so you can focus on what's inside of you rather than outside. It should feel warm, like sitting in a spot of sunshine."

"Okay." Tula squeezed her eyes shut, wiggling where she sat.

Lucas covered his mouth with his hand to hide his smile. Sitting still had always been one of her least favorite things. "Relax, sunbeam," he whispered. "It's just like the Everything Place."

Tula wrinkled her nose, straightening her spine into the meditation posture. "The Everything Place is *hard*."

"I could teach her that much," Lucas mumbled, glancing at Adrian. "...how many of them are there?"

"How many spirits?"

Lucas nodded slowly.

"Dozens," Adrian murmured. "With varying levels of connection to our world. We *are* in a cemetery."

"Yes, but... They don't all just... linger here... all the time, do they?"

"No, they don't. They typically don't stray far from where they were buried or the paths they walked in life."

"It sounds dreadful, being stuck in the same place for eternity. You'd think being dead would be the time to explore. Go bungee jumping."

"They don't stay forever," Adrian told him, his hand resting lightly on Tula's shoulder. "The ones that linger usually have a reason to do so."

What reason could keep them hovering in the same spaces, unable to touch or taste? He'd always imagined his parents were off exploring when they weren't visiting with Tula in the mausoleum. Or... Gods, were they just sitting there? Listless and waiting? Would Lucas do the same when he passed on? To see Tula again, to be there for her should she need it, even if only immaterially...? He grimaced. He could see making that choice if it were an option.

"Oh, I can see the glitter!" Tula chirped. "Papa! Everyone is glittering! Like sequins!"

Lucas bit back the impulse to ask her to quiet, checking the wards that muffled their sound instead with a slow blink of awareness. Still connected. Still protected. "Well done, sunbeam."

"Now look at your father and me," Adrian said, patting her shoulder. "Do we shine the same way?"

She squinted, her nose twitching like a rabbit's. "No. You look like rainbows."

"Like rainbows," Adrian repeated. "Interesting. I'm not certain what that means. Perhaps your talents are more extensive than I anticipated."

"You have lots of colors and they're all swirly," she murmured, staring at them wide-eyed, then looking off to her unseen companions. "Not glittery."

"Well, you can see the difference now, which is the important thing." Adrian tugged on her pigtail lightly. "That's very good work, you realize? It took me three days to be able to see the auras when I was young."

"*Oh.*" She smiled widely, hugging herself. "I'm a natural. Papa says that all the time. What does it mean? How do I make the auras different?"

"You don't make them different, at least not with magic. You see them as they are and sometimes it will help you figure out why a person chose to stay on this plane after they passed or if they're friendly or dangerous." Adrian hummed, thoughtfully. "I've seen auras change, but not often."

"Does everyone have them?" Tula asked, blinking at him with her pupils drowning her soft blue eyes. "All the time?"

"They do." Adrian nodded. "Unless they know how to hide them. I wouldn't go looking around for them all the time, though; you'll wear yourself out and get dizzy."

"Do I have one?" She wiggled her fingers in front of her face. "What's mine look like? Am I a rainbow too?"

Adrian dipped his head, exhaling steadily. When he opened his eyes again, the silver of his irises were no more than thin rings around his pupils. He smiled, touching her hand. "That's appropriate. Like sunlight in midday. You shine like a beacon."

"Papa! Do you see me shining?"

"I always see you shining," Lucas murmured, gazing at them both fondly. "But I can't see auras. I never have."

"Yours is beautiful," Adrian said softly. He blinked and his eyes returned to normal. "As it should be."

"Flattery will get you many things." Lucas winked at him. "I think that's enough for tonight unless there was something more you two had up your sleeves?"

"It's gotten quite late, hasn't it?" Adrian asked, glancing between the two of them. "Shall we say goodnight to our families, since we're here?"

"Tula." Lucas held his hand out to her. "Normal sight again, please."

"It's so pretty." She sighed softly, blinking rapidly until her pupils shrank to normal size again. "I want to show Mada and Grandpop and the smiling man, okay?"

"Yes, and then a well-earned rest." Lucas patted her shoulder, handing her a juice box. "Hydrate. Both of you." He offered one to Adrian. "I don't want to carry you back to the car."

"Yes, sir," Adrian chuckled, tongue in cheek, sipping from the plastic straw. "Thank you for indulging us, darling. I hope you weren't too bored."

Lucas shook his head. "I enjoy watching you work." It was mesmerizing the way he taught so patiently and Tula blossomed when she had an opportunity to actually use her abilities rather than work so hard to conceal them. "Thank you."

Adrian took Lucas' hand, bumping their shoulders together as they meandered through the empty cemetery. "No thanks necessary. I enjoy the excuse to practice."

"So does she." Tula wove and danced between the stones, chattering to people Lucas could not and had never been able to see. "It's good for her to be able to share this. Perhaps it will help her keep it inside when she must."

"That's my hope." Adrian squeezed his fingers. "And that she can discern the differences between the living and the dead and tune them out when she needs."

Lucas leaned against him. "The amulet seems to be helping as well." He could taste the end of winter on the air; the mist around them rose into the night to form low clouds, muddling the moon. "It's a monumental gift that you both have. There are times I envy it."

"I wish we could share it with you. Perhaps we can work on a way."

"I'm honestly not sure that I could handle it," Lucas admitted wryly. "Maybe the gods have reasons for whom they send particular abilities."

"You get used to it after a time." They paused at the gate to the Halpern mausoleum, waiting patiently as Lucas dug in his pocket for his key.

"You've had *years* to get used to it. So has she." Lucas rolled his eyes, unlocking the gate and calling Tula to them. "Come say good night, sunbeam."

She skipped past them down the steps. "I learned to see rainbows, Mada!"

Lucas laughed quietly. "I've never seen rainbows. Not any sort of otherworldly ones, anyway."

"Nor I," Adrian wrapped his arm around his waist. "But I could see your aura. You were very—" He paused, tilting his head to the side, looking past Tula's shoulder. "Hello. It's nice to finally meet you. I've heard all manner of lovely things."

Lucas rested his cheek on Adrian's shoulder, looking in the direction both he and Tula were before he sighed and shut his eyes. "Say hello for me, will you?"

"They can hear you, darling," Adrian chuckled. "Your mother says it's good to see you so happy. Though I think she should be proud for the role she played in our—" He paused, eyes widening. "Seron? What are you—" Adrian clutched his hand tighter, his voice weak. "I wasn't sure I'd see you again."

Lucas lifted his head, uselessly looking around the room as Tula scurried to his side and took Adrian's hand. "Don't worry," she said with a serious little nod. "We'll take care of him. He's the Wizard King, so we have to. Right, Papa?"

"...yes," he agreed weakly. "Yes, for that and many other reasons." Watching them listen to the silence of the mausoleum was suddenly much less charming than it had been out among the stones.

"...I intend to," Adrian said slowly, staring into the space in front of the wall as the lights slowly revolved to send orange flowers and blue hearts scattering across the stone. "I'm—I'll always miss you," he whispered, pausing again to listen. "I understand. I would have found that incredibly hard to swallow once, but now I understand. I love you." His chin lifted lightly. "I'd like to believe I'll see you again one day. When it's time."

"What did he say?" Lucas whispered, wondering if he should say anything at all.

"He's saying goodbye," Adrian murmured, turning towards him. "And thanking you. He stayed... He stayed to make sure I was alright after he'd gone."

Lucas swallowed. "We should—We'll go outside. Give you a chance to say a proper—" Like treading water in the middle of an ocean, this. "We'll go outside. Tula."

"Stay," Adrian asked, not letting go of his hand. "If you will."

Lucas nodded once, palm to palm. "If *you* will."

"Thank you for leading me to my family," Adrian said softly to his lost husband, his voice low and raw. "I should've known you were with me all along. I'm sorry I was angry at first. I didn't—It didn't seem fair to lose you like that. Thank you for staying, even when I couldn't see you. I'll try to make the most of all of your gifts. To put everything you taught me to good use. And—" He shook while Lucas and Tula held him. "I love you. I'll always love you, until the end."

Lucas studied his profile, remembering how Adrian had seemed so broken when they'd first met, and the times before, when he'd watched Adrian making his forlorn pilgrimage to and from the mausoleum. Adrian ached still. He loved still. He would do both, always. For this man that Lucas had only ever seen in photographs. Would it be a fresh wound again? Lucas wondered. Returning to the beginning to heal what had only just begun to scar?

The room filled with a soft, golden glow that even Lucas could see. It could have been a trick of the light, it was so faint, but it enveloped Adrian between them, gilding his skin and making him glimmer. It grew in intensity, surrounding the three of them like a warm blanket, before slowly fading away. Adrian's grip was tight on Lucas' hand, holding him for stability.

"Goodbye," Adrian murmured, dipping his chin. "I hope whatever comes next is as beautiful as you were."

Lucas held onto him, heels rooted to the marble floor. Another loss when they'd finally found each other. Another tear in Adrian's cloth armor. Tula yawned, waving until the light softened around them once more. She turned to look up at them, her eyes sleepy and soft. "Can we have sunflower stories at home?"

"I think that can be managed," Lucas told her gently, holding Adrian against his side. "Let's just be quiet for a moment, alright?"

Tula nodded solemnly. "People go away and it's sad," she mumbled, holding Adrian's fingertips where they rested on Lucas' waist. "It hurts in the tummy place."

Lucas swallowed hard, hugging her to his side. "Tula..."

"It's okay, Papa. It's okay to miss them. There's still ice cream and swimming lessons and stories about dragons. Huh, Mr. Adrian?"

"Yes," Adrian whispered, taking her hand. "Just so. Ice cream and sunflower stories. Shall we head home, then, darling?"

Lucas looked around the mausoleum, wondering if there would come a day when his parents would leave him, too. "Yes," he agreed. "Let's go home."

CHAPTER TWENTY-TWO

ADRIAN

Adrian didn't let go of Lucas' hand until they got to the car and he took it again as soon as their seat belts were buckled. He needed the contact. He needed to feel the callouses on Lucas' fingers and the warmth of his palm. When he closed his eyes, he saw Seron glowing faintly and awash in gold, as handsome as the day they'd wed. Dressed in white from head to toe, with sunflowers woven in his hair—long, careful golden plaits Adrian had only ever seen before in pictures of when Seron was a teenager. It had taken Adrian's breath away to see him again, to hear his voice and realize he'd nearly forgotten what it sounded like. To gaze upon that smile, one final time.

Are you going to stay with them? Seron had asked, standing next to Lucas' parents and studying him curiously. *Are you at home again?* And Adrian had given the answer he'd felt in his heart.

Now Seron was gone.

Truly gone.

Lucas took his hand again at each stop light, the glow blooming crimson through his lids. Twelve lights, then the stop sign, then Lucas' little brownstone. They sat in the quiet of the car for a long moment when they parked, the only sound the slumbering breaths of the little girl in the backseat syncopated by the occasional inhale from her father as though he were about to speak. Four times. Five. Then more silence and the dark of the night wrapped around them all in the car as the motion-detecting driveway lights gave up on them and turned off.

"Are you staying?" Lucas whispered finally.

Adrian dared to open his eyes, just enough to look at their hand clasped on the median. There were tiny silent bells woven into the leather of Lucas' bracelet. There was still chalk on his fingers from the wards. "If you don't mind, I'd like to."

"I don't mind." Lucas held on, warm and sturdy and alive. "There's ice cream in the freezer if you want it. I'll listen to your sunflower stories if you want to tell them."

"I love you," Adrian whispered. "This doesn't change that."

"Alright." That quiet acceptance. The lack of judgment. A gentle squeeze of his fingers. "Come inside. I need to put her to bed. Do you—"

"Hm?"

"I love you," Lucas said instead, squeezing once more before he quietly slipped from the car and collected the sleeping child. "Take your time." The driveway lights illuminated them together as he carried Tula to the door, her cheek pillowed on his shoulder; he unlocked the door and left it open for Adrian behind him.

After a few steadying breaths, Adrian followed him inside the house that had begun to feel suspiciously like home in the past weeks, toeing the door closed and locking it behind them. There was something about returning here with Lucas and Tula—the halls filled with memories of laughter and brand new crayon sketches—that welcomed him anew each time. The stairs creaked under their weight as Lucas went to tuck Tula into bed among her stuffed animals.

Lucas eased the door shut behind him after making sure the nightlight with the dancing bunny was turned on. He leaned against the door. "Big night." His voice was as soft as the shadows around them. "I could use a drink. Can I offer you a brandy?"

"Please," Adrian agreed readily. "In a moment." He shut his eyes. The vision of Seron was already fading again. How much longer would he be able to remember the sharp angle of his chin or the shape of his lips when he smiled? "I need to hold you for a while."

"If you insist." His arms came up around Adrian's waist, resting gently at the base of his spine. "I'll suffer through."

"They're still here," Adrian murmured. "Your parents. In case you were worried about that."

"Thank you." Lucas' voice was muffled against Adrian's shoulder.

"You were right about him." Adrian kissed the top of his head, his breaths uneven. "He was afraid I'd never leave his altar if he appeared to me."

"And now?"

"Now..." Adrian squeezed Lucas' waist. "I have too much I don't want to miss out on."

"What? The sequel of Hannibal's Surprise? I can't imagine it will be very surprising."

"Exactly," Adrian laughed despite himself, gazing fondly into those familiar emerald eyes. "I'm glad you were there with me."

"I'm glad I was, too." Lucas kissed his cheek gently. "Even if I had no idea what was happening."

"I'm sure you got the important bits," Adrian murmured, nuzzling his cheek. "I wonder what it's like, wherever he is. I hope... I hope that it's peaceful. He's had enough fighting for one lifetime."

"So have we all," Lucas agreed, his breath ruffling Adrian's hair. "I always imagined it was sort of a weightless light. Like anti-grav, but warmer and not nauseating."

"That'd be pleasant, I think," Adrian considered, leaning against him. "I hope he's got an infinite supply of spiked lemonade. He used to love that bar that overlooks the water near our apartment; we'd sit outside for hours, trying to see the stars through the city lights."

"Could you ever?"

"A few here and there, when we were lucky enough to have a clear night."

"I'm sorry he's gone, Adrian." Lucas looked between his eyes, somber, fingers brushing back the hair at his temples. "You deserved a life with him."

"Perhaps," Adrian agreed quietly. "Though I'm rather looking forward to my life with you."

"Ah. Well." Lucas looked down, dark lashes brushing his cheeks. "I'm glad to hear that. I would be very sorry to see you go. I've never loved anyone like this."

"I don't intend to go anywhere." Adrian touched his chin, lifting it to brush their lips together lightly. "I'm yours, for as long as you'll have me."

"Come," Lucas whispered against his lips, taking his hands. "Just come and sit with me and drink my brandy and stay until Monday." He guided him away from Tula's door and down the stairs, bypassing the little cupboard with its glassware and amber bottles to curl against Adrian on the sofa, arms twining around him. He tugged the throw over them both, wrapping them together tightly in the dark. "I'm yours," he whispered, barely audible. "For as long as you'll have me, too."

EPILOGUE

LUCAS

C umulus puffs like cotton swabbing whipped by the little air-plane windows, catching the sunlight and glowing. Tula had her nose pressed to the glass, wide-eyed. The only headphones they'd been able to find in her size were bright pink and she couldn't have been more pleased. She'd been talking about the flight for a month solid, leading up to the day, and had insisted that she and Adrian both get to dress up as real pilots, so there Tula sat in bright orange aviator sunglasses and a puffy jacket with patches featuring rainbows and smiley faces and her favorite ponies. Sometimes her taste bewildered Lucas, but it was hers. He wasn't going to ask her not to be herself.

"Would you help me with this lever, Tula-belle?" Adrian spoke into his headset, his voice strange and scratchy through the speaker. "Watch your step on the way up. Over."

"Roger! On my way!" Tula beamed, unlatching her seatbelt and climbing nimbly up into the cockpit alongside him. Lucas' heart eased its race as he heard the snap of the buckle in the copilot seat. "Which lever, Mr. Adrian? Over!"

She'd been using the aviation alphabet to spell everything for a week, too thrilled to keep her feet on the earth for another day.

Lucas leaned forward to watch them together. Like two peas in a pod. His two dashing necromancer pilots.

It was time.

He felt it in his bones; every few days, the words came to him again like a heartbeat.

It was time.

Adrian belonged with them. To them.

"*There* we go," Adrian laughed through his headset. "I'll make a pilot of you, yet. Can you see where we're going off in the distance?"

"The turtle in the water!" she pointed eagerly. "And we get to swim on the beach, right?"

"Just so," Adrian chuckled. "A nice long weekend to enjoy the tidepools and delectably frigid Pacific." He tugged on her pigtail gently. "I'm very excited for you to see the island. And the cabana."

"And join the Polar Bear Club!" Tula cheered excitedly. Lucas was absolutely not going to join them in swimming before dawn, no matter what rewards they cooked up.

They sailed through the air, passing under clouds before finally touching down smoothly on an empty runway. A pair of tanned attendants in board shorts and tee shirts wheeled over a staircase, waving as the three of them disembarked.

"Everything's in working order, I trust?" Adrian smiled, helping Tula down from the final step.

"Your mother left the weekend before last, Dr. Sharp," the taller man assured him, dipping his chin slightly in deference. "Everything has been seen to."

"Fantastic." Adrian always grew a little tense when his mother was discussed, but he was currently buoyed by Tula's dancing. "Thank you for your diligence and your patience with her; I know she can be trying."

"We get to live on an island full-time," the lineman said with an easy shrug. "I can't complain."

"Well, if you ever feel the inclination, send word and I'll try to smooth things over. We'll take an ATV to the cabana and hopefully won't bother you too much."

"Cabana, cabana!" Tula sang, turning a cartwheel on the tiny tarmac. "Can I drive the ATV?"

"No," Lucas laughed, rolling his eyes. "You already flew a plane."

"And I did good!"

"Well."

"I did *well*! Didn't I, Mr. Adrian? Over!"

"You did wonderfully," Adrian assured her with a chuckle. "What if instead of driving, you sit in the back and wave to everyone as we pass?"

"Roger that!" She spun in a circle, hugging him and then racing towards the ATV. "Over!"

"Can *I* drive the ATV, Dr. Adrian?" Lucas asked, slipping his arm around his waist. "I don't want to wave at anyone."

"You may." Adrian kissed his temple. "It's pretty easy to figure out the directions. Hopefully, I'm not too much of a passenger-seat driver."

"I didn't tell you how to fly your plane," Lucas reminded him. "I think you can manage."

An entire island. Not just to visit. A whole damned island. It was madness, even after all the time he'd had to get used to the idea. Not that the whole island belonged to Adrian and his family alone, but it was accessible only to residents, of which there were less than a hundred. Lucas laughed to himself, listening to the chatter behind him as he drove along the path and Tula greeted every single person they saw as though she were an official delegate from the mainland.

Lucas parked in front of the bright yellow cabana and rested his elbows on the steering wheel as his little girl raced ahead to find her room.

"Wait a minute," Lucas murmured, catching Adrian's hand.

"What is it?" Adrian asked, tilting his head. "If you've forgotten something, we can probably have it picked up."

"I did forget something." Adrian was a handsome devil, sun-touched and warm beneath his hands. Lucas tugged him close, brushing their lips together. "That's much better. I love you, you know?"

"I should hope so, or I'd be forced to question... Ah, just about everything." Adrian kissed him again, cupping his cheek. "I'm glad you were able to take the time off."

"Perks of running your own business." Lucas leaned back to study Adrian's face, losing himself for a moment in the glint of silver. "I would never have heard the end of it if she hadn't been able to visit your famous family cabana during summer break." He touched Adrian's chin gently. "It'll be nice to spend some uninterrupted time with you."

"Gods, yes." Adrian beamed, eyes sparkling in the warm summer sun. "Just the three of us. I've been looking forward to bringing you here since almost as soon as we met."

"I remember." Lucas lifted his brow. "Happy, now that you've swept me literally off of my feet?"

"Delighted, yes."

"You fly very well."

"It was a very easy day to fly."

"Not so easy. There were clouds. And wind. And gravity. And a six-and-a-half year old." Lucas winked. "Dangerous forces."

"*You're* a dangerous force." Adrian glanced over his shoulder toward the door, then kissed him long and slow. "There's a double-wide hammock on the balcony of our room."

"Is there?" Lucas laughed, swaying with him under the broad, bright sun. "Do you think one of those would fit in my yard?"

"Just between the cherry trees," Adrian assured him, running his palm down Lucas' chest. "We could try if you miss the one here enough."

"Would you come with it, do you think?"

"Oh, I imagine I would." Adrian winked. "As often as you made me."

"As long as the cherry trees stand. How does that sound?"

"As lovely as a weekend with you." Adrian nodded towards the entryway. "Shall we?"

"Adrian." Lucas clasped Adrian's hand over his heart and held it still. "More than a weekend. Cherries grow for lifetimes. Those have lived since my grandfather's house. They lived in buckets for four moves. It's a big commitment."

"Oh, you're—" Adrian blinked. "I thought we were talking about sex."

Lucas snorted. "We could be talking about both, if you're interested. I would like to keep the sex in addition to..." He cleared his throat, watching Adrian carefully. "This is not how I meant to go about this. I just want you to know: when we go home. After this—It would make us very happy if you would choose to come home with us."

"Home with you?" Adrian paused, glancing between eyes. "As in: *with* you?"

"Home with us," Lucas repeated. "For the life of the cherry trees, at least. Something to think about. I don't... I wanted to give you time to think about it, in case you weren't ready. No princess pressure."

"You want me to live with you?" Adrian asked softly. "To move in with you and Tula?"

"I would be very pleased if you did. So would she. It's been desperately difficult to convince her not to ask you every time she sees you. I know she will this week." Lucas smiled, unreasonably nervous suddenly. "When you're ready, you're welcome. And until then, I will protect you from her."

"Is it—" Adrian murmured, pressing his forehead to Lucas'. "You're certain you want this? It's not too soon?"

"It's not too soon for us," Lucas answered, holding him close. "We've taken a vote, you see. Now it's only a matter of if it's too soon for you. And if it is—"

"No," Adrian laughed, kissing Lucas' cheeks. "No. It isn't too soon. I'd love to. Do you think there's space for the three of us in your brownstone? Would you want to spread out more? I think the districts near the park are fairly good, or if you want to keep Tula in her current school, I'm sure we can find something that suits us—"

"Adrian." Lucas cupped the back of Adrian's neck gently. "Racing ahead again, I see. Come back to me and say 'yes'."

"Yes." Adrian kissed him fondly, laughter on his lips. "Yes, yes, yes."

Lucas breathed in his joy like air, sure he might float away if Adrian let go. "Shhh." He kissed him to quiet him. "You have to act surprised when she asks. I don't care where we are, so long as we're together. On the ground or in the sky or in the realms between. So long as we have each other and the cherries."

Adrian lifted him off his toes, kissing him as he spun in a tight circle. "I love you. I adore you. Yes." He whispered, nudging him with his nose. "I very much agree."

"I adore you," Lucas answered in kind, catching his breath as his toes touched the ground again.

Adrian kissed him once more, taking him by the hand. "Let's take our princess to the beach, hm? We can hash out the details while she wades in the water."

"Details, yes." Lucas' smile wobbled as he followed Adrian to the cabana. *Our* princess. His heart sang. Theirs. A family. A home together.

He was impressed that it took Tula a few hours to slip, sleepily, on their walk back from the beach. "I wish we could live here forever," she said wistfully, swinging between them. "We could ride horses and fly planes and swim and always be together everywhere."

"Is that what you want, Tula?" Adrian asked softly, kneeling on the boardwalk to meet her eyes.

"Would you want to?" she asked, wide-eyed. "Because Papa said there might not be room for all your shoes, but you can put some in my closet if you want to!" She threw her arms around his shoulders. "And I'd be very good! And you could do all your studying and I could be your copilot and we could have ice cream after dinner every night," she added in a whisper. "I know where Papa keeps it."

Lucas bit the inside of his lip with a shake of his head. Her sleepiness had fled in the face of the possibility.

Adrian grinned, smoothing his hand over her damp pigtails. "Your father and I will figure out what to do with my shoes; there's no need to sacrifice your closet space."

"Does that mean you're going to be my dad?" Tula asked hopefully. "And marry my papa and be the Wizard King forever?"

Love and panic warred in Lucas' chest like the crash of waves behind them. What if he came to stay and hated it? What if he lived with them for a year and grew weary of endless questioning and stepping on crayons in the morning before coffee? What if Adrian left them both heartbroken in his wake?

It was time, that heartbeat feeling reassured him, but Lucas had always thought of the worst possibilities before the best. Old habits. But he was making new habits now.

"Your papa and I will need to talk about it, Tula-belle," Adrian murmured. "But I would like to move into your castle and help your papa take care of you."

"Like a dad, though?" Tula asked. "Can I call you Dad?"

Adrian gave in to the princess pressure, hugging her close. "Sure, if you want. That's perfect," he whispered, peering up at him. "So long as your papa doesn't mind. Luke?"

"I..." Lucas began, worried she'd pushed Adrian too far.

"I get a Papa and a Dad!" Tula squealed, hopping up and down in the circle of Adrian's arms. "I have to call Malcolm and Samantha and Marjorie!"

Lucas swallowed as she skipped and giggled her way up the stairs into the cabana, towel trailing behind her like a cape. He felt as though he'd swallowed a bucket of butterflies. He exhaled slowly. "Adrian... You're sure?"

"I have been for months," Adrian admitted, taking his hand. "I'd sign the papers right now if you wanted."

"Which? Donating your teeth?"

"I thought I'd set up a trust for her." Adrian lifted a brow. "So you won't need to worry about her schooling, even without the dental donations."

"So it's a selfish thing," Lucas whispered, looking down at their hands. "Trying to protect your perfect smile. I see."

"Just so." Adrian cupped his cheek, kissing him fondly. "I'm open to other papers, too, once we've all settled in."

"Are you getting married?" Tula shouted from the window of her room. "Mrs. Anara asked Malcolm to ask me to ask you!"

Lucas laughed, lost and found, and wrapped his arms around Adrian. "Mrs. Anara can ask me herself when we get home," he called back. "Wash the sand off, please." He sighed, meeting Adrian's gaze. "Once we've all settled in," he agreed quietly, watching silver melt. "We have time."

ABOUT THE AUTHORS

A.D. Armistead (they/them) lives on the Eastern Coast of the United States with their supportive spouse, their anxious dog, and their cuddly demon cat. Aside from writing, their work involves traveling the world and trying to solve impossible problems. In their free time, they love hallucinating stories either through writing and playing TTRPGs with their friends, doing yoga, and playing the piano.

Austin Daniel (they/them) has been known as an actor, a rogue, a canine behaviorist, and a writer. Their work across multiple disciplines has always been chiefly absorbed in exploring the human experience hidden within extraordinary circumstances. They reside in the Pacific Northwest with their partner, dog, cats, and fiddleleaf fig tree.

ACKNOWLEDGEMENTS

Writing these books has been a labor of love from the very beginning—lines torn from foggy days in forests on cellphones and pencil-crowded notebook papers when the power was out. It was written across a continent, for years, and with such attention that our partners sometimes despaired. We would like to thank them, especially, for their support when all we could think about was this world and its characters instead of what we were having for dinner or when we would do the laundry. We would also like to thank our cats for keeping us company when we were deep in editing, and our dogs for reminding us to leave our computers for stretches of time. Additionally, a heartfelt thanks to our wonderful beta readers who gave us such great feedback and inspired us to dig deeper and turn up the heat. In particular, we want to thank Raleigh and Lillian for reading our little story multiple times and helping us craft the lovely little bonsai tree that is *Spirits & Sunflowers*. We couldn't have done this without you!

SIGN UP FOR OUR NEWSLETTER!

D id you know that we send out a monthly newsletter that contains all of the updates on our writing and publishing, highlights works from other authors, and contains free short stories related to the world of Maligned Magic? In fact, if you join the newsletter now, you can read a bonus Lucas prologue for free that tells the story of how he came to adopt Tula!

You can sign up for the newsletter at www.adarmistead.com!